Leaving Eden

Leaving Eden

Ann Chamberlin

FORGE

A TOM DOHERTY ASSOCIATES BOOK
New York

LEAVING EDEN

Copyright © 1999 by Ann Chamberlin

Book design by Victoria Kuskowski

This book is printed on acid-free paper.

A Forge Book
Published by Tom Doherty Associates, LLC
175 Fifth Avenue
New York, NY 10010

Forge® is a registered trademark of Tom Doherty Associates, LLC

Library of Congress Cataloging-in-Publication Data

Chamberlin, Ann.
Leaving Eden / Ann Chamberlin. — 1st ed.
p. cm.
"A Tom Doherty Associates book."
ISBN 0-312-86550-3 (acid-free paper)
1. Adam (Biblical figure) Fiction.   2. Eve (Biblical figure) Fiction.
3. Lilith (Semitic mythology) Fiction.   4. Bible. O.T. Genesis —
History of Biblical events Fiction.   I. Title.
PS3553.H2499L42   1999
813'.54 — dc21   99-22072
                                                      CIP

First Edition: July 1999

Printed in the United States of America

0   9   8   7   6   5   4   3   2   1

For Virginia

Acknowledgments

I dedicate this book to Virginia Kidd, who graciously allowed me to preface my story with her poem, not to mention all her work as an agent on my behalf. I must also thank her assistants, Jim Allen and Linn Prentis, for their help and support.

My editor, Natalia Aponte, spent hours and hours—until her elbow grew numb—working with me to make this a better book.

Louise Crawford Feaver, waiting for the airport shuttle, dug me out of the pit I'd plotted myself into. Alexis Bar-Lev was always generous and fascinating with her expertise. Again, I'd like to thank the Wasatch Mountain Fiction Writers Friday Morning Group for their support, patience, and friendship.

Marriott, Whitmore, and Holladay librarians never stinted in their assistance. And I must credit my family's ongoing patience while my mind is elsewhere.

Eden

Did they stay and tidy up a bit before they left
Dragging hesitant feet, abandoning what could not be carried —
Having little else to carry, yet unable to transport
A freight of golden afternoons beneath the fig trees:
    The single print of their two bodies in the first grass
    The lane worn by their bare feet to the gnarly apple
    and the giant ash?

Did they try to puzzle what eviction meant?
Or bow their heads, and go in discontent?

The serpent, watching.

—Virginia Kidd

Leaving Eden

One

In the beginning, Adam was lonely.

That's how the clanswomen explained it, anyway. "Adam wants a helpmate," they said, winking.

"Oh, Adam," one of my older aunts, Rachel, said with a dismissive wave. She was the liveliest, the jester. "He thinks he's the only man in the world. He always has."

Loud laughter burst from the group, as it did after anything Rachel said. The great, bare limestone face of the mountain jutting before us, looking and acting like an animal's shoulder blade, scooped up the sound and flung it back on my ears. But then the women dropped down over a low rise and the dance of sound changed on the spring morning air. I couldn't hear who spoke next. I scurried after them, leaving most of the tender green shoots of a clump of yarrow untouched.

It was my father they were discussing, after all. My father, Adam, who was lonely. Whom everyone declared needed "a helpmate."

Of course, this wasn't the first time my clanswomen had discussed my father in my hearing. Fifteen years of such talk had failed to bring them to any agreement, however, or they would have changed the subject long ago.

Fifteen years had also failed to answer my questions.

Why should Adam be lonely? I wanted to ask. Doesn't he have us, nearly as many in the clan as there are days in a cycle of the moon? Doesn't he have me, his own daughter?

We'd sat across the campfire from each other all my life, and my father remained a mystery to me. Less than most daughters, I supposed, could I say what his needs and wants were. Some girls complained their fathers never brought them enough skins. I was grateful when mine said a word to me. Most of the time I couldn't even win a glance.

My father saw me as the cause rather than a cure for his loneliness.

The clanswomen were laughing again when I caught up with them, but I'd missed Rachel's next words. Still, the direction she'd turned her round, flushed face gave me a hint. Her banter today was not meant for me.

It was meant for Eve.

Eve was not a clanswoman.

That is to say, she was new to us and the clan was having an uneasy time wrapping its cloak around her.

And she in accepting it.

In truth, I had known Eve almost as long as I'd known anybody. When I'd seen no more than three winters, she had mothered my motherlessness in the insistent way of five-year-olds who have no younger brother, no younger sister. Then we'd become close friends, for the years between us were nothing when balanced against our fondness for each other.

But—until five, six days ago—I'd seen Eve only at winter camp. Until then, she'd belonged to another clan and had always gone with them in spring. Five or six days ago, by the shores of Mother River, she'd said good-bye to her own clansfolk and come with us.

Eve had not gotten along well with her sharp-tongued

mother and her rough stepfather ever since I'd known her. This was a large part of our affection for each other. In winter camp she would come crying to our fire and tell me the latest argument from beginning to end. Then, if my father was gone—as he usually was—she would sway me to tell her my woes.

Words only came to me when I recited others' trials in the tales of our clan. My father's formless silence had taught me nothing of the sort of sharing Eve wanted. All I could stammer about my own life paled in storyteller's skill beside her insult-by-insult, blow-by-blow accounts.

But, "Tell it," Eve would croon and give me the embrace I found no place else. And in those arms I would tell it, even if only with my tears.

Eve was such a good listener. Certainly when I spoke of my father.

Maybe that's what my father wanted, what I could not be for him. A good listener. But I listened well enough to my clanswomen, didn't I? How else did one become a storyteller if she didn't keep her ears open? And how could I listen to Adam if he never spoke?

He never did speak. To me.

I looked back over my shoulder, expecting Eve to be just at my heels. I was the familiar thing for her in the strange, new clan, the strange, new landscape. But Eve, I saw, had not followed me back to the group. She was still at the yarrow patch, intently tearing up shoot after shoot.

The subject was Adam. That should have interested her. But for some reason, my clanswomen made her uneasy. Why this was I couldn't tell. Surely my clanswomen's recounting of all our members' odd traits was just their way of making Eve feel at home. Wasn't it?

That morning, the last of the other clans had followed

"their" river, the small River of Departure, to the southeast. We followed ours almost exactly at their backs. The Wolf River, the other clans called it. We called it ours, our dwelling place. Already the spring air said "home" to me.

During the wet and cold of winter, the whole tribe slipped like water down to the lowest places by the Mother of Rivers. We camped together, strung like beads along Mother's shores, more clans than there are fingers on my hands, and so many people that even Grandfather did not know every name. I had all I could do to learn the names of the girls near my own age. And of the friendliest boys.

It was always a great time when the tribe first gathered and built the shelters in the late fall, the rains beginning, the fogs rising. One clan after another came down from the hills as the season and the leaves turned. We feasted, told and heard new tales, sought out old friends. The men hunted gazelle in large drives, the women gossiped. As a tiny child, with little sense of time, I'd wondered why we ever bothered to leave the winter grounds.

Now that I was older, I could feel the upward pull of spring as the days began to grow longer. The freshness of many faces wore off. I got tired of slogging through the mud churned by feet numbered like the stars, jostling for clear water where scores of other women had already brought their waterskins. It took a longer walk every day to find enough fuel to burn. The food got worse, overpicked or frightened off by too many singing, shouting voices. Old angers, purged by three seasons out of sight, flared again under these stresses. When my father came to blows with other men four times in half a moon, even a girl of only fifteen winters like myself could feel the pressure in her chest that said, "Time to move on."

So we followed the spring-swollen river on the right. A deer path took the easiest way alongside the torrent, avoiding

the muddy shallows, the thicker stands of trees, and the out-
crops of rock. Like deer, we could have gone single file where
the footsteps of many generations, both beast and clan, had
beaten the grasses into dirt. But the only women who did this
were carrying children—my younger aunts, my older cousins.
Grandmother followed, giving Grandfather a hand.

Those who had no more than baskets and bundles to
shoulder fanned out. We brushed aside dried, snow-crushed
grasses, hunting familiar stands of asparagus, emblems of Father Mountain's vigor. Bunches of raisins overwintered on
faithful old vines we found again as easily, as unfailingly, as I
can touch my own eyes in the dark. We'd spend no more than
half a day walking before we'd reach the spring campsite, but
we shouldn't waste even that. When we laid the fire, those
women who'd been gathering would be able to dump enough
out of their twine sacks to feed us all, even if the men killed
nothing.

I was old enough to find stands without help. I ought to
have been working harder to fill my sack. But I kept braiding
my way back through the taller grasses to the trail, to listen to
the gossip. And Eve wouldn't follow me, though the talk was
clearly for her benefit.

"Adam—" Rachel panted with her plumpness, the walk,
and her good humor. "Adam thinks the gods came down and
breathed a special creation for him."

Her jesting put an amusing twist on the old story of how
the world and everything in it came to be as we saw it now, one
unified being stretched all around us.

I rarely caught a glimpse of our men except for Grandfather. Even when I turned myself in all directions, I couldn't see
them. I looked down the grassy way we'd come, then moun-
tainward on every other side. I saw no uncle or male cousin.
No Adam. Dogs at heel, the men moved in a great unseen

circle around us, warning off any dangerous beasts. And they stalked what game they could before our feet and laughing voices sent it scurrying.

Of course, it was spring. The season of Little Ones. While the breath had still steamed from us early that morning, we'd seen fawns and infant gazelles with their mothers—season-moving, like us, up from the desert. These sights had made the burdened women pull their own infants closer—and me to feel an emptiness, a need to be fulfilled.

The men must have seen these lovely creatures, too. But they had not shot. This time of year held deep bans against what Mother Lilith's sons might hunt. A man's companions would kill him if he were such a fool as to mistake a nursing doe for a wolf or a porcupine, offending the beautiful ache the Mother of us all felt in such a season. Perhaps the men would add nothing to the baking rocks that night. Still, they had to travel as men, apart.

So the women could discuss them.

The older women did not require silence in us younger ones. Particularly not from me—who had already gained some respect as a storyteller. As a second childhood lured my grandmother to its fancies more and more, the clan turned more and more to me. Even Granny knew it and sometimes, when pressed to "tell the one about—", she herself, after a fumble or two in the growing blanks of her mind, would say, "Let Na'amah tell it."

And I was the one who'd have to take up the old singsong, "Once there was—and once there was not—" Even for tales that had happened long before I was born, things I'd only heard from others.

Like the tales of Lilith.

I pulled my mind from the formation of that name, as from the sting of a bee.

In any case, the women already had respect for me, and would not hesitate to hand over any tidbit for use in my creations of the tongue—even blame of my own father. Just so might they bring tufts of goat hair or news of a good stand of withies to Aunt Yael, who was cleverest with her hands. We all delighted to recognize—and yet not quite recognize—our fibers twisted into a new and lovely basket between Yael's cracked and callused brown fingers.

Just so had my clanswomen begun to give me anything they thought I might use and then delight to hear it presented back to them—wonderful and new, worked through a child's eyes—around the next fire. More than a child's eyes. I hoped— and felt—the gift of the tale came with a powerful crone's wisdom. If I followed the gift's call with careful obedience. And did not let things like prideful defense of my own father get in its way.

So I could have asked why my father was lonely and hoped for some sort of answer, not a brush-off as children get. But I was also coming to know my craft better. And I already knew that when the winking started, generous as my clanswomen tried to be, I would probably learn more useful things if I kept my mouth shut and my eyes and ears open.

" . . . all of us know—" Yael was ending a speech when I strode up to walk by her.

"For some of us were there," Rachel threw in from behind. The very lilt of her voice could make a person laugh.

"—that Adam entered this world like anybody else."

"Through the mountain passes formed in a woman's nether side."

And everybody laughed.

I laughed, too. Because Adam was my father, I might have felt shame. Or because of my mother—who was no mother—I might have felt the stranger here. But all the clan was my

mother. And as a female, I knew I would always have an un-
questioned place in the midst of these women. And we could
always laugh together at our menfolk.

I already knew, at fifteen summers, that men had their
own bonds, their own tales, and considered their own sex su-
perior. Men were stronger, smarter, I'd heard it said—but only
by men. Men brought meat to the fire and death to enemies.
Better in every way. I couldn't have been my father's daughter
and not have learned this.

Except that we women thought—rather, *knew*—the same
pride of our own sex. We had the more abiding strength. To
know this I only had to look at my cousin Devorah slipping her
brown breast out of her doeskin smock to give to her little son.
I remembered her three days' labor just before we left the valley of "our" river five months ago.

Or I could look at the sack bouncing on Aunt Afra's back.
I knew more than asparagus and fennel bulbs bulged in there.
Women's herbs, acrid blue rue, probably, and womb root. Wil-
low bark for spring fevers. We all knew the vegetable world
that healed as well as fed when meat was scarce—often. But
Aunt Afra knew it best of all.

Who told the men about the gazelle spoor among the goatgrass? Where boar rooted beneath oaks or mountain sheep lay
to chew their cud? Men couldn't even stalk without us.

Women could also know with a sudden bolt in our hearts
what men could never know, even with months of furrowing
their brows over the matter. And it was through us—"through
our mountain passes" as Rachel so vividly put it—that life
came. And that was better than the death men wielded with
their spears and knives, wasn't it?

Grandfather did not like our female chatter. He might find
himself the subject of a similar discussion at any moment. As

soon as we gave him a chance, he broke in with an unrelated comment.

"There is no snow." Under the gray ridges of his eyebrows, from the nets of their wrinkled lids, his yellowed eyes scanned the slopes rising on our right hand. "There always used to be snow, in the shadows and on the higher north-facing cliffs, when we came to this part of the path. When I was a child."

He had made that same complaint as long as I could remember. And as long as I could remember, there had never been snow in the valley when we came to it.

"There is still snow on the long comb of our Father Mountain," Devorah assured him gently, shifting little Lev on her hip so she could point toward the ridge. Father Mountain was so long, he vanished from our sight at both ends, shadowed and chilled our path in places even so late in the morning. "The bands of snow look like the snaggled, yellow teeth of some fierce old beast."

"And there are more trees," Grandfather complained as if he hadn't heard her. "More little scrubby oaks."

Now I had the sense of this increase, too. But it didn't seem such a bad thing to me, to have more firewood presenting itself for my gathering.

Others talked about this for a while, honoring our grandsire for his age and wisdom. Sometimes I wondered if Grandfather were the storyteller, that he just forgot to frame his tales with the ritual words. It was easier to think this than that the world might really be changing, changing so drastically that the tiny span of a mortal life could see and feel the change.

I looked back at Grandfather's face, as gray beneath his gray beard as the exposed limestone face of Father Mountain. The two old men were such cronies, I supposed they'd grown to resemble one another. I didn't like the pinched look in that gray of mortal nose and cheeks, however. Grandfather must be suffering pain in his walking. It had been almost all he could do to reach the winter gathering last time, but we'd hoped the months of rest had helped him.

We'd been seven days on the springtime path now, mostly uphill, only two days of rest among them. Then came the dangerous, chilling river crossing. These were telling on him. It was Grandfather we waited for more often than anyone, even more than the children—my two little girl cousins, skipping hand in hand—who were making their first trek on their own two feet.

Grandfather pulled the black-brown aurochs-hide robe tight around him, as if with all the sun and vigorous walking, he still could get no heat. The robe swung low, around his knees. When he felt well, he liked his thighs exposed. There was a scar on his left thigh of which he was justly proud, though it deformed the limb like a gouge in the brown trunk of an old oak. Now I saw the lower ends of his legs only, and they quivered with his effort—with pain, perhaps.

I had nothing to say by way of encouragement, so I did what I could do. I fell back and took Granny's place at the side opposite Grandfather's walking stick, supporting him. He put a great weight on me, enough to make me draw in breath, although his frame was smaller, frailer now than what even I, with my short memory, could recall. I hoped he felt he could put more on my strong, young back than on that of his wife of nearly forty years.

We continued like this for a while, following the path where, in fall, dried grasses splintered as sharp to the eyes as if they were white flint-shard in the sun. Winter had swallowed last year's death, leaving black virgin earth, still damp in the hollows, waiting.

On either side, the wheat stood refreshingly green and calf

high, mixed with shorter, tougher goatgrass and with flowers: grape hyacinths scenting the air from their thick, low hummocks and narcissus about to split their sheaths. The wheat smelled, too, clean and grassy, growing with promise, and the damp spring earth had its own sweetness.

Along the river and the streams, the trees grew thicker. Graceful poplars caught the gentle breeze like dancers in a line. Away from such barriers, full, rounded trees dotted every twenty paces or so of the waving ground: oaks in a haze of pale new green, and pistachio.

"See how you can tell the female from the male pistachio even at this season," I said to Grandfather, "by the litter of shells about their feet?"

This was the wrong thing to say. It was an obvious thing to say, but I hadn't considered what thoughts might infest an old man's mind when he heard it.

"So how do you tell a man from a woman?" His voice was quiet and breathy but his crunching weight screamed at me. "A worthless old man who must walk with the women and children and even then have his granddaughter carry him."

Pain and effort left him no words for a few steps. Then, even with me all but carrying him, he begged, "Rest."

"Rest," I called out to the others.

Mothers set down their children, gave the infants a good cuddle and nurse, let the older ones off for a toddle or a crawl. The rest of us set down our bundles and went for a serious forage. Yael brought Grandfather water from the closest stream, ice-cold and clear. She had not bothered to fill her goatskin very full. Its rear legs, tightly thonged at the ends, had none of their usual quivering lifelike quality as she tipped them up for him to drink. But the slick wetness released some of the animal's living smell from the dead skin.

"By Old Father Mountain, I'll not make another season-

move," Grandfather managed to gasp after he'd gotten his beard
wet. The cold was refreshing, but it made him shiver visibly.

I shivered, too, though I'd had nothing to drink yet, and
tears stung the corners of my eyes as if from a slicing winter
wind. Neither Yael nor I scolded him not to say such things. A
clansman never broke an oath made by Old Father Mountain.

I took my digging stick and went after scallions.

By the time I got back, ten-year-old Kochavah was bound-
ing back over the hill ahead of us, followed by her own little
gathering sack, her bouncing black braids, and her mother.
"Courage, Grandfather," she called happily. "It's not far now.
We've seen the Tree."

No doubt Grandfather knew to the step just how far the
way was. But the child's singing cheer gave us all strength. Besides, sitting too long at this season in this spot allowed the
clouds of midges to grow annoying.

I went to Grandfather to lend him an arm up. Once he was
on his feet, however, he said, "Your Grandmother will do for a
while now, child."

Weariness and worry about her mate had made our oldest
crone's feet follow her wandering mind. But Yael soon brought
her back and off we went.

I was pleased to find that talk swung again to the subject
of Adam as soon as everyone relaxed into the pace.

"Maybe it's because he can't accept the will of heaven that
Adam is so—well, lonely," Yael offered with her usual gentleness, but confirming my own mind.

I was thinking men's thoughts mattered very little, even
those of honored elders like Grandfather. I'd learned that long
ago from the chatter of such walks as this.

"A man whom Lilith has chosen should know better than
to nurse such pride," said Afra.

The women threw furtive glances in my direction. Eve

was my friend, they seemed to say, and if she wouldn't listen to them, I must make her hear.

Or maybe it was for my own sake they looked my way whenever anyone pronounced the name Lilith. As if I would make more than basketry with their words once that name was evoked. As if I could work magic. As if I had that mythic woman's ear.

At such times I was glad for my calling as storyteller. It made me think I had a right to these looks. They meant no dishonor but gave me power I didn't otherwise have. I must, after all, tell the tales of Lilith.

My kin had never treated me as other than one of the clan, a woman-to-be like any other girl. But sometimes I could tell this sanction took effort. Sometimes the fact swelled to fill the air between me and the rest: if Adam was the man Mother Lilith had chosen, I was the fruit of that choice.

Lilith is the Mother of us all, I insisted to myself, and turned my concentration elsewhere as the chatter went on without missing a beat. The looks were just fancy. The looks were because Eve was my friend.

"Lilith chooses to make the honored one humble, not to bring him up."

"Let Adam think what he wants."

"Let him puff himself up large like some beast's bladder." I knew without looking that such an image came from Rachel's mind.

"Men must do so," Yael said, gentle as always. "The work the gods have given them to do—hunting, fighting—it rides at the edge of life, like babies on their mother's hips, no longer in her womb. Because Mother did not make them at the center of being, She gave them pride to make up for it."

"Like a man must give a crying baby his finger to suck, a dumb teat," Rachel said.

After the giggles, Devorah said: "Each person should undertake the blessing, the fate, of his life with as much joy as he can."

Perhaps Father chafed at fate because he could not confer and condole with a group of women like this, I thought. Because I had these women, I felt none of Adam's weakness. Or his shame.

Because of these women, I could return and comfort my father in any way he'd let me, with all the fervor my fifteen years of girlhood had to offer. As I could comfort Yael for her lazy Dov, Devorah for her sometimes violent and broody brother.

And Eve for having, as yet, no man at all.

Two

Eve.

No one had said it yet, but wordlessly they were joining the two names together as almost one word: "Adam and Eve."

My clanswomen often looked at Eve when they spoke of my father and his loneliness, of his need for "a helpmate." Because they looked, I looked, too.

So much of the season-move was new to Eve: Afra's stand of fenugreek we greeted like an old friend when it appeared around this outcrop of limestone. Even Grandfather's comment about the snow.

All winter Eve had been at our fire as often as at her own, even sleeping with us. But to switch clans was a serious move. Of course, anyone could do it, if the new clan welcomed her. The most usual shift happened at marriage, for no one could marry within her native clan. Our people usually celebrated marriages in winter, and a woman followed her husband's clan in spring. Or a man followed his wife's, if that clan were short of hunters. Or a woman might return to her native clan with her children if things did not work out with her husband. A widowed sister might return to her brothers, a mother go to help her daughter with little children. Such were the usual shifts.

Eve had no such claim on us. No claim except my friendship.

And my father's.

Something in the clanswomen's winks told me I must in-
clude my father in these thoughts. Something more than
friendship had grown during the winters between Adam and
Eve.

That was impossible, I told myself. I had no mother, but
my father was not free to remarry.

"If Adam were to lie with any other woman," someone was
always sure to say any time Eve drew near the chatting group,
"Mother Lilith would know it. She would come to take revenge on him."

"What is so with any woman is more so with Lilith."

"And as long as a woman has children alive"—always a
telling glance toward me—"her spirit will haunt him."

"Will come to tear his new bride to pieces."

"Or turn their children to monsters."

"Bring her womb nothing but grief."

"How much more so the woman who dares to embrace a
man whom Lilith has favored?"

Truly, my clanswomen had no reason to say such things. I
felt for Eve, alone, travelling away from her kin for the first
time in her life. She knew the force of such traditions as well as
the next woman. All the clans have the same respect for the
jealousy of the dead. And for the power of Lilith. Eve would
not do anything foolish to tempt the spirit world.

Would she?

Again, my mind buzzed when the clanswomen's teeth stung
their tongues in the saying of "Lilith." My mother, as well as I
remembered her, was neither jealous nor violent. She was gentle, rather, and endlessly patient. But then people told me it
was my aunt Gurit I remembered, my father's sister who had

stepped in to nurse and take care of me when her own little son had died. When Lilith, my real mother had —

No child likes to think it, but Lilith *had* gone. Abandoned me, her infant daughter.

If Lilith had ever existed.

I didn't feel resentment. Only the buzz. Mother Lilith was not a figure I could resent, any more than I resented floods or landslides. In fact, in every other tale except that of my own getting, Lilith was a force of nature, eternal and divine. And as people generally asked for the greater, more all-encircling tales, I suspected they spoke more myth when they spoke of my mothering. That I was born of Lilith was merely a poetic way of saying I had been born a storyteller, hearing the voices of the world around me, remembering them and passing them on around the clan fires.

If I was expected to state the strict truth of my experience, I would have said, "Gurit mothered me." And the Gurit I knew would not have wanted her brother Adam to pass the rest of his days in loneliness.

But Gurit had died trying to rid her body of my unborn cousin. She'd known she couldn't carry both him and me on the next season-move. And as Lilith's, I was the child she must save.

This was a thing my uncle never forgave. He had returned to his own clan after Gurit's death and, being childless, remarried and fathered other babies. But he was one of the men my father had come to blows with as the Winter Gathering grew stale.

So, long-suffering as Gurit was in my memory, her spirit still lingered, and with less patience. Everyone knew death could harden any spirit.

I let my gaze follow my clanswomen's now, off to where Eve walked alone along the grassy ridge of the next hillock, out of earshot, her attention on the horizon. Watching for my father? Could it be?

My heart gave a little thump of panic at the thought. It must not be.

No. Eve's reserve was caused by my neglect of her, while I was distracted by the clanswomen's chatter. I must cure this situation at once, I decided. Give Eve's thoughts no chance to wander onto dangerous ground.

So I left the main cluster of clanswomen and their enticing gossip and went to rejoin my friend instead.

As I swished up through the mingled wheat and goatgrass toward her, I tried to look at Eve without the blind acceptance of a friend. I tried to see her as a lover might, as those who'd hung around, posturing with their spears in the winter firelight, must have seen her. (I knew they hadn't come over for me, an uninitiated girl. "Just ignore them," Eve had always hissed in an undertone. "They're only *boys*.") I tried to see Eve as my father might in his loneliness. If nothing else, such a view could serve as grist for my storyteller's grinding stone.

Eve was of medium height, or perhaps a little shorter. I was already two or three fingers taller than she and I didn't think I'd stopped growing. Hers was an endearing height, a height that called out "fragility," enabling her to tuck up under a man's arm, against his ribs, for protection.

She had round, soft features to match. Her breasts, high and firm, swayed with every step, the life latent in them. Brown, upturned nipples knotted the ends. Between the breasts rested a necklace of cowrie shell, centered by a dark blue stone. The white looked fine against her skin, which was brown and flawless as if molded from the richest soil. The necklace was just the length, the bead and cowries just the rounded, open shape, to draw attention.

She bundled extra garments for chilly days on her back.

Careful of them, she now wore nothing but a short skirt of many rabbit pelts patched together. I knew her stepfather had been stingy in his gifts of skins to her, giving the largest and best to her mother and to his own daughter. But Eve had sewn the bunched manginess of the skirt with skill. It tossed with an enticing twitch from hip to hip as she walked.

"Good, broad hips for birthing," had been Afra's judgment. My father, I think, had been within earshot at the time. Maybe his mind did not carry to quite such a distant end, but I don't think he needed a midwife to draw his attention there.

The hair of Eve's head was thick, black, and very curly. It reached her waist as she wore it caught back at the nape of her neck with a thong. Shorter strands had worked their way free and the breeze coming down the canyon lifted them off her face as she turned to smile at my approach. The strands lifted not as the whipping snakes of limper hair, but all together, in rich sheaves.

And Eve smiled, a bloom of full, red lips, seductive, as I approached. For a year or two, before her first child, even the plainest girl has a certain seduction. She cannot help it. It is Earth's way of giving her that first child.

I was a woman, I reminded myself, or almost. But those moments of unnatural beauty have the power to blind us as well as men, in the interest of getting that first child. Did Eve think the same wiles would seduce me? Her friend? Against my gossipy clanswomen she could win me to her side. But I must not allow her to lure me beyond that. Against the world of the gods and departed spirits? No.

My father . . . ? Father is old, I thought, too old to fall for—But, I reminded myself, it is different for men.

I smiled at my friend in return. Perhaps she saw some doubt in me, for her eyes narrowed momentarily with thought. I forced my smile broader and her eyes relaxed to their usual wide, starry blackness, a night sky between lashes. Every morning she outlined her brows and lids carefully with a stick of charcoal from the edge of the low-burning hearth. Men as well as women commonly used charcoal, sometimes ground with sesame oil, against blindness or the evil eye. But usually only older folk worried about that. And Eve couldn't be totally innocent of the extra enhancement it gave the dark beauty of her eyes.

Eve had a full twine sack of gathered foods strung to one smooth shoulder. She would dump it proudly at my father's feet when he came into camp, showing him how well she was adjusting to a new land. But I saw she had been gathering other things, as well, unable to resist the explosion of spring through which we traveled. A wreath of grape hyacinth and early-opening narcissus crowned the light top layers of her hair. The whites and yellows contrasted beautifully, the purple made her hair look and smell the same as the darker flower. She'd stuck more blooms, caught in a rounded spray, into the belt of her skirt, emphasizing the low swing of her hips.

The glories of spring, like the strong arms of the great Mother, carried everyone away. Who did not long to embrace its renewed life and become part of it? I plucked flowers of my own. But did Eve have other motives in her wreath and posies? Love for someone other than the Mother of us all?

Three

The rest of the women were ahead of us and had already begun to gather beneath the Tree. The first trial notes of their welcoming song struck the ear. I quickened our pace and it made Eve's skirt switch from hip to hip with an audible slap at each step.

The Tree was a great fig, the height of four men. It stood in a hollow above a shrubless slope, no more than twenty paces up from the river, its back against a south-facing limestone shelf. Its branches were thick and spreading, excellent for climbing as we'd all learned when we were children, as Kochavah and Boaz were learning now.

The Tree was still leafless, the splitting buds, faintly touched with pink, just visible on the closest branches. Two or three storks' nests rocked winter-roughened and deserted in the upper limbs, waiting for the return of their builders whose presence there would have marked any tree as sacred.

Fallen leaves and pulped figs blanketed the ground beneath, sending up a rain-damp, moldering, fruity smell, rotting, yet somehow delicious. I imagined the earth salivating over this season's meal. There were signs that deer, goat, and ibex had fed here over the winter. Half-ripe figs still dangled among the dark gray branches. Warm days might swell and sweeten them within the month, and then the new figs would come. We'd harvest them with proper rites when we returned in the fall.

In the meantime, the clanswomen greeted the Tree with the special, joyful song we had for it, naked as it was. I heard Eve's voice raised beside me. Her tones were sweet and sure and she knew the words. Her clan must also have the song.

A twinge of jealousy slipped beneath my breastbone. This was our Tree, our song. Mother Lilith was ours—was *mine*. But no, Lilith was a myth. She was everywhere. I should not claim her for myself.

I looked at the Tree again and felt a deep wisdom coursing beneath the smooth gray bark. Yes, there is knowledge here for everyone, I thought, and smiled generously at my friend, thinking she might be homesick.

"Tell us the story of the Tree, Granny," someone said.

Granny licked her lips, took a breath or two, then said, "Let Na'amah tell it."

So I told it, after I'd moved to Granny's side and taken her hand, whether for her support or for my own I'm not sure. Eve moved with me, sitting at my right hand with her feet folded neatly under her. I glanced at her once, the sun-moistened, melting edges of her beautiful form. But she was looking elsewhere. To the Tree. But beyond the Tree. To my unseen father.

I began the tale.

Once there was—and once there was not—

I told how, long ago, in the beginning, the Tree came to us in the early spring, in just such a season. The River roared like bulls, carrying it. (I myself had never heard the sound an aurochs bull could make.) The Tree, then no longer than my arm, had seemed like a dead thing. But Mother Lilith had waded into the biting cold of the River and fished the branch out, and showed its wonders to her daughters.

Mother Lilith.

I said the word "Lilith" and magic began. Thinking or hearing the name always brought an insect buzz to my mind, but actually speaking the word, here, in the shadow of the Tree—It was as if I had called a child to me and here she came, skipping. No, someone more obedient than a child. A lover.

I knew the Tree had something to do with what I sensed, for I felt the breath of power from the net of limbs cast above my head. A web of knowledge held me fast while also spreading my mind wide.

"The born storyteller conjures worlds with her words," Grandmother had always told me. "That is her power, to have no power. To be the tool of the spirits of other times and places and let them overwhelm her—so she can pass them on to her hearers."

And I felt what Grandmother meant in every story.

Now, the Tree conjured forth by the name Lilith took my words, combined them with the roar of the present river, molded, deepened them into the River of the past. My words wrenched a tree limb out of a far-distant bank and sent it swirling down the white spring foam. Lips and throat and teeth and tongue dancing together filled the air and our nostrils with the sharp, cold scent of rock-volleyed spray.

The moment I said the two beats of "Lilith," all the commonplaces of storytelling shifted for me. The tumble of my tale changed from solid earth to quicksand in a step. And suddenly I found myself—

Mother Lilith brought it to us in the springtime of the year.

I kept talking but, removed from my body like a beast skinned from the nose backward, my insides left the pelt of what was Na'amah. They wafted off in spite of me, away from the circle of my hearers.

I found myself in an expanse of sand that stretched as far as my eyes could see, sand hot to the touch, blinding with glare. Then I was in a land where plants I had never seen before grew as dense as the densest thicket, up to the edge of sight and farther than I could walk in all directions. The smell of life was urgent in that place, as strong as the whooping, echoing calls of animals I couldn't name.

Then I bobbed like a rotted acorn in a world where there was only water. But was it really water? It tasted, when a wave pushed into my mouth, of the soil out in the desert where my people go to gather salt. It tasted like sweat.

I looked around the circle under the Tree, into the familiar faces of my clan, Rachel's sweat-basted plumpness, Granny's wizened gray sinking back into a childishness, Yael's placid calm. Suddenly they all seemed only water-splashed variations of my own face, compared to what the visions gave me.

There were different sorts of people in all the places where the vision led. People I could never have imagined on my own. People black as night and tall. People brown and no higher than my shoulder. Pale people, not the accident of one birth but clans of them. They passed on their paleness or their narrow eyes or their thick lips, as mother passed heavy nose and curly hair to daughter around the circle of the clan that faced me. These innumerable strange clans spoke tongues I did not know—and yet, with the new ears my journey gave me, I thought I might, in time, draw sense from the babble.

Trying to make sense of these other moving lips made me panic for a moment, thinking I had forgotten my own. My clanswomen waited patiently. I set down one word. It was my native tongue. I set another next to it. They matched. I set another. The story edged painfully on.

"Mother Lilith" entered the story again.

Was the power of that name potent enough to turn me into the great Mother Herself?

I remembered once asking Grandmother about the craft.

"I am afraid," I had whispered to her. "I am afraid of the power of words on my tongue."

Grandmother had patted me on the head as if I were only a child. She did so now, as we sat side by side under the Tree.

"There is no fear in the calling. Only honor."

But then she had admitted, "You are Lilith's daughter."

"Aren't we all Lilith's children?" I had asked. "I feel no different from any other. 'Lilith's child' is said of anyone; it is simply a form of speech, as we are all children of Mother Earth."

"That also is true."

"Then why do I—?"

"You are Lilith's own."

No more.

Now Granny's hand felt light, dry and brittle as wheat chaff in my own. It shook as if the breeze were at it. I held it for support, for the strength to carry the simpleness of the story on through the tangled web of what my insides saw and felt. But instead, I felt called on to warm, moisten, still, her hand with my own.

The pull of the word "Lilith" at my innards drifted farther. I found I had left a thin membrane of self across the new lands I entered, like the fall of dew before dawn. Or like birth skin that covers an infant as he leaves his mother's womb.

And as my being settled dewlike over the face of the earth, I found myself fused to all creation, as beeswax may melt in a fire's heat and fuse to hafting fiber. As brains and tannin fuse into new-scraped skins and make them different than they ever were before, supple, soft, sweet-smelling.

Then the Tree was not outside me, but part of me. It was

my own skin, rough as sand and parched, scalding to the touch. I myself rolled and heaved and sweat saltwater, teemed with fishes and floats of brown, palmy foliage. From my own breast, the great trees of the forests shot toward the sun, and my heart squeezed the sap of life up to the loftiest branches, took them to myself again when age felled them.

In this state, I could feel every thrust of every woman's digging stick in my own flesh. Every spearing of gazelle or deer was the death of one of my own children. I heard their screams as if they came from my own lungs, tasted their blood, still warm but rapidly growing earthy, as my own belly accepted it within.

Not to mention the lives of all these varied, living, laughing, loving, weeping people . . .

I drew back in terror from these visions. All life gurgling through my intestines made me heave with nausea, brought on a fever. I felt every clanswoman's eye on me, waiting. The rest of the story—where was it? Surely they were restless with impatience.

I had come to a point where I must pronounce my mother's name again. I approached this as one might approach licking the glowing end of a fire stick. I could feel my hearers around me, waiting for the next word-beats. Men have the ban against speaking the names of the animals they hunt lest the beasts get warning of their advance. Any person may receive signs from the spirits that they are to avoid such and such a word or thing. Lilith, I thought, must be my avoidance.

But a girl, before her initiation, is not old or wise enough to know what phrases she herslf ought to leave alone. To adopt a personal ban out of season is to exalt oneself; jealous spirits punish such deeds.

And how could a storyteller, of all people, avoid the word "Lilith"? Every other tale of the tribe featured that Mother of us all in its lines. I clung to the ridges of the veins in Granny's hand, felt the blood like fig sap in them, felt the gnarled knuckles of her years of work. I wanted their strength. But Granny did not seem to understand what ailed me. Had such knowledge, such terror, never affected her? Or had her wandering mind merely forgotten what doubts she had suffered when she was my age?

Or was I, as Grandmother said, truly "Lilith's own daughter"?

Perhaps Grandmother was mistaken when she had chosen me for this calling. Perhaps I wasn't strong enough to be a storyteller. Like the fissured yellow stone so common in our Valley, I would crumble under the use to which the spirits put me.

On the other hand, a sort of temptation swirled in the midst of my fear. Just so, men are tempted to fight the fiercest beast. Longing and fear struggled together between my ribs. Just so, I imagined, the wrestle with a man would be when I came to lose my maidenhood. I would burn with desire, yet throb with fear, every sense sharpened as the unknown rolled in upon me . . .

So I took a deep breath and bent my tongue toward the glowing stick. I spoke the name again — "Lilith" — and went on with the story, no matter how I felt my skin swell and burst and rut and bloom and birth.

Once there was — and once there was not — on the banks of this same river, Lilith showing our mothers the roots of the fig, the lifeless branches. Then she showed our mothers — her daughters — how to dig a hole for the roots with their digging sticks in this protected place.

I felt the thrust of those sticks in my skin, but pressed the story ahead.

Our mothers fertilized the soil, the Great Mother's body, with their

*own bodies, then sealed the roots in Mother Earth. Miraculously, the
dead thing sprang to life before their eyes. And so the Tree has stood and
grown and spread ever since.*

*Such is the tale. And within it are contained three apples, one for
you, one for me, and one for the story's magic. May each catch in her lap
the meaning best for her.*

"Thank you, O Mother Lilith," the women murmured
when I'd finished. Even the children quieted with awe. Did
everyone, then, have a glimmer of the self-rending power when
they spoke that name?

I'd told the tale exactly as I'd always heard it. The pauses
that had seemed so eternally long while I struggled to find my
bearings in a world that had sprung beyond familiar horizons—
these pauses had come to the clanswomen as only moments for
accent. What had seemed an endlessly long recitation had
merely slowed to just the right pace to counteract my usual re-
action to nerves, a rattling haste.

The pressure of Granny's hand confirmed my gift, as did
the silence in the awe that followed.

Why, then, did I find the gift so uncomfortable? And why
under this Tree in particular?

Four

Mother Lilith understands us so well, she gave us the Tree to love when we cannot love our men."

Rachel found something to amuse even in the wonderful. The sight of her plump good nature reaching halfway around the trunk to give it a welcoming squeeze signaled the end of the story's spell, the start of the shifting and scrambling to move on.

I sighed out the story air, replaced it with more mundane breath. Granny's hand had slipped from mine and she was up and walking, her mind slipping from her just as easily. And I — I was one of the clan again, not even Lilith's own. I set my hands against the fig-leaf litter to help myself to my feet.

But then Eve held me back. She lifted up her pert and perfect rounded chin and brought it toward my shoulder. From there, she murmured in my ear, "Our clan also has such a tree. In our spring lands. Mother Lilith planted it, too."

Her tone suggested support, even thanks for the welcoming unity my tale had given her. But as the one who must wield the tools of tale-telling, I had gnawing doubts. Did this view of other clan-worlds shove the matter firmer into the hands of the gods — or more onto the windswept changefulness of life?

As the rest of the clan shifted to their feet, Eve pressed me further. "Were you at the planting of your Tree?"

That seemed a silly question to ask. "Of course not."

"Was your grandmother?"

"No more than I."

"No one can remember the event in our clan, either."

"Granny only learned the tale, as I did, from the teller before her. I know this for certain, because I once asked her for details and she replied with no more than a teller's catch phrases."

Eve nodded and side by side we sat and watched the clanswomen, Hadassah calling her son Boaz to come on down from the Tree now so we could move on, Kochavah pressed to take little Ilanit into the bushes to relieve herself. The clan hated to leave the Tree, and both Eve and I knew there was no hurry. Our friendship—our questions—could linger.

"How can I believe that Mother Lilith—who fetched the twig from the spring runoff before my father's mother was born—how can I believe that Mother Lilith birthed me? If such a woman had been alive when I was born, she must have been the most ancient of ancient crones."

"Yes," Eve agreed with me. "There could never have been such a person except in stories. She appears too often, in too many tales, throughout all the clans of the tribe. I have heard the name at every winter telling."

But now the flesh crept along my arms. It was one thing for me to say this, to have disturbing visions I couldn't even begin to tell my best friend. But for Eve—

"My father must have known her," I began again. "He must have married her, or else the ban—"

"Or else the ban against his remarriage would have no meaning."

"Did he tell you so?" I heard my voice grow too loud when I said this. Some of the clanswomen dropped their glances to us. "Did he?" I repeated, but in a whisper.

" 'The name Lilith means "night wind," ' he told me once. ' "Female wind spirit," ' no more."

Jealousy burned in me. My father had never told me even so much about my mother. It hurt that he had said such things to Eve, who had no right to know.

Still, this was no more than I had come to believe—in spite of the clanswomen's never-failing word that they had seen and known my mother. My father's silences must have been what made me believe the place of my mother was a blank. Some dark and hated thing rested in that place for him. His silences made that clear to me. No worn myth could fill that mystery any longer.

And that's all Mother Lilith was, a myth, an image from poetry. Who should know that better than I, a storyteller? Certainly there was no reason why I shouldn't use her, and use her lavishly, as an image in my tales. Like Mother Earth, who also figured in the story of the Tree.

And yet, the images of Lilith were so real. The words of the tale conjured precisely her dark legs, wading into the frothing fury of the stream. I could see those legs turn blue-white beneath the hitched-up skirt of serpent skin, the muscles bunching with the cold. Those legs became my legs. The roar of the stream deafened the hearer, now as in ancient times, to any sound but its own. Bursts of spray filled the breath.

"I have as much respect as anyone for the power of the storytelling gift," I told Eve now. "But I—we all—can see the many hands reaching from shore toward the daring woman in the tale of the Tree too clearly. It can't be just a teller's fancy. Those hands have names. Ancestress's names." I couldn't let Eve lure me any further down this path than I'd already gone on my own.

"And there is the testimony of the Tree," I continued. "Here it is, the only fig in the valley. No matter where she stands, a woman can always pick out the darker, blue-green leaves when she comes from the other, paler growth. Her eyes fix here by themselves."

"It is so in our valley," Eve said.

"And the fruit—so like the blood-lined insides of a woman herself. The leaves, five-fingered like human hands. It's uncanny. And doesn't the very air around the Tree seem to enter the lungs and line them with pure spirit?"

"But—the Tree is just a tree, after all. It's not eternal, not like Father Sky. Can't your grandmother remember a time when it was smaller than it is now, not so tall and spreading? A time when she could see the River easily over the top of its full-leafed branches if she stood on that stone shelf at its northern side?"

"That's true," I murmured. Granny had told me so. It was in my story.

"The tallest of men couldn't do that any more if they came here. Adam couldn't do it." She gave his name—and his height and all his myriad charms—a caress. "The Tree, like the one in our Valley, sheds those hauntingly human leaves, bears fruit in season, just as our mortal bodies have their seasons."

I shook my head to clear it of visions. I had dreamed the power "Lilith" conjured from the branches overhead. The Tree was just a tree.

"Isn't it possible that this Tree, long as it has lived, might be prone to disease or blight if that is how the seasons turn?"

"Mother forbid it," I said.

Eve pressed on. "It might even die of old age."

"Yes," I agreed, with a sad glance at Grandfather.

"A woman can come and pick the fruit of the Tree, after all. We turn its flesh into our own. There is no ban against this."

"Except for men, to whom the fruit is forbidden."

Eve shrugged this off. She had already seen past other bans—imagined marrying Adam—to which this was nothing. "A man—not a woman, for we do not use such tools—but a man could come and lay adze to the bark, sink stone to the growing heart, haul the wood to his camp, burn it, reduce it to ash."

"It's evil just to think of such a thing. No man I know is so ungodly as to dare."

"But your mind can imagine it. Your storyteller's mind."

I nodded, my neck rigid with horror as if I'd never made such a gesture before. That imagining removed the whole matter from the eternal safety of unchanging gods and spirits. It *could* happen.

Fortunately, we hadn't any more time to pursue such thoughts then. I can hardly connect the two events, for her words went no farther than my ear. But at the very moment Eve spoke, a snake slithered out of her winter burrow under the litter of leaves at the foot of the Tree.

This was not such a remarkable thing. The creature moved slowly, however, cold-drugged, and gave time for everyone to see the silver pattern to her scales. She so startled little Boaz that he jumped out of the Tree—or tumbled, rather—farther than he would have had the courage to do on his own. He scurried, whining and rubbing his stinging shins, to his mother's skirts.

And Eve. I already knew Eve had a dread of snakes. She'd spoken of her fear to me before, and I hadn't forgotten. This was odd, since she had just been whispering worse horrors into my ear. And she'd actually been named for the creatures. That is one meaning of her name, at any rate. Now, in spite of that, she clung to me, whimpered and buried her face in my shoulder.

They said snakes lived forever, if they were not killed. And no one would knowingly kill one because he would be

banished from clan and tribe, even if the deed were an accident. The key to serpents' eternity was their ability to shed
their skins. They were favorites of Lilith—shed skins made her
skirts in every version of every tale. Sometimes, when I had
said her name very often in one tale or another, I could actually
feel the fragility of such husks on my thighs.

Everyone also knew that snakes carried secrets of healing
and dreams; they could bring messages from the spirit world to
the open-minded, for they moved like spirits, silently, without
legs. Because of these powers, one of the snakes' honorific ti-
tles was Eve—just as my friend had been named at birth—
"mother of all living."

"It is a good omen," Granny assured us, her mind brought
to itself by the event.

Eve gave a hiss of disbelief and clung to me tighter.

"A good omen," Granny repeated. "The serpent welcomes
us to our springtime home."

The clanswomen nodded and Granny herself drew the
stone knife from her belt and cut a lace of leather off the hem
of her skirt. This she tied to a low branch of the Tree, to mark
the event.

"Thank you for making us your welcome guests in this
world, Serpent-Eve, mother of all living," Granny said.

One by one the clanswomen stepped forward to touch the
strip of leather where it dangled snakelike, and to repeat
Granny's words. With this token, an animal that could die grew
to resemble the eternal spirit of One who could not.

By the time I took my turn honoring the leather lace, however, I could hear Grandfather fussing on the tumble of stone
he had made his seat. He had never drawn near the Tree; this
was a woman's place. Had we been at the cave near the upper
end of the Valley, the men's secret, sacred place, stones under

his bony hips never would have made him so impatient. But here he could not help his unease.

Even little Boaz felt it, and had left the cover of his mother's skirts as the simple rite went on, escaping to his grandfather's side. He convinced his little self, no doubt, that at the next season-move he must be old enough to walk ahead or behind with the men, out of sight of such dreaded magic.

"Come, clanswomen," Yael said then as the rite-power dwindled. "Let's go on to the campsite." Lengthening shadows streaked the afternoon sunlight in the same direction as she pointed. "We'll return to the Tree soon. It's almost the dark of the moon."

Yael was right. The last fingernail paring of an old moon was about to set over the line of peaks across the river, retreating from having to share the blue field of the sky with the more constant sun. A cloud of starlings momentarily shadowed the moon from view. The birds' beaks were still dark for winter, and a dull yellow spangled their green-black plumage. Their busy, noisy cries welcomed us.

These promises—and Grandfather's discomfort—made us pick up our bundles once again and move on.

We left the deer trail now, taking the even steeper way in a direct line from the Tree toward the mountain—and the caves it contained. By the time the moon had vanished, we were halfway between the sacred sites. Here we easily found the rock rings that marked last fall's hearths. Winter rains had sludged the ash, and goatgrass had already grown up between the rocks in stubborn tufts.

In the midst of a thrust with my digging stick to get the worst of the tufts out, I paused. I looked down the Valley, our

Valley, the spring place, where I had been born—no matter
who my mother was—and all my ancestresses before me. Joy
surged from the pit of my stomach to tingle at my shoulders before its beauty. How clear was the air, like ice. How fresh the
water, how painfully green the new spring growth on every
hand.

I whispered the name of this Valley as the beloved might
whisper her lover's name, this place of purity, of changeless-
ness, where the gods dwelt and walked in the cool of the day.

The very name of the place, in our ancient tongue, meant
"delight."

Eden.

Beside me, Eve was also no longer digging. She'd straight-
ened her spine, set it in its seductive curve, and was looking
back down the hill. Of course, even unleafed the Fig attracted
the eye, no matter where one was in Eden. But in Eve's face I
saw again the deep, in-bred fear caused by the sight of her
namesake, the serpent.

Five

We camped where we had always camped, by the scars of our old fires, on the first terrace above the river, near the spring and the water-carved gully. Grandfather took the honor of striking his flint and setting the spark for the new fire to our kindling. When that was done, the clanswomen left him and Boaz there, warming themselves in the sun like dozing lions, amidst our cast-off burdens. We went to perform the next rite that had to be undertaken upon our arrival, even before we prepared the food.

Aunt Afra led the way. We clambered after her, farther on up the hillside, stretching our already weary legs from stone to stone, using the laurel shrubs peculiar to our spring valley as handholds. The laurel berries were as yet unopened spikes of yellow-green, and bruising the leaves released their almond scent to the air.

We arrived at the Great Cave after a climb that left us winded. This was not the men's cave, which was much smaller and farther up. This was a great triangular maw, at least five times the height of a man at its peak, nearly as wide and deep. Here lay most of our ancestors, near the rear of the cave, although a few were at the front, marked by stones and memory.

My mother was here—or rather, Aunt Gurit. I knew the

rock that marked her resting place. I remembered standing
there, suddenly motherless, suddenly the charge of all the clanswomen as I was ever after—which felt like the charge of none.
I remembered the rampant smell of yolk-colored groundsel
and pink and crimson hollyhocks filling my nose as my three-
year-old mind tried to comprehend the "no more" of death. I
stood in the same place now and set a bunch of hyacinths
there, as I had done every year since.

All the other clanswomen had their stones to visit, mop-
ping at misty eyes. Every woman but Eve, that is. Eve sat
barely within the cave's mouth, toying with the brown rabbit
fur covering her lap. Her eyes kept darting away, downhill,
toward where my father must be.

Or toward the Tree.

We sang the dirge for the dead and then the song of memory, with its echoing parts like the voices of the dead singing in
response. Eve knew the words but seemed not as affected as
the rest of us. Perhaps this was due to the newness of the place
to her. The Cave of the Dead had yet to wrap its tendrils
around her heart.

After the songs, every woman had a chance to recall one of
those resting here to our minds with her memory.

When the circle came round to Eve, she looked away and
said, "I don't know anyone."

"You could recall someone from your own spring burial
grounds," I suggested gently.

But she kept looking away and only shook her head.

My clanswomen seemed relieved they didn't have to share
this time with her, but I thought that a mistake. She would
never connect the past, present, and future if she did not take
part.

"Please," I persisted. "You must tell us something. It is tra-
dition."

Eve remained firm, however. She even made sharp gestures of refusal with her hand that seemed like the cut of a
knife, cutting herself off from any past. So the circle skipped
her.

The clanswomen let me go last, knowing my gifted words
would bring some sort of end to the rite. The voice of the Earth
came to me that I must not confine my words to Gurit this
time. The very personal feelings of emptiness and loss that
enveloped me whenever I saw groundsel shedding its corpse-
white seed or spikes of hollyhock jutting against the sky—
these were for another time. I had to say something that would
capture Eve and bind her to this place if she were ever to sit
comfortably within our clan.

Once there was—and once there was not—

When those traditional words left my lips, I knew this was
not going to be the usual memory tale. I was not much closer to
the "ever after" ending before I realized it had very little to do
with the dead at all. This tale did not rest in the traditional cycle of tales. The word of Earth was urging me to tell of my own
conception, here where we thrust the seed of our dearly departed in the Mother's womb to await rebirth. Many, many
walks spent tagging alongside my clanswomen had given me
most of the story as snippets of gossip. Now I would tell it
whole.

A storyteller knows well enough not to turn her back on
the voice of Earth when it comes.

*—A man called Adam, named for the red-brown earth his skin so
resembled.*

How did I dare to speak about my father? I who knew him
so little. And Lilith. I could already see that in order to please
my hearers I would have to make Lilith real to them. I, who
couldn't believe in her myself. Who felt so unlike her, I, who
was said to be her daughter. But tell this I must. Eve must

believe this if she were to live with us. And perhaps the telling
would help fill the void I felt in this place, too.

From the time he was a very small child, Adam sensed himself pe-
culiar. Chosen. Though he himself didn't know yet what it might be, he
knew his was a tale storytellers would rehearse around fires kindled gen-
erations and generations from now. He had, after all, heard how his
blood father had been killed—claimed by the Great Mother and the au-
rochs—before Adam himself was born. Who could say he was not the
spirit of that great man renewed? Perhaps the dead man had requick-
ened his own wife's womb with spirit, spirit thickened in the process as
blood stew thickens over the fire.

From his earliest childhood, Adam was always getting into scrapes
and fighting with other boys. And when he could do none of these things,
he would dream dreams and report them, bragging of every exploit and
forgetting the humility a single man must hold in the face of the greater
good of the clan.

In his nighttime wanderings in the realm of the spirit, Adam would
see how the world had been created new for his sake. In his vision, this
miracle of many faces had taken but six days, from the splitting of the
great original monster of formlessness into sky above and earth below,
to the creation of Adam himself. And he saw every animal given for his
use, those the Mother protects for Herself as well as those She allows to
fall to the arrows of men for their meat.

A great spirit, taking the form of a bull or sometimes a mountain,
told Adam to name all the beasts according to his own names. This
meant the sacred names full of awe and fear and kinship with our species
that the beasts have always had, but which hunters speak in whispers, so
the hunt isn't spoiled by disrespect. Adam felt that some god had given
him leave to speak to the rest of creation as others would only speak to
infants whose bottoms they must still wipe.

This runs against all we have ever known. Our mothers have
taught us that Earth's creatures hold ancient wisdom and the secrets of
eternally renewing life in the movements of their lives' dances. Men,

hunters in particular, do not feel the secret rhythms within their own bodies as women do. That is why men must always listen very carefully, and never show disrespect for sacred names.

"It's only youth's energy and high spirits in the boy," the elders' voices soothed. "Wait until he is made a man. That will settle him."

"If that's the case, the sooner he's made a man, the better," urged some, and wanted Adam to go with the boys to initiation before the first down had appeared on his face.

Fortunately, Grandfather's wisdom and that of the other elders held sway and the tribe put up with the willful youth for another three years until the proper time should come.

And the time came, in the great gathering of winter, as it always has. Without flinching, Adam suffered the new-chipped blades that carved his boyhood shape into that of a man. The boyhood basket caught his severed foreskin and blood. The healing poultice of leaves, which he had shed like serpent skin, went in there, too. Along with the blood and boyhood of the rest of his age group, the elders sealed these things with mud and left them to molder new life — "seed and sons," as the saying is.

Adam suffered the whips and the fasting, the all-night vigils, dancing and singing to the point of pain, that prepare a man to shoulder the charge of an adult. All of this Adam took well. Better, the elders said among themselves, than most. So they held great hopes for Adam's manhood.

All that remained of the initiation was the fearsome Time Alone, those three days and nights when, without food and water, an infant man must sit in the loneness of the unborn, to hear nothing but his inner self. He must give himself up to be tormented by demons or blessed by spirits as that self may be — and come to terms with what he finds there, with which he must live for the rest of his life.

"These are not things of which women may speak freely," I admitted to my hearers, "having our own initiation. But who can hold her tongue when it comes to Adam's Time Alone? It has had effect — and continues to have effect — on all of our lives."

Rather than provide unity, the Time seemed to shoot back at him, like an ill-strung bow in a child's hand before he has learned which fingers to loosen first.

The world was created in six days. The Bull of Heaven rested his harrowing horns on the seventh. And set Adam in the world with no other purpose than to tend the place. And to subdue it. Rather than, in the end, to learn submission to the Great Mother's cycle.

This was Adam's man vision.

Which would have been one thing, and no others hurt. Except that he began to try to get the rest of the newly initiated to forget what they themselves had learned in their own Time Alone. He began to gather hearers about him. First he spoke to those young men whom, by accident of birth, fate had decreed always to be close to him, in the same age group. But his words soon attracted others, both older and younger than he. He began to preach (a word our tongue had never known till then and which comes from words meaning "to Adam-speak"). And with this Adam-speak he began to lure many men to a new vision of the world. They turned a deaf ear both to the words of their elders—and to the wisdom of the beasts, whom he taught others to rename, as well. And some Adam-spoke with their fists.

But there is more. More than the sons of men, Adam began to entice their daughters. His was a man's body now, with a man's needs, but still with the spirit of a willful boy, the spirit even the cuts and blows of initiation had been unable to purge from him. His wild ways, if not his words, drew the tribal daughters to him like moths dancing among the fire's sparks. And many were they whose wings were singed. Take note, those of us who live today.

I let my storyteller's glaze break for a moment to look pointedly at Eve. But her attention was elsewhere.

"Yet would he marry this one?" I said. "Would he marry that one? He made no answer to the young women's troubled fathers. One was not enough for him; all not too good for a man breathed upon by the gods."

Eve was looking not at me as the rest of the clanswomen were, but out the cave entrance, down the hillside slope, and into the late afternoon sunshine where it hit spring green with an almost painful glare.

So I gave up and forgot Eve, submitting, as a teller must, to the tale.

"And then," I said briefly, "Mother Lilith came."

I said the name; I shivered. I felt the tilt of the earth gone out of balance beneath me. I felt the Tree's wisdom creeping up the hill and into my voice again. And I tried, with the magic of my voice alone, to bring Lilith similarly into view for my hearers. They would want to know what she looked like, how she wore her hair, her snakeskins. But now I found I couldn't imagine these things. I, who felt so acutely the lack of a mother, could not set any human traits into that void as I drew near to it.

So it was no mortal woman, this I conjured, but something rolling on a dust cloud with the wind. I met Grandmother's eyes, and those of other, older clanswomen, caught in webs of memory. Women who had been there, who had seen my mother. Those eyes told me I had her image right, in all her divine void.

I went on.

With Lilith magic, our Mother had sensed disruption in the world's balance. And so she came. On vulture wings.

"Sons," she called to the men of our gathered clans, "my sons." In the voice of the turtledove, the voice of the winter blast. And her beauty, as she stood before them, was the beauty of the quiet dawn, the beauty of thunder's roll.

"A contest I present to you," she said, "a divine match of human strength. And the first of you, my sons, to reach me shall gain secret knowledge of the Mother of you all, and a child of my body to claim as his own."

The moon hung full-bellied in the sky. The wolves on the Mother's plain howled in recognition, like women come to their time.

And in the winter shelters of our people, the men echoed the howls, until they could no longer resist her, Mother Lilith. Out of the shelters she drew them, howling. Young men, old men, fathers of many sons, it mattered not. Even men who at the last full of the moon had taken new brides, these wives who even now stretched out the winter hides toward them, even these men Mother Lilith's call drew out and up.

I stopped again for breath and Rachel offered me a drink of water. I looked over the hair-tufted waterskin at the older women, and they all nodded: "Yes, it happened exactly as you tell it." The younger ones believed the wisdom of their elders. Only I, who saw the loose reed ends buried in the back of the work, found the whole still difficult to fathom.

And Eve.

Eve, who could not, or would not, meet my eyes, but looked out the great lighted triangle of the Cave of the Dead to the still-bare-branched trees with the season's first flowers at their feet. It was as if, by clinging to those open-air sights, she sought desperately to draw a line between what was real and what was not. And my words she committed to unreality.

Her disbelief urged me forward, convinced me of my own worth by her very resistance.

Up, out of camp the howling beasts of men came, slipping over the rocks, their skins sesame-oiled by the moonlit night. Each ran as fast as he could and, beastlike, clawed even the full-blood brother who chanced to get in his way.

"Mother Lilith. Mother Lilith," throbbed the drum of each man's heart. Even when he fell behind, a man did not, could not, give up the chase. He bounded on, baying, like a dog after his bitch.

Handfuls of dogs there were. And but a single bitch.

And Adam, alone, ran out in front.

There was the night. The cold. The dark. There was the rocky way.

But yet more obstacles Lilith planted than nature would have had it. Boulders. Fallen trees. Demon shadows not to be pierced, turning the bowels to water. Yet more trials to prove her man.

The moon set, but fire lit the way, an unquenchable fire before which many quailed. Still Adam ran on, through a stream cold-crusted with ice. The ice gave at every step, yet in he plunged, up to the knee. His winter leggings and foot bindings stiffened with the cold and weighted with the wet, but still he did not falter.

For Earth had gifted him like no other. If there was a prize to win, he'd be the man to win it.

Now came the test of the realm of plants. A briar, its thorns winter-stripped of leaves, unsheathed, gnawed hungrily through water-weakened leather. It left his skin crusted with laces of blood. But his heart remained undaunted.

Finally came the fiercest test of all. Adam came to it in the half-light of dawn, when night's shadows seemed most malicious. Now Lilith strewed the way with terrifying forms. The carcasses of a lion—could it be?—a heifer, of a she-goat and a ram; she had split them down the middle. A man, his heart thumping, had to pass between a canopy of the skyward-yearning ribs to reach her. And in the midst of this tunnel rilled the spilled intestines, as well as the bodies of turtledoves and voles and rabbits, death-rigid, unparted but their necks broken.

On hands and knees, the man crawled down this space, gore assaulting his nostrils, as in first light vultures descended to this meal. The dreaded birds settled with a rustle of wings, those grim-eyed, death's-head creatures that are Lilith's best companions, twisting life and death together in confusion along with her snakes.

Her snakes—Adam could not tell, in that light, whether he crawled through curled tubes of she-goat belly. Or fire-fanged vipers.

Now between the arched frame of carcasses passed what seemed a blazing torch. And climbing, choking smoke, stoked like green wood. But Adam waved his arms against the vultures and held his breath against the smoke and plunged ahead.

If there was a prize, he must win it. The gods favored him above all others.

The passage closed about him, pulsing, as does a woman's passage in the throes of love. And there crouched Lilith, naked. Howling. In a cave. A cave, like this one here, that made her howls assault the ear from twenty ways at once.

Against all others Lilith shut the cave. Against all but the victor Adam.

And so pride won him the prize.

And Lilith performed her own initiation on him.

Mother Lilith fell on him, devoured his novice manhood in the power and wisdom of her unnumbered years. For five full days the earth shut them up so, Adam fasting the initiate's fast and forced to feed Lilith's woman-greed without rest both day and night.

No flinch crossed the older women's faces. Even when I said such things as these, they knew them to be true. The younger women, new wives, they flinched. But they didn't disbelieve.

As the full moon passed, five days and nights later, the bones of the carcasses lay all picked clean and the vulture magic drew off to circle elsewhere. Another day passed, during which Adam had to mend, the divine having likewise eaten his mortal strength.

Frenzied heartbeat had hammered new, cold, echoing spaces in his chest. His mind was fogged and infantile. Long lances of crippling stiffness shot down the muscles of his legs from buttocks to toes, result of love's unnatural rigor. And all within his loins was such a weakness, they seemed a reed mat well worn, the edges turning to dust.

Soon, plied by Lilith's restoring food, Adam could walk again and the couple returned to mortal life. The monster was subdued, brought back tamely on a cord as any young goat may be when a man has killed its mother and hopes to raise the offspring to eating size among the clans' fires —and to delight his children.

But who was the monster tamed? Lilith, within whose divine belly now grew a mortal child? Or Adam, who allowed the bonds of marriage to settle firmly on his shoulders?

Adam was a man, born, so he thought, to be different from all others. So he had won Lilith for his wife. There were tales of this happening in times past, when the tribe was curled-fern new, but never within human memory. Now that she, the Mother of us all, was here and loaded with a child—his child—the unnatural glow about his life must surely brighten.

For nine months, Mother Lilith lived with us, lived as any mortal woman, following our seasons and our times. For nine months, and the one month of birth's holiness, she carried, bore, and nursed the child.

But when the holiness was over, and the child presented to the clan as is the custom, Lilith spoke anew.

As if divinity had been weighted with the mortal all those months, it now shook itself free.

"My time with you has been a blessing," said the Mother of us all, "but the world teems with other children among whom unbalance threatens, whom I equally long to bless. Much as I would like, I cannot spend more time with you."

Besides, rumor ran, Lilith would no longer allow Adam to know her as a husband knows his wife. Adam had to learn that if he wanted superhuman favor, superhuman demands would be made upon him.

"In the Name of Mother Earth," Lilith said. "I give the child, whom you call Na'amah, into the hands of Adam's sister Gurit, to comfort her somewhat for the recent loss of her own son. And to you all, I leave my blessing."

When asked where she would go, Lilith replied, "To the Red Sea." But a place with such a name was beyond the ken of any tribesman.

Beyond the ken of kinsmen, but not totally beyond my ken, I thought. This was not the first time that speaking those words along with the name Lilith had evoked a place where barren, leather-colored hills met turquoise water. My insides shifted as the turquoise swarmed with jewel-colored fishes, forming, it seemed, a necklace tight about my neck.

But I spoke none of this to my clanswomen.

What did Lilith do in such a place? "No doubt she went there to birth other children, 'a hundred a day,' as the saying is." Other children. More important than I. Mentally, I broke that necklace of fishes from my throat and tossed it away. "Never have we of Eden seen her since."

And Gurit died and was gathered to her mothers and lies buried here before us in this cave as a witness to the truth of these things of which I've spoken. Such is the power and wisdom of Lilith that no clansman has heard a word of Adam-speak since the days of her coming.

My father had never spoken to me of these events—nor of his bull of heaven. And the nods of my clanswomen told me they hadn't been bothered by his preaching, either. The loss of their menfolk for a single full-moon long, long ago seemed an easy bargain in return. And I found my words had somehow convinced me, their maker, as well. For something out of the ordinary must have actually appeared and made a deep, physical impression to turn my father's course. The thing that had given him fifteen years of humility was more than just a storyteller's image. It was more than could be contained in my awkward and struggling mortality.

But Eve turned to look at me now for the first time, telling me with her eyes that I deluded myself. *She* had heard Adam-speak. My father's fights with other men at the end of winter meant he was finding his tongue again.

No stone stood in the cave as solid witness of Lilith's existence once among us. I was the only testimony of her visit. And I felt hopelessly meager for the task.

"Such is the history of Adam." I firmly drew the conclusion against Eve's hopes—and my doubts. "And why he must not take another wife. For the jealousy of a mortal woman who leaves her husband with their children while she embraces death is one thing. But it is as nothing compared with the jealousy of Lilith toward the mortal she takes in marriage."

I saw satisfaction gloss the eyes of my hearers as after an abundant feast. So I brought my story to its traditional close:

Such is the tale. And within it are contained three apples, one for you, one for me, and one for the story's magic. May each catch in her lap the meaning best for her.

What meaning did Eve catch? I wondered.

Six

The songs sung, the stories told, there remained one more rite to fulfill at that season in the Cave of the Dead. Aunt Afra led us to the rear of the cave where the lowering spring sun barely reached. Here were three more gray stones, like gravestones, only closer together. The stones were slabs, easily moved by two women working together.

In everyday terms, I knew what those slabs concealed. I'd helped to dig one of the covered pits myself, using my fire-hardened digging stick to the depth of my mid-thigh. I'd hauled up some of the fine clay from the river with which to line the pit. I'd watched the fire laid in the smoothed container, helped to rake out the coals when the fire burned out and the clay was baked hard.

But the spirit of the place, that spirit prickling over us all now, is more difficult to describe. It bated our breath, chilled our spines where the sweat of our climb was drying. I can only say in everyday terms what Aunt Afra did there, not hope to match the effect her actions had.

"Remove the center stone," Aunt Afra told Yael and Devorah.

They did, and revealed the pit filled with dull brown kernels of wheat. The clanswomen had gathered and stored the grain there at the end of last spring's stay in Eden. Aunt Afra murmured ancient, secret words of praise, then brought forth a basket, daubed with mud mixed with bitumen and fired, that we kept near the storage pits from year to year. This daubed basket was round, with a narrow neck.

Afra's words taught us in the way of ancient lore, by saying, but not saying, which always makes a deeper impression than telling a thing outright. In this manner she taught us that this basket was the shape of our own inner womanhood, if we were to cut it from ourselves. We had all seen that part in butchered animals, sometimes full of tiny, pale young, in which case the Mother required a special offering for their killing.

Into this womb made of the reeds and clay of Mother Earth, Afra gestured for each woman to drop a handful of grain scooped from the storage pit. We did, feeling the cool kernels, seemingly lifeless as only so many small pebbles. Yet they hinted, in their fragrance, at life—like mold beneath the Tree.

Afra spoke words evoking bolts of lightning, the plummet of rain, the embrace of men, as she poured water from a skin into the vessel's narrow neck to cover. Then she swaddled the neck with a dampened scrap of hide. The vessel was too heavy now to return to its shelf of rock. We left it in the dark corner.

"Now we wait," she concluded, "for Mother to work Her magic, as each daughter can work her own bit of life magic with time and the Mother's blessing."

By the time my clanswomen and I made our way down to Grandfather and the camp once more, our men were straggling in, one by one or in small groups.

My uncles Ari and Dov had killed a porcupine and carried

it between them on a pole. They laughed as they worked their way through the spines to the pink flesh and soft, warm organs. Their wives each claimed half of the quills, which would make graceful necklaces and dangles to their favorite baskets. Ari and Dov cut strips of meat at once and threaded them onto thin green sticks of wood. They burned the first strips almost black in hungry haste.

Other men had caught smaller things, rabbits, birds. The game in the Valley had forgotten what the scent of man meant and there would be plenty to eat that night.

By their men's sides, the women started their own work on the garnishing vegetables and herbs. The sweet smells of chives and asparagus rose on the clean spring air along with the contented babble of conversation.

Last of all my father came. I felt the darkness, the tension, his presence always brought. I felt it settle on my shoulders before I actually saw him. Then I saw him in places the sun had already deserted below. He took the rise at a lope, a pace he'd plainly kept up for some distance.

"He thinks he's the only man in the world," I remembered Aunt Rachel saying, and the memory made me shake off the tension and greet him with a wider smile than usual. I tried new eyes on him, storyteller eyes. Or eyes such as Eve might blink at him over the crackling flames. I didn't see that he noticed. In fact, he didn't look at me at all.

Ari and Dov made a place for their brother between them and Adam dropped at once to his haunches. From the distance he had covered, the muscles of his thighs quivered visibly beneath dark hair and skin. Dov handed him the new-grilled stick of porcupine flesh and my father took it. But I noticed he ate thoughtlessly, neither tasting the food nor honoring his brothers on their success.

Adam was a thick man, especially about the shoulders and chest, covered by a dark pelt of his own hair. He was tall, too. Tall enough to tuck a little thing like Eve cozily up against his ribs.

He was no longer young—how could I think so when he was my father?—but he hadn't yet seen forty winters and the worst blow the years seemed to have dealt him was the loss of his left dog tooth in a hunting accident. The gap showed in a rather endearing way—like a boy missing a milk tooth. All his other teeth were sound and straight. I saw that well when he smiled, when he bit the blackened porcupine tasting of smoke and green wood carefully on the right side of his mouth, and the juices ran.

His hair was still thick, but curling back from a forehead higher than it had been when I was a child. The last of the sunset caught in the tangle of his hair and beard, emphasizing the reddish highlights there and concealing the first few strands of gray.

Adam had said nothing since his arrival—not even a "thank you" to his brother Dov—but he kept smiling quick, quiet little smiles to himself. Some of these shy stretchings of lips and moustache seemed to be directed at me, so I returned them. But then a weight against my right shoulder reminded me Eve was at my side.

"All right, come on now, Adam," Dov kidded. "I can tell. You've got something to tell us."

My father smiled but said nothing. Eve shifted on my shoulder.

"Yes, what kept you so long?" Ari asked.

"You bagged nothing."

"But—"

"But?"

"What did you find in the Valley, brother?"

"Nothing." Adam shrugged, and gnawed his meat.

"Don't tell me you found nothing," Dov said. "I know that look of yours."

"Well, maybe. Maybe something. A very little something."

Ari's and Dov's eyes met over their brother's shoulders and caught orange from the fire. They knew it was something, all right. Something big.

Ari and Dov began to pound Adam on either side, shouting, "Tell, tell. We'll beat it from you."

Adam fended them off with his fists and empty cooking stick, laughing. The trio rolled back from the fire like puppies. Devorah slipped swiftly behind them to move her baby—whom she'd set to sleep in a furry bundle—out of harm's way. The rest of the men and some of the women chose sides and shouted their encouragement. From my right shoulder I heard a quiet "Adam." Then, as he took a blow, another "Adam," pitched higher but no louder, with concern.

Outnumbered two to one, my father soon gave in, laughing. "Let me up. Let me up, you two wolf cubs. I'll tell. I'll tell you. Just let me up."

The three men scrambled back to their places by the fire. Dov dabbed at a cut on the cheek he'd received dangerously close to the eye. Red blood and black soot from Adam's cooking stick came off on his fingers. Aunt Yael tried to spit on the wound for her husband, but he waved her away.

"I found . . ." Adam said, pausing to make sure everyone was listening. He had the entire clan. "I found a pile of dung."

"A pile of dung?" Dov burst out. "Is that all?"

"You're a pile of dung, Adam," Ari said, and took to roasting more porcupine. "You looked in a pool of water and saw yourself."

"Show it to me," Dov said, "and I'll rub it in your hair for you."

"Ah, but this is no ordinary dung."

"Dung is dung," said Dov. "You can't eat dung."

"No," Adam agreed slowly.

"If your dung is so fancy I'll make you eat it," Ari said, catching spattering hot porcupine between his own strong white teeth.

"It is large, flat pats. I think," Adam said with another pause during which he took a look at Eve, then shifted to his father. "I think it's aurochs dung."

"Aurochs? Aurochs!" The word circled the fire like the hiss of hot sap and the pop of sparks, never mind that the beasts might hear their given names and be frightened off.

"Yes, I think it is aurochs," Adam repeated, high on the wave of the word's effect. "Father, I'd like you to come and take a look, tell me for certain."

Even Grandfather had been roused from his doze with the word "aurochs." He pulled the dark, worn robe closer about him and blinked his rheumy eyes against the heat of the fire. Or perhaps against tears.

"I can't go stalking on these legs of mine," he said sadly. "The horned one took his due of me many years ago." The name he chose to give the beast held more respect, more prudence, than Adam's "aurochs." The old man tenderly rubbed the thigh that held the memory scar.

"I'll carry you to the place," Adam insisted, "on my back all the way."

"I won't be carried like an infant," Grandfather snapped.

"But you have to see the spoor, Father. I must have your judgment. Is it the aurochs for certain? What does this mean? Have the aurochs come back to our hills after all these years?

Do the spirits favor us once more? And if so, then I must hear your opinion how best to follow him."

"I'll come with you," Ari said.

"We have to see this dung." Dov's words stumbled on top of his brother's.

"We'll carry Father—"

"Not like a child, but between us."

"Then we'll help you with the tracking, Adam."

"The aurochs is mine," Adam stated.

"We'll hunt him together."

"You can't hunt the horned one on your own."

"They're very dangerous beasts, even with arrows."

"The aurochs is mine," Adam repeated, fiercely. And the offhand way he said the beast's name seemed to confirm the point. "Mine, do you hear?"

Everyone did hear and fell silent. My father's dark eyes caught Eve like a spear shot over the fire and I felt her make hardly a struggle to avoid the shot.

"Father? You'll come?" Only Adam dared break the silence he'd clamped on the clan.

"It's too late to go tonight, son," Grandfather replied.

"There's still light," Adam pressed.

"Twilight. It's clear to me you've come a long way since finding this spoor and my old eyes can't track in twilight. And it's the end of the old moon. No one can track by an old moon, once the twilight's gone."

"We could take tinder," Adam said as hopefully as a small lad. "We could hunt by torchlight."

"And scare the beasts away? No, son. Tomorrow is soon enough. Rest tonight and tomorrow—tomorrow we'll see how these old bones of mine feel."

Adam nodded and shrugged his obedience. It was the only

reasonable thing, after all. He helped himself to more meat and scraped the last of the asparagus out of the cooking skin Yael handed him. For tonight he must content himself with such gestures, with the looks all the clan turned on him.

But tomorrow—I read it in his eyes—tomorrow he would force the looks to even more wonder.

Seven

"Tell the tale of the great horned one, Mother," Uncle Ari said.

Boaz had been prodding his father to make this request almost since Adam had first said the word "aurochs" that evening. And the boy, finding himself ignored as the men debated the more vital issues of the dung's existence and meaning, had crept to my ear more than once to beg the tale from me. The child's claim flattered me. It unnerved me as well because it proved that my storytelling had come to rank over Granny's in the sweep of his short life. I didn't feel ready for the burden.

"Hush," I'd said, and, "In a little bit." I had not wanted to miss a word my father addressed to anyone else even when he wouldn't speak to me.

But now the request had come from Ari.

"Yes, Granny, please," Boaz echoed, his eyes bright with firelight and the fight against sleep on such an exciting night.

Granny's "Let Na'amah tell it" saddened me. This was not my story. Granny appeared as a character in it herself, as a young woman. But at the word "aurochs," our crone's mind seemed to have wandered back into that time completely, and couldn't bring anything back up to the present for all the clan to enjoy.

Tales of the hunt made me cower—especially in front of men, who knew the magic. But the telling of the tale was my magic, and I had to learn that I bound even the greatest hunter by it. I began:

In the high and far-off time, in the winter season when the breath came off Hiddekel, Mother River, to mate with Father Sky's rain, once there was—and once there was not—a herd of aurochs.

Storytellers are allowed use of an animal's magic name, because the power of our craft can contain them. Yet I spoke the word carefully, aware of binding the power to me.

They came down to the plains where the entire tribe was camped. A mass of red-brown and black they were, those huge, fierce cattle, stretching as far as the eye could see on the opposite bank of the river. The herd appeared through the mist like the dark underbelly of storm clouds, yet shot with the tawny colors of the choking dry winds that come from the southern desert. The clans could hear the thunder of the beasts' hooves even over the sound of the river. The creatures came down—bulls and cows with new calves at their udders, skittish yearlings with tiny horns itching for use, and shy, young heifers—all came to drink at Mother River.

And all the tribe stopped whatever they were doing to watch, for such a sight had not been seen in recent memory. The elders told of a time when the aurochs had been common, when rather than following the seasons, the clans had followed the herds, and the herds undertook the spring and fall moves before us. In autumn, on the downward track, there had been beasts enough to stampede through the drainages with torches and yelling. The entire tribe had once helped in these drives and the elders still pointed out the cliffs where, just above Mother River, the foothills wedged their heads against the sky. The cliffs over which the tribe once drove the aurochs to their deaths.

At the foot of these cliffs had come the butchering for winter stores, the meadows strung with drying racks, all the tribeswomen laughing and singing together at their work and the promise of full stomachs throughout the season.

The day this certain herd came, only the elders remembered such times of plenty from their childhoods. The autumn drives no longer happened. The clans moved, whether cattle showed them the way or not. And there were children who had never seen an aurochs at all.

"Like us," Boaz broke in, joined now by his cousin Kocha-vah.

Like most of us living now, I thought.

"Tell us of the aurochs," Kochavah and Boaz then chirped together. "I mean, the horned ones." Cuffs from their parents made them mend their plea.

"'Tell us of the aurochs,'" I had the children in those long-gone days beg, even as they looked across the river and saw the great herd with their own eyes.

"Hush," the elders said. "You must not speak an animal's name in its hearing. You must call him 'horned one' or 'black four-legs.'"

But having given this warning, the elders obliged the children, and in guarded tones told of the ferocity of the beasts. Of the black bulls that stood higher than a man at the shoulder, longer than two men together. Of the savory flesh, of the strong, huge hides. Of the tails excellent for fly whisks and the balls like the plump gathering sacks on women's backs. The hooves made excellent rattles, the bones decorations for clothes or, boiled down, they rendered a glue for hafting spear points and arrowheads.

But the greatest of all the aurochs's goods were the horns. Any men's sacred place displayed skulls adorned with great horns, or it had no claim to sacredness. The largest man could not reach the span of those knife-sharp points with his wide-stretched hands. And a bull could gut him with a shake of his great head.

The man who braved such death gained more than all the solid wealth a bull represented. The man who single-handedly killed an aurochs bull gained the power of life so ample, he could ease the jealousy of a first wife. Whether she was alive or dead, he could take a second. Then, no matter how many children already clustered around his fire, he could get more.

The present power of my words echoed in my heart. He could get more. *Adam* could get more. Children other than me.

I looked up from my tale now to see the same wide, fire-awed eyes that must have been turned on storytellers in Grandfather's youth. I felt a momentary shiver at the eternity of this gift I carried.

I saw Grandfather's hand stroke his aurochs hide in deep thought, almost greed. After all these years, the hide, though thinned till I could see through it in places, still held the beast's power to thicken and strengthen an old man's bony fingers. But without my words, its power lay asleep.

Then I shifted my gaze to my father's face. He wouldn't meet my eye. His lips narrowed as if to conceal their nakedness between beard and moustache. And, at my side, Eve lowered her eyes from the sight.

Eve's clan had its tales of the aurochs, I knew, and brave slayers of the beasts of their own. But she was not in a mood to find our heroes wanting in any way.

That day the great herd came to the Winter Gathering, it had been years since the beasts had been seen in such numbers. The men with second wives could be counted on one hand, and in the secret places, the men merely dusted off and repainted old horns year by year. No new trophies came to refit the displays.

The aurochs were dying. Either dying or moving off as the winters warmed and the scrub oak and pistachio crept in upon their traditional grasslands.

And without aurochs flesh to soothe it, the jealousy of wives grew. The willingness of mothers to expose their daughters at birth grew, as well, for fear that, without aurochs, many would find no husbands when they were grown. Better to let the little girls be reborn at another time.

When the gods saw fit to bring back the aurochs in numbers high
enough so men could, if need be, take second wives.

And then—then the herd had come.

An owl hooted. Bats, newly wakened from their winter's
sleep, hunted out of our caves. A rabbit screamed as he met his
fate in the jaws of a fox or wolf. All creation, so it seemed,
waited for the story's next verse. I looked toward Grandfather
but found no voice of Mother Earth in his shriveled from. I
looked away to the void of night and only then was able to see
the story's young hero in my mind's eye.

He was already married at the time, young Shimshon, and the father of two young sons, but unmarked by the spirits in other ways. The
moment he saw the herd slipping through the mist that morning, he blew
up a goatskin to cross the river after them.

Two score and two of the tribesmen also pulled themselves up on the
westward side of the Mother, wet as infants newborn from Her womb.
The herd had broken the reeds on this bank, trampled some beyond
recognition. The mud held the beasts' countless prints like the face of the
pox-cursed man. The mud held their smell, as well, the smell of their
urine, sitting in glowing pools. The sweet, grassy smell of fresh, trampled dung.

During the tribesmen's swim, the herd had shifted itself off, westward again, up a still-dry wash to higher ground. The men flattened the
sharp, deep hoofprints with the balls of their own feet in their winter
wrappings. The ground was open here, offering greater vistas than in
any season save summer on the mountain peaks, and the men set off after their prey at the easy, steady hunter's lope.

Before the men, and to the right hand, north and east, fallen snow
was already making the mountains one with the clouds. The peaks un-
coiled with the rising light, weak with the season and the threatening
sky. Flocks of ducks spearheaded across in sharp contrast. The ground
the men took continued to rise, slightly but steadily, into new grass
greening under the summer-blasted stubble—perfect aurochs fodder.

The herd had grazed, but not long. Nor had they stopped to chew their cud.

The men's steady breath steamed like masks in front of their faces.

"They head west now," one of the men in the lead called out.

"West?" echoed his neighbor. "Do you think —"

"They head toward the land between the four rivers?"

"Certainly so."

"Great Mother whispers to them that they are being hunted, that they will find refuge between the rivers," panted one, slacking his pace as if already defeated. For, as everyone knows, the land where the four streams spread like the Great Mother's Hand smoothing the hide of the land — this place is sacred to Her and may not be hunted in any season, even for hunger. The land there is often low, marsh or meadow, perfect for the raising of young of all kinds, fowl and beast, and men may not step there, on pain of death.

"Maybe we can turn them before they reach Mother Hand," cried a man who had a good view from a rise blue-white with slumbering thistle. "If we speed up. Our great four-footed brothers don't know they are pursued yet. They move slowly."

"If Mother calls to them, we'll waste our efforts. No man can thwart Her will."

"But it may be Her will to let us overtake and turn them."

"Yes," agreed a third. "Mother wouldn't taunt us, Her children, with the sight of such a herd when we haven't seen one in so long."

"When so much depends on them," agreed more than one widower.

So ten of the swiftest, among them Shimshon, broke out of the group to circle the herd and turn it if they could.

The wind blew in snow-chilled gusts off the mountain peaks. The clouds overhead folded in on themselves like cowrie shells, green-white like the petals of spring lilies. Water- and wind-whittled nests of rock infested the ground now. The herd moved faster over such poor land, nothing luring them to pause and browse. Shimshon in the forefront panted his way up the final rise.

They're here! he gestured to his companions, his breath too far gone for speech, the herd too close.

The herd, the thunder of their countless hooves, the fire of their combined breaths, were, indeed, just there. He could feel their heat.

But the Mother's first Finger was also there. The lead cattle had already lumbered their way across to refuge as if warned by an omen.

Without a backward glance, Shimshon and two of his companions got their second wind and set off down the slope. The spirits in command of the air were for them, blowing the breath back into their faces and filling it with the overwhelming sounds and odors of damp cattle. Still, the Mother drew her beasts on, as if the winds blew hostile instead.

The hunter's song, calling his quarry to him, throbbed in Shimshon's mind, hand in hand with the splitting of his lungs. But he began to hear the Mother's song louder than his own, louder than his could have been, even if he'd had breath to sing aloud. He began to realize they couldn't reach the herd in time to turn a single one. Even now, the path through the Mother's Finger was the direction all the beasts would jump when fear hit them.

Shimshon heard his companions' pace slacken, too, and he didn't know whether it was his heart or his lungs that were about to burst. But then he saw that the man to his left, Caleb of the strong right arm, had stopped running only in order to slip an arrow out of his quiver and fit it to his bow. Now, this Caleb put more power behind his pull than any other in the tribe. And he knew, besides, a magic in his arrow-making that called the flight of the birds to the ends of his shafts most wonderfully.

Shimshon saw the prayer of flight twitch Caleb's lips and repeated it himself. Caleb pulled, then held his breath so jagged panting wouldn't jar his arm. Shimshon held his breath, too, in fellow feeling.

The bolt sailed true. A young bull calf crumpled down on his haunches and bawled in pain. His coat was the beautiful russet of aurochs young, without any white markings as yet. Like children in every clan, he had refused to hear the Mother's call. He lingered on the shore outside her refuge to charge at a tussock of dried grass with his little buds of horn.

At first, when he saw the result of Caleb's work, black wrapped Shimshon's heart. Why go for so young an animal when there were larger beasts —even bulls —still on this side of the River of Refuge? But then the blackness lifted as he realized that even Caleb could not have been sure of his shot at such a distance.

The slayer of so young a beast could not claim the honor of a bull. Nonetheless, this hit not only brought up the calf, but his bawls soon brought the anxious cow to her son's side. Until that moment, she'd been intent on the Finger crossing, already having reached a pebbly center shoal and so safety. She'd probably been relieved that her son had found something else to tease and run at, something besides her long-suffering self —until she heard his cries.

The rest of the cattle bolted to a stampede and the Great Mother took them up into Her grasp. But shortly Caleb sent another arrow into the cow, and Shimshon's second companion, his brother-through-marriage Eben, followed with a bolt that killed her through her wild, rolling eye. So by Caleb's cleverness, the hunters had two carcasses where any other move could not have assured them of even one.

Of course, none of these arrows brought the almost magical honor of a bull, but here was good meat for the whole tribe: aurochs flesh, succulence few had tasted. Beyond that, these were the beasts the Mother had brought to their hands.

A look at my father halted the storytelling energy in a breathless pause. The power spoke through me: "Much as every man dreams of joining the realms of myth, the ancestors rarely grant it. With the dwindling of the aurochs herds, the granting is even more rare than before."

Then I looked away from Adam and the story picked up again:

The three hunters loped up to finish off their work with their chipped chert knives on the Finger bank.

The cow's knees had folded under the weight of death so she lay as one in prayer. The foam pink with blood smeared the black-brown fur where tender muzzle skin joined her face. A final gasp for breath had left her mouth open, her teeth set in a grimace. Her unharmed eye had rolled back in her head so mostly white showed.

The calf still lived and struggled on his good forelegs, bawling. But it was a simple matter for Caleb to recite the prayer for taking life to send the little spirit off—willing it to return again soon in another body—and then slice the big vein in his neck. Blood cascaded and festooned the leather-yellow soil like dense carnelian beadwork. The little fellow's hooves pawed twice, three more times, his eyes went tallowy. Shimshon thought he actually saw, out of the corner of his eye, the shadow of life break the terrible lure of earth and rise skyward.

And then a scream pierced Shimshon's ears. When he turned to look at the shadow straight on, he saw no shadow at all: both scream and rising form were Caleb's. The three men had been too occupied with their dead aurochs. They had assumed all the rest of the herd were in the Mother's Hand. But they were wrong.

Unseen and unheard over the sounds of the retreating animals, a great black bull had answered the woe of his wife and child and turned back. Caught neatly under the rib on the great horn, Caleb rose. He of the strong right arm probably never knew what hit him. He was dead when the bull threw him down like no more than a tuft of chaff and wiped him off his horn with a hoof almost as big as a man's head.

Shimshon hardly felt himself a hero now. He stood up from the carcass of the cow, groping to replace his knife with his cast-off spear in his right hand. But even armed, he felt naked and helpless. He felt, in fact, as if life were already ebbing from him as Caleb's was. Even when he stood, the bull had several hands on him at the shoulder hump. And heavy bone, Shimshon knew, braced that hump to provide a sturdy lashing for the knots of muscle that could hit a man like a rock face—especially if that rock face had the feet to get up a good gallop behind it.

Worse, the bull's muzzle was close enough for Shimshon to see its gleam of moisture, feel the heat of its offended snorts. Only three body lengths—Caleb's, the calf's, and the cow's—separated Shimshon from the horns, and those bodies were crumpled very close together, almost as a single form. More space separated the tip of one horn from the other.

The pierced-gut odor of Caleb's deep red wound overwhelmed Shimshon with nausea. Mingled with the fumes of the bull's vigor, it was the smell of his own death. Shimshon shivered, feeling the clammy weight of his leather clothes, and thought his own flesh would soon be much the same.

Then he spared thought for Eben, Eben who had been at the cow's hindquarters, down closer to the river just at Shimshon's right. Eben had also gotten to his feet. Shimshon couldn't free his eyes from the hold of the bull's small, fierce round ones, but he saw Eben raise his near arm in a gesture. Whether he meant that they should try to make a run for it up from the river, to divert the bull, or something else, Shimshon never knew.

The bull's obsidian-spearpoint ears flattened against his head, the muscles over his great humped shoulder bunched. He tore dust and grass up with his left forefoot. Then all four feet left the earth at once; the animal charged straight over the corpses.

Shimshon must have spun in his attempt to get out of the way. The horn caught him inside the left thigh and opened the flesh from knee to groin.

Shimshon crumpled with pain, and a faint gray narrowed his vision to the smallest of awl bores. But somehow he saw—or felt, perhaps—how the great head turned from him to Eben with no more effort than a girl tosses the hair from her eyes.

Eben hadn't been able to recover his spear; he'd thrust it into the ground near the cow's head when they'd thought only tidy butchering lay before them. He had nothing to hand except his knife, but he did have the extra half a heartbeat of Shimshon's goring in which to position himself. Refusing the reflex to run, he used the time to move into the bull and, instead of cowering, reached up, up, to sink the chert blade to the hilt between the beast's shoulders.

Shimshon winced at a glimpse of his own leg — and with the knowledge that Eben's hand's length of bone-hafted stone would go nowhere near anything vital in such a beast. Indeed, it didn't. It only maddened the bull; he bellowed and leaped against the pain. Shimshon thought that surely anything within a body's length of that fury would be rent to leathern fringe.

But Eben stuck close. He stuck so close, he was within the circle of the horns' squeeze. He stayed there, and kept from being knocked under the knife-sharp hooves by clinging to the curls on the beast's forelock and shoulder. As Shimshon watched in a stupor of wonder, Eben even managed to swing one leg up and over, tucking it firmly under the bull's dewlap. With that hug freeing a hand, he caught up his knife and stabbed again and again. He slipped a shoulder out of his red-deerskin cape and used the loose garment to try and blind the bull.

Shimshon, for the first time, began to feel like a hero. Or at least he began to feel that he had no choice but to act with more heroics than he had shown until that point. He struggled to his feet — or foot, rather — using his spear as a crutch. Then he took off his own cape and began to flail in the beast's direction, croaking hoarsely by way of a yell.

Obligingly, the bull turned toward him. On one and a half feet, feeling his own blood pool about him, Shimshon tried to steady his spear. But Eben's cape and a chert cut near the bull's eye made the charge bad. Shimshon couldn't move fast enough to improve the aim. His spear no more than grazed a flank.

The butt of the spear drove back and down into the dirt behind Shimshon. He used it to swing himself clumsily out of harm's way — then heard the awful snap.

"By the Mother's sacred Hand," he swore involuntarily at himself. He'd mistrusted the knot in that length of ash wood, and now it proved itself false. Shimshon crumpled to the ground once more, amongst the splinters of his ruined spear.

The bull turned and trundled off, paying no further mind to what he must have taken for a fourth corpse. Apparently the cape had shifted. The beast could see better now, or perhaps the Mother called him, for he moved straight toward the river and sanctuary, carrying Eben with him. Eben's knife had finished its usefulness. Shimshon saw its broken haft not far from him, red with blood—not all of it the bull's. Weaponless, wounded, Eben could do nothing but cling to his foe—and be carried off into the forbidden Mother Hand.

A man who broke the sanctuary suffered a vague but terrible fate. But what if the man was borne there in spite of himself? Shimshon didn't think it mattered. Mother must claim him for sacrifice. She couldn't allow him to live. Spirits of horror filled Shimshon until he could feel them throbbing all the way up to his nose. Mother's Hand actually came up and grabbed him by the hair at the nape of his neck. Before he knew what he was doing, he was on his feet again. On his feet, and—not hobbling—running, totally ignoring his wound.

He drew Eben's cast-off spear out of the ground as he ran and used it to prick the bull's rump. Shimshon didn't think the bull was in the forbidden water yet. In any case, his hind legs were not, Shimshon's legs were not. The bull turned in fury, almost in place and, lowering his head, charged. Shimshon murmured the hunter's prayer and stood his ground. The spear slipped in just behind the curly head, driven in by the creature's own monstrous force, up the shaft, right to Shimshon's hand.

His arms felt broken with the impact. He sank to his knees, then his knees wouldn't hold him. The great horns seemed to take him in an embrace. A shudder, like the climax of love, and the bull died, his heavy head on Shimshon's breast. Only at the edge of consciousness did it occur to Shimshon: the shoulders into which he'd plunged the fatal blow carried no Eben.

Other hunters arrived, dragged the bull's head off by the horns, and *let Shimshon awaken as fresh air filled his chest again. One man lifted Shimshon's head and gave him water from a skin, another stanched the wound in his thigh, found yarrow shoots to help the healing and bound it—for the moment—with strips of his own cape. Some ran up and down the river looking—in vain—for a sign of other straggling aurochs. Others went back for women to help with the butchering and carrying. Yet another cut out the beast's heart and shaved off a bit, raw and still warm, for Shimson to eat. And all the men exclaimed over and over at the wonder of the triple kill.*

Only later, much later, near nightfall, indeed, when he saw Eben's body laid out next to Caleb's, did Shimshon realize through his own pain just what the three aurochs had cost.

Grandfather broke in to my tale. "Eben," he whispered, reliving the old pain. "My wife's sister's husband—"

"*My* husband," Grandmother echoed and slipped closer to Grandfather's side.

"*We found him facedown in only an ankle's depth of Finger River water,*" *hunters told Shimshon. "We fished him out with forked sticks, although some felt we should have left him. For the Mother. May She grant no curse to follow us for wanting to reclaim our dead."*

Shimshon saw what had happened in his mind's eye. The bull had finally shaken Eben off and, in the process, the man had hit his head. Unable to rouse, he had drowned in the shallows of the River. There were otherwise no more than a few scrapes upon him.

"*But no,*" *the other man insisted. "The Mother Hand simply reached out and claimed him for Herself. No man can touch Finger water and live.*"

I paused and considered the fireglow of tears on my grandparents' faces, on several of the others. The urge for the final cleansing purity of the story seemed to enclose our camp like the petals of a nighttime flower.

I told of the march back to winter gathering, of the three biers led by the bull's head with its great horns borne in triumph on two men's spears. I sought for magic words to bind thoughts of male vigor to images of those horns, to speak of the horns piercing women's jealousy, but at the same time, to twine the Mother's blessing on them like garlands.

I told how Grandfather, with those horns, claimed a second bride. He took Eben's widow. That seemed to be the match the spirits wanted, as Granny was great with her first child and needed a hunter. Grandfather's first wife was also her older sister, and it's known that what women's jealousy an aurochs can't cure, sisterhood can.

For some weeks, the clan feared Shimshon might die and leave two widows behind, that the exchange Mother extracted might be three aurochs for three men. But the younger sister sewed the gash up most skillfully with her fine bone needle and strands of her own long, thick, black hair. And tended it afterward so the fever broke on the power of herbs and he lived. The hero carried her son, Adam, when he was born and claimed him as his own at the Reckoning.

And so they lived happily ever after and begat sons and daughters.

Such is the tale. And within it are contained three apples, one for you, one for me, and one for the story's magic. May each catch in his lap the meaning best for him.

In the firelight, Grandmother thoughtfully touched her hair. It was white now, not black, and too fine and brittle for dressing wounds. Her sister, Grandfather's first wife, had slept up in the Great Cave for years.

Grandfather smoothed the aurochs skin about his shoulders, but more from cold than pride. Even he seemed to be led, by my words, to believe that the hero in the story must be a different man. A man to whom great deeds were natural, who thought nothing of wresting an aurochs bull from the Mother and presenting the horns to our men's sacred cave.

Grandfather was the last man ever to do so. Now that the forehead curls had sloughed off the great trophy's bones, young men had only my words to tell them what the beast had looked like in the flesh. Grandfather had grown, in his old age, to depend on the same reminder.

Only Adam, it seemed, imagined a world beyond my conjuring. Perhaps because he carried in him the blood of a man whom the Mother had snatched in Her Hand. The fire etched his features against the night, like flame himself.

"Tomorrow," Adam murmured into the fire. Perhaps he meant the word for no ears but his—or his and Eve's. But it served to close up the clan for the night about the low-gleaming coals.

"Tomorrow *I* will go and hunt the aurochs."

Eight

"I'll go in search of the aurochs, too," Eve declared the next morning.

Nobody replied to her announcement for a while, however doubtful their looks. Women shouldn't go hunting; it would spoil the magic. But Adam, to whom the magic of this outing was very important, also said nothing. He didn't even look doubtful. He seemed to expect Eve would go with him. I had to do something.

"I'll go with my friend," I finally spoke up, and took Eve's hand. "I'll show her that side of the Valley. And we'll gather firewood."

"Firewood" swayed the argument. After the first night around one hearth, the clan would divide into family groups— build separate fire pits, make small lean-tos against the rains that were still likely—for more privacy between couples. Firewood would be a constant concern of the women, and if we were willing to go farther afield to bring in our share, the rest would not stop us.

So off we went, my father and his brothers carrying their father between them, sometimes singly, sometimes in pairs.

We crossed the river on a great felled log where the gorge narrowed. The water, white as the ice from which it sprang,

roared so far below I would have fallen five times my height
before I hit it—if I lost my balance. My father carried Grandfather jigging on his back over this bridge. Adam's feet urged
us all to a good pace. The dogs trotted alongside, tongues lolling.

This side of the mountain got most of the sun in the morning,
but was still shadowed and chilled in its green folds. Although
tight-woven peaks also bound our sight here, the mountains
were neither so high nor so rapidly rising as on the home side.
Between river and slopes, some level ground offered room for
our feet, room to spread out before the steepness.

There were nonetheless waterfalls from time to time that
silenced Eve's chatter and mine. Away from the force of the
clanswomen's talk, we were best friends again. Still, sometimes
I shivered at a sort of forced gaiety I heard in her. That's meant
for my father, I thought, and didn't like it.

Father didn't like it, either. He remembered, too late, his
hunting magic. More than once he turned to scowl—at me;
nothing was Eve's fault. And once he spoke: "How can we
hope to take this honored beast by surprise if we are joined by
such a racket?"

"Women who always gather in groups but are unarmed
know no other weapon than our voices," Eve retorted.

"With their gossip's sting," said Dov.

"Our noise will only keep away the bears and the mountain cats."

"Don't say the given names of such honorable creatures
aloud!" Dov hissed. "You will give them our power."

Hardly shamed, Eve got in the last word. "So far we've
seen more of their dung than of the—of the great horned beast
you seek."

Dov smiled crookedly, but he didn't dare scold her if Adam
didn't. Adam had let her come in the first place. This was Adam's

hunt, a dung hunt. If it were a real hunt, he would have left the girls—and Grandfather—at home.

So only the fall of water echoing off the close rock walls of the gorge had the power to silence us. Mother Earth's stern voice and the heavy fall of Her white hair over sharp, narrow shoulders gave signs of Her presence before vanishing once more into the underslopes of scooped and pitted limestone.

There were only the blades of narcissus here yet, no blooms. Only snowdrops, crocuses, and violets flowered, tucked into the curves of the terrain. Eve picked them and tucked them into her own curves. I saw my father watch—with approval—and then hurry our pace as if even one heartbeat more or less could make or break his chances with a storyteller's beast.

The oaks were blooming in their sweet, quiet way. The small tassels begged to be brushed away like yellowish-green crumbs, like mistakes or shavings in basketmaking or like insect damage. They added their own earthy smell to the crisp, never-breathed air.

Eve and I found the best deadfall under the oaks. We broke it and carried it in small, workable armfuls, then left these where we could gather them easily on our return. We had no desire to pull out our binding cords and be burdened by great loads until later, when we'd be going downhill.

Moving wood also revealed tribes of gray snails, often with their soft white clutches of eggs, waiting for warmth. Eve and I tried to brush the eggs off carefully, though this was difficult and the slightest pressure tended to burst the infants to lifeless ooze. Those we recovered we took care to preserve with leaf mold, remembering that if we were gentle to the children of other species, the Great Mother would be gentle to our own—when we should have them.

But we did take the adult snails, those that had yet to break their crusty winter-sleep membrane. We slipped them in our gathering bags until every step we took clattered with shell. The snails would be delicious cooked with garlic and parsley.

Then we hurried to catch up to the single-minded men.

Its light dropping like a weighted fishing line to the bottom of the gorge, the sun hung at its springtime height before we reached the place. A pair of lately returned white-tailed eagles inspected their aerie from a high, effortless soar between the crags. Even higher, cranes flew homeward, too—in formation like a woman's careful binding stitch in leather.

Under such omens, we reached the place.

With an imposing gesture toward the ground, my father revealed the dung, glorious between two stately poplars.

"Yes, it's aurochs," Grandfather wheezed more than announced. Even carried every step, he had had to beg to rest frequently. And now he remained on the rock where Adam had set him down, eyeing the spoor impartially. Every joint in his old body must have ached too much to give attention to anything else. He didn't even bother to use the beast's name with hunter's caution.

My father and uncles, however, studied the stuff as little boys study the wonder of life in a lizard they've caught, pulling off its tail and hunting it into burrows with their sticks. Each man had to take a trial kick at the heap. The dung separated easily into layers, a cross section of the live, warm bowels that had created it. But the dung was pale and dusty, dry, burned by frost, flushed by rains, and baked by the sun. The dogs took one sniff and went off after fresher scents. The holes of beetles and their wriggling white young riddled the whole mass. Undigested seeds sprouted now in the rich decay.

A woman's mystery, I thought, but didn't say aloud. Men shouldn't be told such things, even when the Mother presents them right under their noses.

No more than woman should view a hunter's mysteries. I hung back and pretended, like the dogs, to find other things of more interest elsewhere. Eve, on the other hand, had had enough of fallwood and snails.

"The stuff is old," I heard Dov say.

"Four, five months at least," Ari agreed. "Probably before the snows."

"But it *is* our great horned brother," Adam insisted. "There have been cattle — may we honor them — in our Valley of Eden. It's a sign."

"This doesn't look like a herd."

"No," Ari echoed. "It's only one beast."

"A rogue, perhaps, Father?"

Grandfather nodded as if the action hurt his neck.

"And rogues are always male?"

Grandfather couldn't even bring himself to nod in response to this. The men took his silence as proof.

"This is a bull, then?" Adam could hardly contain his eagerness.

"I think so." Grandfather nodded again. "The trunks of the trees look as though the beast used them for whetting his horns. See the scars? A rogue, yes, most likely. Driven off by stronger bulls during the mating and forced to make it on his own for a while. Some time has indeed passed since this creature was here. Summer is the usual time for mating. Like women, they carry nine months and birth in the spring. But sometimes a cow will enter her heat in the fall."

"So this *is* a bull?" Adam repeated, grinning. "And a rogue, all the more easy to take the beast."

"Cows are never away from a herd; bulls only sometimes, and when they're too weak to get wives of their own."

I'm sure only weariness made Grandfather careless in his words, but Adam took his final statement as a personal challenge. He did nothing to reproach his father, but began to speak at once, and with furor, of tracking the aurochs. A little farther up the slope, where the land flattened out at river level, there was more dung and tree trunks the bull had taken on in his frustrated defeat . . .

"No, you won't set off tracking today," Dov called out to Adam.

"I've no interest in spoor five months cold." Ari agreed. He chewed on the greens of some onions he'd found. This was how we were all taking the edge off our morning's hike.

"Besides, you're the one who insisted on bringing Father with us."

"Father is the last man ever to have set trophy horns in the sacred place," Adam said, justifying himself. "He deserves the honor. And the wisdom of his eyes has told us every hint this place can reveal."

"Very well, but there's no use bringing him on such a diffi- cult hunt."

"Such a hopeless hunt," Dov muttered.

"We must take him back to the comfort of camp now. And since you brought him, you must help us carry him back. You will not set off on this hunt now."

"Or what?" Adam took a defiant stance, planting his feet wide.

"Or I personally will break both your legs so you never hunt again."

"And I'll hold you while he does it." Ari grinned, green onion on his teeth.

They were out of earshot of the old man.

"Besides, it's the dark of the moon," Dov said.

"You can't set off on an overnight hunt at the dark of the moon." Ari stated the obvious.

"It's better to do hunting magic at this time of month,"

Dov concluded, and Adam, with a glance in Eve's direction, nodded submission.

So in the end, my father returned. He didn't fear for his legs or the dark of the moon as much as he realized that to set off hunting now would dishonor his father. And honor toward that man in the aurochs hide mattered most of all.

But Adam addressed a prayer to the place before we left and tied a deerskin fringe from his loincloth to one of the oaks as a sign. By such means he begged the place to preserve the spoor for him until he could return. And he bent to scoop a good portion of the dung up into the gazelle-skin bag he wore about his neck.

Return he would, soon; this he swore.

Then we retraced the morning's steps. Ari went off when his stint with Grandfather was done and came back with a small rabbit, just so the entire day of four adult men should not be wasted.

Then, at one of Grandfather's halts, we stayed longer than usual. This was near the river, where the land leveled and a band of smooth cobbles five or six paces wide bordered the water. Father spent a great deal of time scouring the wash for weapons material. Ari and Dov contented themselves with the first likely stone or two they came upon, but Adam tried and rejected flint after flint—and flint was not common in these mountains.

He hefted one stone then another, wet them in the river to note the color changes, studied their fabric in different lights, even squatted and chipped off trial flakes. He tried the edges he produced against clumps of dried grass, against the leather of his loincloth.

Eventually he declared, "I've three of the best rocks in creation." His joy must have made hunter's magic tremble.

Adam was, after all, hunting aurochs.

I, however, flinched. Who would have to mend those rents he made on purpose in his loincloth, if not his daughter? Eve . . . ? Eve must not claim such rights.

Not until Adam brought back aurochs horns.

While my father worked, Eve and I took the chance to set down our growing bundles of sticks and wash a little in the numbing shallows where the water lapped quietly. Eve worked loose her hair thong and washed her hair. I could see she was conscious of Adam's gaze on her when it wasn't on his flints.

I studied my own face in comparison when she let the water still. A father might ignore such a face, very like his own. And where it differed, it was different from any other face in the clan, any face I had ever seen. The heavy brow, the darker skin, the small, hardly existent chin—was that Lilith looking back at me? That stranger's face, livened by the movement of the surface of the water. I shivered, in spite of the heat. Is this what my father saw when he looked at me, a past that threatened to strangle his present?

But Lilith was only a story.

And a shadow on the water.

Eve had climbed away from the river and sat on a flat, sun-warmed stone. I shook myself free of the vision as of the water and scrambled up to join her. I carefully stowed our snails in cool, damp shade and watched her hair fluff into dryness again.

A triumphant shout from my father drew his brothers to him to consult on a cobble, and Eve's eyes followed, with their own form of interest. Confronted then by nothing but the black silent back of my friend's head, I turned my glance elsewhere, across our jutting rock of a seat and to the river.

As I did, I saw something that made my heart stand still.

Eve's thighs were bare up to the edge of her rabbit-skin skirt. Gooseflesh raised the soft dark down on the earth color of the limbs, glistening still with river water. Along the inside of her thigh where it sloped slightly to match the rock ran a trickle of blood. It grew while I watched in frozen fascination, branching here and there as the hairs diverted it. If one were able to watch the growth of scammony root, many times faster, even, than the natural speed, and if it were the color of dock root instead of the scammony's strong-smelling though anemic white, that would be the sight I saw.

She has come to her moontime, I thought. This was not what surprised me, nor what kept the breath uneven in my lungs. I knew well enough that my friend, unlike me, had come to women's initiation over a year ago. But because she'd been initiated, there was no reason why she should be doing something so openly disrespectful. She shouldn't be here, casually exposing her womanness to the company of menfolk when the Mystery was on her. It would deaden the Mother-power— power to create, power to hear the secret will of the Earth— within her.

And she most certainly should not be watching hunters about their work, especially not their weapon-making. Their work would prove as changeable as the moon.

Nine

Seeing Eve make straight for the Tree as soon as we crossed the log bridge lightened my heart with relief. She left her pile of wood outside the holy space and begged me to carry it and her snails up to camp for her. Then she slipped under the spreading branches to join my aunt Rachel and cousin Hadassah who were already there.

The women of the clan bled together, at the dark of the moon. Some started earlier, others as much as three days later. They came down to the Tree as the Mystery overcame them. Hadassah and Rachel had been first this time. They'd already taken off their skirts so they could bleed directly onto the earth. They had a fire going, and were erecting a small tent of skins in the fig limbs and against the stone outcropping. Once they finished these tasks, they must do nothing else during their moontime but sit and chat and bleed beneath the Tree.

My aunt and cousin welcomed Eve friendlily enough and asked her to lend a hand. I scurried off after the men, meeting Yael on the way. The Mystery had come to her this moon although she was almost a crone and did not always have a moontime any more.

But no one saw me as I took Eve's snails and freed them in a damp rock crevice filled with leaves. Her bundle of wood I scattered here and there. Although women could make a fire for their own comfort during the moontime, everyone knew the wood they gathered would burn noxious smoke. And food they collected during that time would make anyone who ate it sick.

Surely, I thought, Eve must know these bans. I wanted to forgive her, thinking perhaps her clan had different ways. But I knew this couldn't be true. All the tribeswomen retreated together to a longhouse made of wood and stone and thatched with reed during the winter. Their songs and laughter filled all the moonless nights down by Mother River.

If Eve's ways were the same, the only explanation I could find for her actions had to do with my father. Even if, in her youth and inexperience, she had not been aware when she awoke that morning that the Mystery was about to overtake her, she must have known it long before I saw the trickle of blood on her leg. Either she had not wanted to leave the company of my father when she should have—or she had been ashamed to let him know, which amounted to the same thing. Shame of the Mystery sometimes overcame girls at their first time. But initiation was supposed to cure that, if the days of unburdened female companionship did not. No one should ever be ashamed of anything to do with the Mother.

The idea that my father's company could make Eve deny the Mystery unsettled me. It seemed like the effects of Adamspeak.

But after my return to camp, there wasn't much time to think about Eve nor what I should do about her, if I should tell. The coming of moontime always laid a great burden on those of us who didn't bleed: the younger girls and me. The men, of course. Grandmother and Aunt Afra, who were crones. And Devorah.

Devorah did not bleed because she was with child, a very

sorry case for her, because the baby at her breast couldn't even crawl yet. She'd missed the previous month as well, which meant all her efforts to rid herself of the growing blood clot within her had failed. She spent a lot of this dark of the moon consulting with Aunt Afra as to what herbs or spells she might try next. No woman can carry two children on the season-moves. Until the firstborn can walk the long distances on his own, a woman must give any other child back to the Mother, telling Her to send him back to her to raise later, when she can do a better job. And such a painful, heart-wrenching task is easier to do before the Mother has given the mite shape and the spark of life. Anything is easier than having to expose a child beside Mother River just after having gone through labor and birth.

This state of affairs kept me very busy, indeed. I did most of the cooking, although men will try to lend a hand this once a month, encouraged by the fact that their traps and bows bring in most of what is served. I then had to carry the meals down to the retreating women.

And I had to take care of every child who wasn't still at the breast. This often meant trooping down to the Tree with a howling tot when only his mother would do. But all the women would join me in shaming a child when he demanded such attention: "What? Are you such a baby that you must disturb the peace of the Tree?" Then I'd have to troop on back up the hill with the child when he had sworn to be a bigger boy in the future.

I know the moontime is, among other things, the Mother's way of reminding men what they owe to their women. I, for one, could hardly wait until the Mother called me to Her and even, when I was very tired, had the brashness to ask Her aloud what was taking so long. Men, at least, have the luxury of escaping the chaos of dark-moon camp to perform rites of their own.

By chance, I watched the men's rites at this moon. There was no harm in this, or in telling what I saw, for a girl may see what she may see before she is initiated, the same as a boy. They said initiation wiped the memories of childhood from the mind, but I know that in the present world, the power of initiation is gone. Anyone who may hear my tale will be as a child, and still, in a way, innocent.

It happened one of the nights of the dark of the moon that when I had settled all the children in the lean-tos around the fire, I counted one missing. Sometimes simple counting was the best way to keep track of them those days of the Mystery, counting over and over again to fill the fingers of one hand as fast as I could. But when I found the little skin-wrapped figure that must match my thumb was missing, I knew it was Boaz.

No man sat about the fire except Grandfather, who'd dozed all day, but was now awake and restless. Grandmother was doing her best to settle him, though her mind wandered. Afra and Devorah were off somewhere trying yet again to give that blood clot back to the Mother. They could not have gone anyway, being initiated women; for I had a pretty good idea where I would have to look for him.

In all the chaos of getting twenty-two mouths fed at suppertime, I remembered six-year-old Boaz's questions above the rest of the clamor. "Where is my father?" "Where do the men go at moon darkness?" And "Why?" I hoped I'd given clear enough answers to the first two inquiries. I doubted I had to the third. I trusted he'd gone off to find out "why" for himself. On that hope, I took a torch—glad that Uncle Ari always saw to it that our camp had plenty of bundles of tallow-soaked reed—and thrust it into the fire.

By this light, I took the uphill trail through the moonless—almost starless—night. I didn't know this trail well, having taken it only once since our arrival. I climbed slowly, seeing no more than the yellow light dancing a step in front of me. I whacked the edge of this light with a stick, to warn the brother and sister animals of my approach. And from time to time I called Boaz's name, lest he had wandered from the path in the dark.

The hike took a long, stumbling, sometimes bone-jarring time as shadows fooled me with depth where there was none. At last my heart leaped once with relief and then calmed to see the little form huddled black before the brightness of the men's secret cave. If Boaz hadn't been there, I don't know what I would have done. I might have called his father out from the rites to help me look, perhaps, but I would have felt very uneasy breaking the men's magic like that.

How close to womanhood I was showed in the discomfort I felt as I neared the blaze of light and warmth from the cave. Boaz had no such problem. He squawked a protest when I sat beside him and suggested we leave the men and go find his nice warm skins.

I'll wait till he falls asleep, I thought, then carry him down. Carrying the torch and a six-year-old's weight for such a long, dark way was not a cheering thought. Perhaps his father, when he finished— But I knew how men were after their rites.

For the moment, I settled next to the boy, shared my fur and my shoulder with him, and turned, like him, to watch.

The contrasts of male and female struck me at once. While women stayed out these nights, unafraid of the naked face of the universe, men cowered here in their cave. While the women embraced the darkness, the men were burning everything you could imagine in an attempt to defeat it. Ari's rush lights and hollow stones full of grease combined with three large fires to make the cave seem a great stone lamp itself, glowing even through its thick rock sides.

And finally, while women's bodies at this time brought them to wisdom, whether they wanted it or not, the men resorted—frantically, desperately—to a herb.

Hemp was the only plant in which men took an interest as great as that of women. Both sexes appreciated the fiber, women for everything from baskets and mats to cording, men for hafting points to their arrows and spears. But in spring, even before the plants were ready to be used for fiber, men visited the hemp stands and plucked off the yellow spikes of clustered flowers. These they spent hours pounding with red-deer antlers into hemp matting until the delicate flowers were reduced to hard brown lumps of resin. I wondered if, in the vigor of their pounding, the men were conscious it was the female bloom that held their attention.

The season was as yet too early for much sign of hemp in the fields at all. But throughout the year men kept the lumps of resin in the magically decorated fawn-skin bags they wore constantly about their necks. And when they entered the great heat of the cave, they shed capes and loincloths, everything but their hemp pouches. The pouches stood out with dark accent against their oiled and sweating skin, and echoed the natural male display dangling from their loins.

The laws of the tribe were firm that, for all the care he gave the resin, a man must only indulge in his herb at certain times—and then only in the company of other men, women not allowed. But you could see their longing for the rites when, from time to everyday time, you caught them loosening the strings on their bags for a tempting sniff.

The flower resin was not the only part of the plant the men used in their rites. Bunches of dried stems and leaves swagged the roof of the cave even as Boaz and I sat quietly watching.

The herbs blended with the garlands of roof-trapped smoke, identical in their gray-green. Men always saved these cuttings from their fiber work, and a woman could relax after a long day soaking and beating stalk. Some man would certainly come along after her, whisking up her tiniest leavings with a handful of dried grass.

Men called hemp the Father of Plants. And as we sat there, the sweet, grassy smell, almost inseparable in my mind from the odor of male sweat and energy, billowed visibly out upon us. I remembered the smell from my childhood, when I would awaken in blackness for some reason I could not say. Then the smell would fill my head and I would know, with neither sight nor sound, that the men who'd been gone at bedtime had returned. I could turn over and go back to sleep. All was well.

The men within the cave ate their hemp resin. They ate the dried stems and leaves, tossed bunches of the plant on the fires, burned it in every stone lamp set about the cave. They curled hemp up in the leaves of other plants and smoked it. Clouds of the smoke wafted out upon me in drifts, yellow, like the light. It tightened my face with its strange, cloying sweetness. My head grew light. My lungs seemed bruised with the effort of breathing it—and I was able to turn my face to the clear, chill night from time to time to refresh myself. The men had no such option and seemed not to want it. They were wreathed in the stuff—and ecstatic.

The herb affected men in different ways. Some, I knew, disliked using it and joined in only because the spirits required it of them. These men sat sullen, blinking, moody, at the edges of the gathering. I wondered if the spirits really prized rites made with such a lack of heart.

For most men, however, hemp was a freeing thing. They laughed louder than usual, shrugged off their normally con-

trolled conduct, talked with vigor, if not always connection—
that was the spirit in them.

The odor of hemp and men throbbed in my head. But the
plant had help in this rhythmic marking of its power. Men had
pits in their caves, but they did not fill them with grain as we
women did. Men left their pits empty, then covered them at ritual time with the well-tanned hides of whatever animals they
wished to hear. Stretched tight and weighted with rocks, the
skins resounded deep in the earth and spoke to the very marrow, when struck by knobbed sticks or animal bones.

Men's rituals demanded that these instruments of the spirits be given voice throughout the events, so if one man tired,
another must replace him. I heard nothing but the pulse of
sound, at odds with my own heartbeat. But often men said they
heard the animals tell them where best to hunt or promise them
success if this or that was done. They must never miss the
chance of gaining such a message.

Each animal and earth drum had its song, each song an
opportunity for the spirit-guided men to let loose in roars or
growls or lowing, as the beast commanded. Each rhythm had
its dance, as well: The straight, stately poses of the cranes, led
by whistles on flutes made from the bird's hollow bones. The
herded springing of the ibex and goats. The solo stalking of the
panther.

There was no aurochs skin left among the men with
strength enough in it to be made to speak. But the dance lingered, in the minds and in the limbs, as if it were something
they got from their fathers in their mothers' wombs, something
beyond learning.

And Adam called for the aurochs.

He twirled to the middle of the cave floor where the soil,
for some reason, was different from that all around it, a yel-
lower clay.

"Aurochs," he announced, his voice high and reedy, his cheeks flushed with the drug like a child's. He could use the word now, in ritual.

The earth drums fell silent. My father took the skull, Grandfather's aurochs skull, from its place of honor on a shelf cut into the center back of the cave. Magic symbols, parallel zigzags and circles, marked the snout of white bone in red ocher. And from each of the mighty horns dangled tassels made of dried hemp and vulture wings. It must have been a heavy load, but Adam never faltered as he carried the burden and let it lead the dance.

With no drums to mark the beat, it was up to Adam's voice and his feet, stomping heavily, to keep the time. My father would sing out one verse—about the aurochs bulls' bravery, about the dust they raised in the summer heat, about the calving or the mating—and the whole line of men forming behind him would repeat it, word for word. They all linked up—even the drummers and the glum ones—hands on shoulders, and did the herdlike steps. The dance made their upper bodies seem heavier; their legs plodded.

And the mind of the dance circling out from the aurochs skull was the mind of the herd.

My spine prickled as I watched the change come over them. The eery sound of the unaccompanied voices echoed around in the smoke and light, swung off the curves of the cave like a stone from a sling. The sounds settled heavily, awfully, in my chest—like the lowing of cattle. The words were exactly what aurochs must say to one another in their own tongue.

My father wound the herd in a long, coiling chain, in and out and up and down the cave until dust rose, coating them first to the ankles, then to the knees. He started them at a slow, stomping gait. But presently, with time and as the verses began to speak—first of the hunters and the drive to the stampede,

then, in the bull's own words, of the mounting of cows in the
dry heat of early fall—the steps moved faster and faster.

Dust rose. The dancers whirled. I became aware that one
or two of the men were aroused, a startling sight for an uninitiated girl. The growth at the base of their bodies seemed magical, unnatural, and I couldn't pull my eyes away, even when
the thought occurred to me that this was something I should
not be witnessing.

I thought the arousal was just an accident, or the chance
effect of the hemp. But then I saw my father, whose manhood
was more erect than any, go with the skull at some who were
delinquent. Then, whether from fear or from the tickling of the
vulture feathers, the spirits soon drew every man into a similar
state.

The dance whirled faster and faster, the circle closed tighter
and tighter around the yellow clay in the center of the cave.
The men raised arms in unison, stomping, tossing their heads,
lowing, and then, with a final bellow, they pounded to a halt.

The men grasped themselves and groaned. Seed shot from
them in great arcing ribbons to combine in the yellow dust in
the ring's center.

So I had seen it. My father's nakedness. It is not forbidden
to a girl as yet uninitiated, but still the very notion cast a spell
of awe—or dread—over me.

The combined male breath escaped in a single sigh. Then
each man laughed or clipped his companion on the back or
sulked, as his nature was, and drifted off for food or drink.
Some almost tripped over me and Boaz, now asleep, as they
left the cave for the bracing air and to empty their bladders.
One of these was Ari, the boy's father, who greeted me in the
heavy voice hemp gives, deep, throaty, slow, and full of holes
between few words. He decided it was time to carry his son
home.

Only Adam remained in the center of the cave. He set the skull down so its empty sockets would have a good view. He shook out his arms from the weight, then squatted to the dance's fulcrum.

While Ari scooped up his son and made his farewells to those who would sleep in the cave, Adam scooped up the seed-moistened clay. I crouched frozen, watching. I watched Adam knead the clansmen's semen into earth, then form two figures, a little bull and a little human. All the while he muttered words of deepest sanctity. I caught these: "Dust you are and to dust return. The gods formed man of the dust of the earth." And finally, "The gods breathed into his nostrils the breath of life." As he said this last, Adam breathed upon the tiny figures in his mud-caked hands.

The figures did not live, of course, but he took them up and set them gently in the place of honor, on the shelf at the back of the cave, as if he might disturb some life in them.

Then I felt the spell break from me. I found I could move again. And I had to hurry if I wanted to catch up with Uncle Ari.

I had been proud of my father, leading that climax of the night. But now, I was only sad. Perhaps the spell affected me, the spell of the forbidden which, as a daughter, almost initiate, I didn't know if I'd be able to forget.

No, it was more. Such honor was a pale substitute for what Ari knew, bundling his flesh-and-blood son up in his cape and striding down the mountainside that snored with the year's first cricket song.

Every child made mud figures by the riverside and let them bake in the summer sun. A man wanted more.

And I, a daughter, was not enough for Adam.

Ten

Five days later, the moontime ended. The women remained under the Tree till the last had finished her bleeding. Then they bathed together, dressed in their best, and snaked their way up the hill back to camp, singing and dancing.

"We are the mothers of your sons, o men," were their words.

> *"We are beautiful and pure*
> *And our power has been renewed*
> *By the Mother's hand.*
> *Welcome us now, welcome the Mother's daughters."*

Their steps were light, jigging, suggestive even. I watched my clay-molding father watching Eve in the middle of the line. My friend swished her hips happily. She wore a crown of golden narcissus in her hair and had painted the tips of her breasts with ocher. I watched my father watch other men embrace their returning wives. Then I watched Adam pick up the weapons he'd spent the moon's darkness creating and whistle his dog to him.

"Farewell," he announced. "I'm going to track our great horned brother."

As a last act, he knelt before the old hero and begged, "Your blessing, Father."

Wordlessly, Grandfather shifted the aurochs hide about his shoulders and gave it, but no one said much more. Everyone had expected this parting.

Less expected was the talk the women brought back to camp with them. All the shadow of the Tree, they reported, crawled with snakes this year. The women had taken to poking any place they wanted to step or sit with a stick first, and liked to squeal together as the creatures slipped off like spilled water.

Once the live ones were gone, reminders still lingered. One had only to shift the fig leaves around a bit to uncover white, breath-fragile shed skins.

"And dead snakes, as well," Tzipporah said.

"Nonsense," Grandmother snapped. "Snakes can't die. They are like Mother Lilith. They merely shed their skins, both of them, Mother and snake. You found just another shed skin, symbol of the power of endless life."

"If you say so, Grandmother." Tzipporah shrugged. But when the older woman was out of earshot, she insisted: "A snakeskin comes with a fine comb of white bones all up and down and a skull and fangs? I don't believe it."

Nobody was hurt; these were not a poisonous variety.

"It is a good omen. An excellent omen," Grandmother began to chant over and over as the story grew in details.

But even she had to admit the event was "Strange." "Unheard of." And "To be wondered at."

I wondered if the snakes foretold my father's chances of finding the aurochs. His departure saddened—and frightened—me. My eyes stung every time I thought that I and the memory of my mother couldn't be enough for him. No one said it aloud, but their thoughts were almost plain enough to hear.

"Lilith." That name had power enough to echo through the

camp silences from which my father was now missing. "Lilith." Lilith drove him from camp, even though no one of our tribe had seen her for years, not since I'd been born.

Lilith, who shed her skin like snakes. Was Lilith in the strange signs under the Tree? And what of the dead snakes Tzipporah had seen?

"Lilith." The name, though unspoken, conjured.

True, my father being around my friend Eve had been making everyone nervous. Even thoughts could make a dead wife's jealousy dangerous—to the whole clan. No wonder Lilith seemed to walk among us. It was best that Adam go hunting. Lilith all but drove him on.

Still, Adam was, after all, the only parent left to me, the only one I'd really ever known. I hated to think of losing him.

And that's what this quest after the aurochs seemed to me to be. In order to prevent forbidden unions, the laws of the tribe would drive tempted men away—to meet their doom at the end of the earth, sent there on a fruitless search. We would never bury my father next to Aunt Gurit in the clan dust in the clan cave. It did not seem fair, but then, that was the way of life.

The way of Lilith, my mother.

I tried to keep my spirits up and hope against hope that Adam might find what he sought. That would be better than to have him not return at all. And when such hopes failed, the clanswomen diverted me with their talk and their work. I felt closer to them, in any case.

Directly after the dark of the moon the days lasted precisely as long as the nights and the constellation of the ram rose. The time had come for all the women to hike back up to the Great Cave. There, Afra brought out the soaked wheat she had been tending all the dark of the moon. While we'd gone about our everyday work, she had drained it and spread it in a covered basket. Now she brought out the basket to where we sat in a circle, drew off the lid with a flourish, and showed us the miracle. The grains, like only so much gravel when last we'd handled them, had sprouted with new green life.

We sang the secret songs then, the songs that only women may hear, the songs that instruct us, like the wheat, to soak up water and sunshine, to let our small, hard bodies swell round with new life.

"How proud, how glorious the wheat kernel feels," say the words.

> *"When she lets the first little white root*
> *Split her brown skin.*
> *The Mystery of life.*
> *Of wheat.*
> *Of women."*

Then each woman around the circle—even those of us as yet uninitiated—took a few sprouts between thumb and two fingers and ate. We chewed thoughtfully, carefully, averting eyes from one another. So we ate the food men must not eat or they would swell, too. The men, unable to split, would die horribly. The smell was damp and had a green tint to it. The taste was sweet and earthy, the taste of spring with the crunch of hull and soil. The taste swelled up inside until a mist formed in our eyes at the wonder of it.

Our hearts swelled, too, close to bursting with forgiveness and love. A deep link swelled to those of our clan who had died and slept, like wheat grains, in the soil about us. We remembered their names, their deeds, and knew they were with us still, reborn in our young and on the tongues of our storytellers. The blessing of sprouted grain extended not just to the dead but to the living.

Every woman embraced every other. Even those who had feuded—not speaking though they'd shared a fire—made up. As the saying is, "When a broken string is mended, the two ends come even closer together."

The embraces Eve received were the most cordial of all, no doubt because everyone had been so slow to accept her before the mystery. "Water reflects to the depth that it sees," the old saying runs.

When Eve and I embraced, I knew we would return to being best friends. At the time I felt it must be the wheat. But perhaps the fact that my father had gone was every bit as much the source.

Afterward Aunt Afra tossed the remnants of the wheat into the tumbling stream outside the cave; "tossing the year's cares with it" were the words of the song we sang then. We could hear the men's songs as a faint accompaniment to ours. Farther on up the hill, we could smell their smoke. They would be burning brush, heavily laced with hemp, to leap over the flames as part of their new year's rite. My father—I couldn't help but think, and embraced Eve again. My father was missing out on this cleansing altogether.

———————

After the wheat sprouting, the other currents of the season drifted around us, each with its special songs and rites. There was rhubarb to pick: stalks as wide as Kochavah's wrists grew under the bushy shade of their own great leaves where the soil was sandy. We always gave the leaves back to the plant when we took the stalks, so nobody's tongue would swell up and burst.

There was digging of the lily bulbs.

The best time for bulbs is in the early fall, when they have bloomed and stored all their energy for the next year. We usually visited the stands near our summer camp then, just before returning to Eden.

But we dug in spring, too, for we wouldn't disturb the lilies of Eden in the fall. In spring, armed with digging sticks, new and well weighted with drilled rings of stone transferred from the old implements, all the women went out among rocks and spring meadows. We went to the spots that clung in the old women's memories as the lilies themselves would cling, two or three months later, like low-floating clouds on the mountainside.

We sang as we came near, careful to have drunk as much water as we could, and carrying waterskins besides.

"O bulb, root of the Lady Lily, be big," we sang as we squatted to the telltale bursts of green lying as yet low to the ground. (In fall, there'd be only dry stalks to go by.)

> *"O bulb, be big for me and mine;*
> *Be a big bulb, as big as my two hands."*

This was a joking song, and we laughed as we loosened the soil about the bulbs. Married women spoke of their husbands in low tones between the verses and laughed louder.

"O bulb, you have betrayed me," a woman sang when she found each loose-petaled root. It didn't matter if the bulb really was the biggest she'd ever seen. A woman had to shame and insult it, so it wouldn't grow overproud. Like good hunters. "You naughty, naughty bulb. You've grown so little."

Then she broke the bulb in two, putting most of the purplish, shell-like petals in the sack on her back but replanting the rest.

"Return where you came from and do better next time," she said as she scraped the loosened soil back over the bulb. Her final punishment for the lilies was to squat over the spot she had disturbed and urinate on it. Hence the reason for the waterskins and the full bladders.

We always had plenty of lilies to dig in the spring in those days. But a woman could only continue to dig as long as she could properly punish those bulbs she gathered. Women who'd had children often couldn't last as long, even with deep swigs from the waterskins. Their weakened muscles made them lose more water at each urination. But the old women told us young ones the practice strengthened us for future childbearing. The lilies helped us this way, as well as by giving us the sweet, nutty, gelatinous mush when properly roasted with savory and chives.

Eleven

Another month passed, a month without my father. Apples and pears bloomed white, the pistachios pink over the brilliant green at their feet. The spring scents sharpened. There were partridge and hoopoe eggs to gather and bake fragranced with thyme. We scrambled them on hot, flat rocks with spring greens in all their variety.

We ate bear meat then. The men, prohibited from the hooved creatures during their time of little ones, killed that beast and other predators instead. The Mother smiled on such actions—they helped to protect the ewes and does and their offspring as much as the ban did.

The initiated women spent the dark of the moon under the Fig, whose pinkish buds had burst and put forth new leaves. They put forth their caprifigs, as well, and the women had plenty of time as they sat and bled to observe how the tiny black fig wasp females crept into those capsules to lay their eggs.

"That's how the fig gets with child," said the accompanying song, always hushed, with heartrending overtones, for everyone knew what cost childbirth could extract from any female.

"But what thanks does the wasp gain?
The caprifig is so narrow.
It tears off her airy wings when she enters.
The wasp must die so the next generation
—Both fig and wasp—
May live."

By now rings of bluebells marked the high mountain springs. Vines were showing their new, pale green leaves and we gathered them. The older women instructed us just how to cut the vines, and never too much, so as not to disturb the tiny white blooms and so they would grow back more vigorously. Sometimes we would prop the long tendrils up with forked branches so the grapes, when they grew, would be off the ground, away from mice and snails. We always left enough for the animals, though. Then we would stuff the leaves with meat or vegetables, and the fragrance of the warm leaves was like the grape harvest before its time.

Wheat was the best stuffing for grape leaves, with mint and basil. Fortunately, the seasons overlapped. Several weeks before the grape leaves grew too tough to chew any more, the wheat, mixed with companionable plants, barley and goat-grass, covered every flat expanse of Eden and stood hip high. It grew a beard, softly at first, like the fuzz of a youth, and the soft green kernels began to swell.

Then we women made our sickles—a new one each year or the harvest would be cursed, so the custom was. The jaw-bone of some beast, usually a sheep or a goat, made the best sickle. When she'd removed the flat, grinding teeth—some set aside to be drilled for a necklace later—a woman could make the perfect setting for tiny, fingernail-sized chips of stone from such a bone. The litter of men's tool-making gave plenty of such small slivers, which the women retouched as they pleased. The more exacting could strike their own. Then the women set the tiny blades in beeswax along the shallow curve of the jawbone. Even so young a girl as Kochavah made a sickle, with her elders' help.

As soon as her sickle was finished, a woman could begin the harvest, a little every day. Harvesting began while the wheat kernels were still soft and green: we enjoyed their milky soup cooked with onions, plenty of salt, and perhaps the scraps of the men's last kill.

We also enjoyed the splendor of deep red anemones, in contrasting shadows at the feet of the wheat's green stalks, and the banks of sweet-scented iris arcing from the blades of their spearlike leaves.

As the days grew longer and warmer, the wheat whitened. Sometimes the merest touch of unskilled or thoughtless hands would send the grains shattering out of their dry hulls to the ground. "For the Mother Who feeds us," we would say, and leave them for Her. But a skilled reaper knew how to get her basket under the spikes before she swept her sickle around them.

Poppies bloomed now, bright scarlet among the whitened stalks. Thistles and lilies, sun shades of yarrow and the yellow groundsel, found their way into Eve's hair and belt, though I felt such decorations had an emptiness for her, now that my father wasn't there to savor them. Eve, I noticed, left much grain for the Mother, when her mind drifted in the warm sun. I hoped the Mother was grateful, and would lead my friend away from dangerous thoughts.

While still bearing a hint of green, the grain was best set near the fire, or in warm ashes, till it popped and burst its tough outer hull without any other work on our part. The children especially liked this treat, rolled perhaps in a little salt and flavored with grease. The smell alone was delicious.

And when a kernel of wheat was too tough and brown to chew, the harvest moved into another method.

We emptied the pits in the Cave of the Dead and used that wheat first. We got the men to cut down a new log, stood it on end and hollowed it out a bit. Then women took turns, in pairs, pounding the old wheat with heavy wooden mallets. Between turns at the mortar, other women helped to parch the new-gathered grain, to loosen the hulls so it required less pounding. Or we would boil the grains first, set them in the sun to dry with a child to frighten away ravens, and then remove the chaff. Everyone knew what bellyaches the greedy got at this season if they ate too many handfuls of grain without removing the hulls.

When the chaff came off easily, we brought out the grinding stones. These stones were too heavy to carry from place to place with the season-moves, and Eden was the only stopping place where we needed them. We stored them in the Cave of the Dead, next to the wheat pits. It was the custom for a pair of partridges to nest in each one, but the bird families were raised and gone by the time we needed the querns. We had only to shoo the most backward of the offspring out, then rinse the speckled quartzite clean of feathers and bird lime and drag them to the more pleasant open air to begin our work.

Any river cobble served well enough as a grinding stone. The more fussy woman might peck hers with another pointed rock into a shape that matched the hollow in the quern better. But long grinding itself usually did that sooner or later. And until our hands remembered the movements, the action ground our knuckles and nails, as well, leaving smarting grazes as it tried to get flesh to conform.

We didn't grind to powder in any case. We kibbled the kernels, a process the pounding in the log began. Different women preferred different levels of coarseness. Once ground, it was served either soaked as a cold salad with parsley, onions, and meat drippings, or cooked as a gruel. I preferred the sweetness of honey in the gruel—there would always be a hive to raid by this time in the season—or the early figs with a little anise seed. Some liked a savory gruel, to which we could add lumps of grease and a little meat.

This might sound like a lot of work, but indeed it wasn't, not with ten or twelve women lending their hands and their company. There was no purpose, anyway, to gathering, pounding, and grinding more than the clan could eat in a day. We couldn't carry wheat with us to the next stopping place, and in the fall, when we returned, there'd be plenty of other foods: apples, pears, acorns, pistachios, grapes, figs, game. We only stored enough to perform the women's sprouting secret of the season of equal days and nights. So there was plenty of time to take days off for another dark of the moon, and to sing and chat and play with the children, until the weather grew warm.

The weather grew so warm that the beeswax grew soft in our sickles. This, along with other signs, said it was time to move on.

Slowly, the clan began to prepare for the move. Once we'd used the pit wheat up, this year's wheat replaced it, carefully covered to keep out small animals. We could eat this year's wheat, but never very much, never enough to use up the vast fields around us that shifted with every breeze blowing through Eden. Before there was any danger of that, the nights became unpleasantly warm and mosquitoes began to bite. The men grew anxious to start hunting hooved beasts again, after the peace of the Season of the Little Ones when, so they said, even the lamb could lie down with the lion.

At this time, a day or two before we left Eden, Adam returned to the clan.

His figure rising out of the twilight into the glow of the fire startled me late one evening. I thought he was a bear, or a spirit. Eve and I had been laughing together in one of our uncontrollable sessions where our sides ached and tears rolled. We both stopped instantly the moment we saw him. The silence throbbed in my ears.

How gaunt my father looked, how worn, how haggard. There was dust in his beard, gray, I thought. A hollow blackness surrounded his eyes. No dog followed at his heels. He said nothing, but squatted opposite us, letting the firelight give his skin a glow its burnt husk did not otherwise have. So much dealing with grain made me see him too in images of chaff and mortared core.

Without a word, Eve got up and handed him the last of some wheat gruel. The two of us were fed up with such fare, but one couldn't throw wheat out except, when breaking camp, with ceremony into the running water. So the gruel had sat by the fire on a fig leaf, untouched, for two days at least. Soured gruel was another clear sign of the time to move.

"That's a fig leaf," I began. "Maybe a man shouldn't eat off a fig leaf—"

Then a look at my father's exhausted face made me pity him and I didn't care.

The leaves of the Fig had grown large enough to hold food now, and weighted by the gruel, the leaf had sunk in the center on the uneven ground into a sort of cup. Adam folded the leaf into a funnel and let the soured, foaming brown juice run off the mess and down his throat first. I watched the lump in his throat under his beard work ravenously at that, and then the fingerfuls of gruel afterward. Some people—men especially, I'd noticed—liked grain when it had reached this slight, bubbling sourness. Adam closed his eyes and sighed so deeply it made my insides quiver.

He chewed and swallowed, scooped, chewed, and swallowed again.

Then he sighed, a dreadful, defeated sound. "How I love the taste of wheat," he said.

Twelve

"No, I will not season-move with you this time," Grandfather said.

For the three moons of the spring Eden-stopping, the old man had sat, dozing in the warming sun. He was comfortable enough, we'd all assumed. Grandmother or one of his sons would help him when he had to relieve himself, and sometimes he'd hold his belly and moan slightly when he thought no one was looking. Otherwise it was easy enough to think he was re-covering his strength — for the next long haul.

Then this.

And his words were not just the grumbling of a surly old man as he saw the grinding stones rolled back into the cave, the gap-toothed sickles discarded, the leftover grain given to the river, the bundles of belongings made up, hefted for weight and balance, remade. He must have thought about making this statement for a long time, whispering of it to Granny under their skins at night.

For Granny too had carefully prepared something to say. "I will stay with him. I know my mind is burdening you all. It gives me no pleasure to be so forgetful and surely none to those

I love. I never wanted to get this way, to let this happen. I will
stay with my husband."

It was the most lucid statement we'd heard from her for
the season. We had to give it respect.

Nobody said anything, feeling the heavy awe due ancestors and letting the loss drag at our hearts, honoring the old
people with our wordlessness.

Then suddenly, Adam broke the somber moment fiercely.
"No, Father, you shall not stay."

Adam hadn't spoken of his hunt beyond the disappoint-
ment we all saw in his face. Fruitless though the journey had
obviously been, it had nevertheless rekindled his regard among
the clan. He had traveled farther and seen more of the world than
any other. His were words to be listened to—and he knew it.

But not now, and not on this subject. Grandfather shook
his head. "Son, there comes a time in every man's life when—"

"But not for you. Not yet. You've got years."

"No, son. I cannot make another season-move. And the
summer move? When there are sometimes steep rock faces to
climb? I cannot make it."

"You can."

"I say I will not. I will not season-move again."

"We will help you," Adam insisted, his body tightening
into a crouch like a wildcat before it springs. "We will carry
you over the rock faces."

"Like you do the babies," Grandfather scoffed, a shadow
of the old, heroic vigor returning.

"You can make it. It's only a two-day trek. Three, perhaps.
We can go slowly."

"I don't want to go slowly any more. I don't want to go at
all." The old man's face, lined, almost gashed with wrinkles,
had the settled firmness of bark under the blue-white thistle-

down of his beard. "The pain is more than I can bear." He rubbed his sunken belly.

"Afra can give you something for the pain. The poppies are going to their pods now. Poppy milk will—"

"I don't want milk like an infant."

"But Father, if you stay here, you and mother, without hunters—"

"You can't frighten me with tales of hyenas, starvation, and fevers. Frighten me, Adam? Me, who killed an aurochs?"

Adam skirted the name of his fear. "You will deny us the chance to give rites due to a great hunter like yourself."

"And you wish me to die, not like a hunter, facing the threat head-on, but helpless and pained and mewling like a child. Your mother, Adam—" And the old man took his wife's hand gently. "Your mother is the widow of a man whom the spirits took to themselves on the horns of a bull, the wife of the bull's slayer. And in her own flesh she did not flinch to look at death three times, each time she bore one of you children. You cannot wish a lingering death, this slow, numbing fading of the wits, for her, either. There comes a time, son, when a man must embrace death as he has embraced life. The one is meaningless without the other. To love life and not to take death in the same embrace is to leave dark and evil shadows behind yourself. I will not do that to my clan, whom I have loved above all else."

All of the women were weeping now and not a few of the men had covered their eyes.

"Sing your mother and me to the spirits before you set off," Grandfather said, speaking in the tones of a young warrior, "and we will bless the clan from the world beyond."

Rubbing my eyes, I failed to see what happened next. But I heard the clatter of spear butts and arrow reeds. It jarred the sorrow from me. My father had dropped his weaponry to the ground.

"If you stay, Father, I'm staying with you," he announced.

"The spirits haven't called you to death yet, son."

"No, I don't think they have."

"Don't tempt them."

"I will defy them. For your sake. And for my own."

Clansfolk hissed out air all around me, then sucked it in again at the horror of my father's words. Women raised their hands with three fingers extended either before their own faces or before the faces of their children, to ward off the evil.

"Adam, Adam, that's unheard of," Grandfather said at last, his voice old and frail once more.

"I'm going to do it," Adam insisted.

Adam's brothers dared to enter the talk now. "A man who doesn't heed the Mother's call to move with the seasons is cursed," said Dov.

"The game deserts him," said Ari.

"He starves."

"The heat of summer melts his marrow."

"Mosquitoes riddle his flesh."

"He dies of the yellow summer fever."

Adam said, "I will stay with my father until the Mother claims him. Nothing can stop me."

The brothers looked from one to the other and knew it was true. Adam, it appeared, had gained no wisdom during his long absence but only a sort of madness. And to try and stop such madness was likely to make the ill luck spread through the family.

There are lures on the one hand and threats on the other to sway a man to stay with his clan in the usual round. But he is free to listen to his own heart, and if no word or tale moves him, the clan cannot force him to join them. It was, after all, a season away from the clan that had already done much to break the remaining ties of kinship from my father. I'd seen how his brothers threatened with as much force as they could and my father hadn't even shifted to regain balance.

It was as if he'd taken a knife and cut the entire net of claims, duty, and love any man is swaddled with at birth in a single pass. The only rope hindering Adam now was that, one might say, bound at the other end to the aurochs. He thought he was free when he followed the pull of this one cord which dragged him along unmercifully.

That was why he couldn't bear to take a last look at his father. Not because he loved the old man more than his brothers, nor because he was a more dutiful son. The opposite was probably closer to the truth. Though Grandfather was the only man he'd ever called "Father," the blood of Eben, dead in the forbidden river, flowed in Adam's veins.

Adam could not even allow a sick old man to return to the Mother when he heard Her call, all because of the yank of the aurochs-hide cord around his spirit. Grandfather was the last man left alive to have killed an aurochs bull. In fact, he was the last man to have seen more of the beasts than an empty skull or a heap of weathered dung. Grandfather was no longer able to hunt. But some spirit power lingered in that shriveled frame, some power that Adam sensed. And my father's single-minded bondage would fight heaven, earth, clan, and spirits before he would let that power pass from this world without finding a way to claim it for himself.

"You do your mother and me no favor." Grandfather spoke quietly. "With your stubborn care, our lives will linger. With your strong life you will frighten off more than hyenas. You will delay the Mother's approach. That is not what we want."

"It is what the voice in my heart wants, bellowing with the voice of the aurochs," Adam concluded. "It is what I must do, stay here with you until the Mother claims you, then sing your spirits on with due honor. I will call on the spirit of the aurochs to go with you, as they must go with one who mastered them. I will call on the aurochs, then, when they are close to earth. I will call on them to return to us."

Thirteen

We clustered our season-move burdens at the mouth of the Great Cave of the Dead, but we stood in the stale, dust-ladened air within. Grandmother and Grandfather sat side by side on the grave markers they had chosen and that their sons had moved into place for them near the back of the cave. On Grandfather's other side lay the mound of dust that marked his first wife. Each of us placed flowers in the withered old hands and sang the parting song, thick with both echoes and tears.

"Come to our clan again, when the Mother wills.
We will wait for you in the summer meadows."

At last the golden daylight crept farther into the cave and would wait no longer. We all gave Grandmother and Grandfather one final embrace, then went to claim our bundles. We shifted skins and tools more comfortably to our heads or backs, then set off, still singing when tears did not totally overcome us.

My father did not come a single step with us in his stubbornness, but stood where he had from the first, at the mouth of the cave, neither mourning nor mourned. Nobody said much to him, not even I. And only Eve touched him. She lingered behind the rest so she could take a hand and press it, unseen. I saw them together, my throat welling with nausea. I heard my father murmur what he thought only Eve could hear: "Soon. Soon, my love. I will catch up with you in the summer meadows, bearing a bull's head in triumph."

I stuck close to my friend's side after that, and was glad to be leading her out of Eden and away from Adam. This thought eased the loss of my grandparents somewhat.

Rooks and starlings, black among the gold, were taking their turns at the wheat harvest. Their shiny jet eyes blinked back at us, their voices chirred and croaked escort to our dirge.

We left the easy slope of the valley and its greenness and began a steep climb of naked rock, side by side with a clan of mountain sheep. One of them, an old ram with stiff joints, stumbled, then, on the next leap, fell. His kin stopped to bleat mournfully at him once or twice.

Then our men went to claim him for themselves. They took his death as a sign that the Mother had given the life of this creature to us, a sign that she had lifted the spring ban. Just so might the hyena clan claim us when we die—if we did not bury our dead carefully and beg the Mother to return their spirits to another clanswoman's womb.

I thought of my father and his father and mother, and thought that nothing good could come of trying to make our lives any different from the way the rest of Earth's creatures lived. The Earth had not made Herself any other way and no man—nor even an entire clan—was big enough to counter Her in anything.

Then I had to turn my attention to Devorah, lending her a hand up the pass with her load and her baby. Two more dark moons had still not rid her of the second infant in her belly. We could put off thought of such things during the comfort of a spring stopping place, but not on the move. I could see she was far along: her doeskin skirt was belted high and the breasts she left naked in the heat were brown and swelling. Her condition threw her balance off badly. We women and some of the men passed her squalling son from hand to hand between us over the difficult stretch, then turned to help her, too.

When Devorah stood at last where the way eased up a bit, she closed her eyes a moment in weakness and clutched the bottom of her belly, breathing heavily in the thinning air.

For a moment it must have crossed her mind — as it crossed mine — that the clan might have left her behind as they had left Grandmother and Grandfather. In her exhaustion, however, she couldn't be roused from such a fearsome thought even to take her infant, and little Lev was now red in the face with screaming.

Soon, however, breath and life returned to her. She looked better and gave her baby the breast. But when she moved on, Devorah fell in step beside Afra and the two women spoke long and earnestly together. I understood better what desperation had driven Aunt Gurit to attempt means drastic enough to kill her rather than continue a pregnancy that made her fall behind.

A breeze lifted the sweat-heavy hair off my neck and I shivered. I smelled an odd sharpness in the air. I thought at first it must only be the welcoming breath of the summer meadows. Each season had its own quality of air, and each of them felt fresh and a little strange when first met. The uplands' rarity in particular took some getting used to. But another gust turned my head toward itself like a schemer's tap on the shoulder.

Looking down the long way we had climbed, and out, farther west and south, I had a view over the ridges. Brown and bunched, they rested overlapped and side by side like lovers' resting limbs, almost down to Mother River. But black and stacking clouds pressed the horizon from sight. These were the source of the wind, and unhealthy color flushed them like a man who's tried to raise a fire by blowing when his tinder's too wet.

Others noticed the clouds, as well.

"Looks like rain." Rachel stated the obvious.

Nobody stated the other obvious, that we almost never got rain in summer.

Nor did anybody else remark on how like a fast-moving herd the clouds looked. I had never seen aurochs, but that's how I imagined them, black and rolling. And sweeping forward with the low thunder of their bellows, the lightning flashes of their horns. Nobody said that Adam and his single-mindedness had called down this stampede upon us. But I felt it as clearly as if they had.

I looked about for Eve. Perhaps her clan had summer rain and she could tell us about it. Then I discovered the most heart-stopping thing of all.

Eve was no longer with us.

———————

My mind raced, trying to sort out when I'd last seen her. I couldn't remember, and this sent me scurrying from clans-woman to clanswoman.

"Before the rock face." They had no better answer than I had.

"If a woman reaches that age and doesn't know to keep up with the clan, she deserves . . ." How the threat might have concluded I could only imagine. The women let their voices drift off, their eyes wander warily to the gathering storm. Then they set themselves with purpose to their walking.

The rock face, I thought, which the men had climbed with us. Eve had vanished at the rock face, while the fallen ram oc-cupied the men. They were not then bringing up the rear and urging a slow one on, as they did through most stretches of a season-move. Distracted, they could not protect a straying woman from beasts—or from herself.

I wondered about the cord that must be tugging at my friend's heart, to make her refuse the safety of the net of the clan around her. I even wondered about the cord that might be strangling my own heart—but not for long.

"I must go back and find her," I said to the women about me. "She has never moved with us before. She doesn't know the way."

"She knows the way," Rachel said sourly.

For once, nobody laughed. My aunt looked off to the west with a dark pucker between her brows, whether at the gathering storm or where she imagined Eve might be, I wasn't certain.

I was leaving the clan without a storyteller. The children would want stories of brawls in heaven to soothe them when they scurried to shelter from the storm. As the saying is, "The people without a story has no loincloth." But my clansfolk didn't seem to mind. I suppose they assumed, as I did, that I would be back soon—certainly before nightfall—if not with Eve, at least with a new story to tell.

I passed my uncles, bringing up the rear of the clan, carrying the fallen ram between them. They were not as far behind us as hunting men usually travel. They already had their catch, of course, and the storm gusts hurried them along to help the women and children instead.

"Eve!" I shouted to them over the storm's noise and pointed. They paused a moment with concern, but then shrugged and let me go.

Fierce gusts of wind stopped me at the rock face. Evil spirits wanted to hinder me, worse, to pick me off the mountainside and fling me, like the old sheep, onto the rocks below. I huddled and watched the swift-moving clouds bruise the sky. Again they made me imagine what I had never seen—aurochs. Triple-pronged lightning lanced the mythical beasts to a frenzy, blew their hot breath in my face, and I could hear the faraway growl of answering spirits.

Once the storm hit, the gusts calmed somewhat. I knew I must attempt the rock face now, for storm beings, whether aurochs or not, hate those whom pride sets on high, exposed places, and delight to strike them.

The first drops were huge and oily. When they hit the rock to which I clung, climbing backward, water spattered up into my face with many drops of a more normal size. It seemed to be raining up as well as down. The moisture released a warm, wet rock smell around me, released the smell of my own leathers and of me, mingled together in one being.

Rain slicked the surface. I found the climb more terrifying than I'd ever known it before, even as a child when my little legs could hardly make the longer stretches from foothold to foothold.

Then came the hail. The pebble-hard pellets left red marks where they hit me and rolled and bounced around as if they had spiteful little lives of their own. No men had posted themselves from point to point along the route to call out the best way to go, to lend a steadying hand.

After a time that seemed twice as long as the climb up, I reached the bottom of the cliff. The sudden level ground jarred my legs all the way to my hip joints. I stopped to catch my breath and get my bearings, then looked around for Eve. I had vaguely hoped to find her here, afraid, perhaps, to make the climb. Perhaps her clan knew nothing of rock faces. That hope was better than my suspicion that even spiritual things, things more fearful than the mere mountainside plunges, did not daunt her.

I called my friend's name, but the storm blew the word back in my teeth.

Eve wasn't at the foot of the rock, where I remembered seeing her last. I went on, retracing the clans' footsteps that the downpour had first washed from the dust and then buried in the hail's white dried peas as if they'd never been. Rain was coming down now like hangings of ill-tanned roeskin, making all the world a lurid yellow. Earth had already pulled in on Herself against the summer dryness and absorbed the rain slowly. It ran from Her like waste and pooled, making my footsteps treacherous. Just so did the water pour from my own brown skin, grown cold and goosefleshed. My bundle, which I shifted to my head, and my leathers, seemed to soak up twice their weight. And mud webbed heavily between my toes.

The clan would have found shelter by now. My mind wandered back up the mountainside toward them with longing. I had to force my attention downward instead.

I paused where the path turned sharply and a lip of overhanging rock offered a view of almost all of Eden, where the riverlike sky did not deluge the river at the bottom of the gorge.

I could see our old camp, already mere shadows of inundated fires and lean-tos washing away. Mother Lilith's Tree on the terrace below remained more fixed than anything we mortals set upon the earth.

Even as this thought crossed my mind, a flash of light blinded me for the briefest instant before the most dreadful noise I'd ever heard split creation from the sky to the center of my brain. I dropped my bundle and buried my head in my arms, helpless to do anything else.

Presently I dared to look up, but only when my mind took hold of the thought that the evil spirits alive in this storm must have vented their rage in a bolt of lightning. Once the ringing cleared from my head, I went over my own body to make sure I hadn't been their target.

I smelled the smoke first—then saw billows from deep in the heart of Eden. We usually expect lightning to blast the heights, but the sight that met my eyes confirmed that spirits may strike where they will. The Lilith Tree seemed to have grown remarkably, burgeoning gray-green leaves halfway up the mountainside. A second look, and the action of the wind, told me the leaves were smoke. The tulips and anemones blossoming in unnatural confusion at the root were petals of flame.

The sacred Fig was on fire.

Fourteen

I hardly dared pick up my pack to take one more step toward so awesome a sign. And when I did, I could not do so without tears of terror twining with the rain on my face. But stumble on I did.

I found them in the Cave of the Dead, my grandparents immobile as the stones on which they sat, plucking in bewilderment at the grave flowers still in their laps. I tried to speak to them, but I'd never spoken to the dead. And they'd never spoken as dead before, either.

While we were still stumbling with greetings, Eve joined us in the cave. I supposed she had gone to study the disaster from a better viewpoint. I looked at her as hard as waterlogged eyes would allow, expecting at least sheepishness in her face for all the trouble she'd caused. I saw only beauty, unmoved, placid, warm—and almost dry.

Perhaps she and my grandparents could not see from this spot what the gods had blasted. Close-standing oaks and pistachios stood in the line of sight as well as a knife-sharp outcrop. But surely they could smell—now see—the smoke.

"It is here. It is now. It is our Lilith Tree!" The effort to keep from screaming gave my voice a storyteller's distance.

What, after all, is here and now with the dead?

The living Eve turned from me and stood in the doorway of the cave. From time to time, more lightning haloed her form with ivory. But the pursuing thunder never made her flinch.

"It is a sign," she said presently. "Adam says it is a sign from his God."

"A sign of serious displeasure," I protested.

"A sign of a new way to come."

"An evil way."

"Adam saw the bull his God in the storm."

So I was not alone in what I'd seen. But in finding meaning—? "It can only be evil."

"Adam doesn't think so."

"That is the Lilith Tree burning."

"Adam says it is a cleansing. And good."

And perhaps, I thought, the bull in the clouds was not the messenger. Perhaps the Tree had called the storm to itself. I thought of the mother I had never known and hoped that the message, no matter how dreadful, might have come from her.

Another flash made Eve seem to tremble like moonlight on moving water. But by the time the crash came, she was clearly unmoving, and would give me no other answer but this—this and her back.

In a panic I looked to my grandparents. Grandmother's mind seemed to have escaped the storm by going on a particularly distant wandering. Grandfather spoke lucidly, but said only, "I think perhaps the storm is letting up now."

The cave was dry, warm and out of the wind, although it was still the place of the dead. I shrugged off my pack and the wettest of my garments, but I couldn't shrug off my concern with such ease.

"Where is my father?" I asked. My voice was quiet and hoarse. I moved as I spoke, trying to set myself in Eve's line of vision without getting out in the storm again.

I must say I was relieved not to find him with her. It didn't much matter where Father was, as long as he was not with Eve. And I hoped speaking of him would not conjure him to us. But when Eve gave no reply, nor even sign that she understood me, I tried again.

"Where is Adam?"

My question hardly mattered. For my words seemed to fall into a pit of silence. Even birds sheltering in the scrub oaks seemed to have forgotten their squabbles. Then, as my words died, a low rumble began all around us.

My first thought was that this must be yet another lightning strike. It didn't crash into the earth all at once, however, but started low, like no more than thunder beyond the foothills. Before I could comment on that, the earth below us shook with a violence so long and fierce that in the end, the thunderclap seemed a mere flash of grease in a fire. Now not only the cloud-riding spirits were angry.

The very dead below us and Mother Earth that held them shook restlessly against us.

"Mother!" I cried as the shaking brought me to my hands and knees. I heard Grandmother say the same thing, and I thought, with what space the clouds of terror had left in my mind, Yes, it is the Earth Mother that calls the sky and not the other way around. She on Whom we all call, old crone, maiden who has never known a mother, and everyone in between.

A cave is a good haven during a storm, but not in an earthquake. I knew the full cycle of tales about how solid rock ceilings had come crashing down on cave dwellers until our ancestors had taken this as a sign to leave such places to the dead, who were buried already.

The rocks that shook loose from the cave roof this time were small, and mostly from one fissure on the other side of the opening from where we crouched. A great deal of dust rolled up or tumbled down, but this soon cleared once the Earth Herself settled.

Whatever message the Mother was giving us, Her anger was not spent—not yet. These were only words of warning.

The silence that followed, breathless in its emptiness, filled the world with more awe than the shaking. The birds had yet to find their voices again, the very grass seemed turned to stone. I waited until it no longer seemed blasphemy, then I got to my feet and brushed the dirt off both knees and shoulders.

I began quietly to recite a verse meant to soothe both Earth Mother and unsettled spirits in their wrath. When I heard Eve chime in, I knew life would continue, though I wondered how we dared until we had untangled this message of Lilith, message on message.

Because I failed at this untangling, I sent my thoughts in a straight line instead. Straight, over the lands I traveled when the spell of stories was upon me. "Mother," echoed in my mind. "Mother, we are out of balance here in Eden. The heavens blast, the earth rocks like a mother's arms. Lilith, please—"

But I felt I spoke only to myself.

"We should help the elders out of the cave," Eve said to me. Hers were the first words outside of ritual, and a distraction from trying to figure out what our Mother's anger might be.

I looked back at my grandparents, covered with dust from the roof of the cave as if from blade bones full of burial dirt. "But we have sung the funeral songs for them. They should stay in the cave."

"The earth might move again," Eve insisted. "Rocks that have loosened this time will fall from the ceiling next time. Big rocks."

Grandfather overheard us and was already on his feet, ignoring his pain in his effort to get to the open. He had dropped his funerary flowers into the dirt and shuffled carelessly through them. Eve took his arm and helped him.

Grandmother was harder to move. She got as far as the place near the cave mouth where the rocks had fallen, where they lay new and white. Though she had followed her man all her life, she now wanted to stay among the rocks. She spoke the names of kin who were gone and moved as if to embrace them among the fallen stones. "Mother, Mother, come again and get me. Don't leave me behind. I want to be with you." Then I heard "Daughter Gurit" like a stranglehold around my heart. Other, less coherent things slithered out of her thin, parched lips.

Eve came back to us and was firmer than I wanted to be about bringing the old woman out. It was still raining; Eve settled them in as sheltered a spot as possible, under a cluster of walnut trees. The walnut leaves were hail-shredded, and small, hard, round fruits untimely knocked from the limbs beaded the ground. I was beginning to feel nauseated, as anyone might who had unburied the dead. I could almost smell the decaying flesh; my skin seemed to crawl with maggots I'd caught from them.

Then, there was an aftershock. Not nearly so strong as its parent, yet its tiny added effect served. The back of the cave let loose, as if a child wantonly toppled the stack of rocks he'd earlier so carefully set up. When the dust had cleared, I saw that had we not moved my grandparents, they would now have been quietly buried, no agonizing wait for hyenas or starvation. Our Mother Earth was, in fact, endlessly merciful. And we had thwarted the Earth's will—

But Eve didn't seem to see it that way. She exulted at having saved these lives and might have been difficult to bear except that she kept glancing up the hill behind us.

"Adam," she said, in tones so like Granny's they made me shiver. Then she said, firmer, "Your father, Na'amah."

"What of my father?" I asked. "Where is he?"

"Up in the other cave."

"The men's cave?"

"Yes. We should go and see . . . see if he's all right."

"We should not. Women at the men's cave? Aren't the spirits angry enough already?"

Eve considered this, but not for long. "We should go," she said, quiet but stubborn.

"I could go," I admitted. "And just look in, perhaps." I remembered when I had done that before. "I am not initiated."

In the end, Eve would not stay behind with my grandparents. I couldn't stop her. Her rounded legs, stroked by rabbit fur, carried her up the sodden hillside, in spite of my wishes.

"Stay back here, out of sight," I told her when we reached the place. "I'll go in alone."

She did, so I drew a deep breath of relief. And went forward alone.

"What is it? What's the matter?" Eve demanded when I returned to her.

I'd tried to wipe the sight from my face at least, if not from my mind. Obviously I had failed.

"Is he there?" Eve insisted.

"Yes." I found I could say that much.

"But he's hurt. He must be hurt. I must go to him."

"Eve, you must not. You are an initiated woman."

Eve waved that off as nothing. I tried to hold her but she broke easily from my grasp and pushed ahead.

Even Eve stopped at the mouth of the men's cave, though whether from awe of the place or at the sight it held, I couldn't say. The aurochs skull sat unmoved on its shelf of honor, its eyes black pits, but steadily fixed—on us and our boldness. Father lay where he'd been squatting, before a small ritual fire and the aurochs skull. His temple closest to us was blurred with blood and the stone that had caused the blow—big as two fists—lay nearby. A fine layer of burial dust seemed to cover him as it had my grandparents. The cave smelled of hemp—and new blood.

So this was the Mother's message. I was to lose a father as well as grandparents on this dreadful day.

"You must go in and get him," Eve said, the place squeezing even her words into a thin whisper.

"I must not," I hardly dared to hiss back. Tears wet every part of my face, mouth as well as nose and eyes.

"Na'amah, how can you refuse? You, as you have said, are uninitiated. And Na'amah, he is your own father."

"He is my father. But it is clear the greater law of the Mother has him."

"Look—he's moving."

And we heard a groan. I found it harder to bear the idea that he might still be suffering than that he had already gone from me.

Eve grew more frantic. "He's alive. Na'amah, you must go in. So we can tend him. He will not survive such a wound if we do not tend him."

"With such injuries, it is death to move the victim."

"But we cannot tend him in the men's cave."

"The Mother must tend him in Her own way, Eve. If he comes out to us, we will rejoice. But if She keeps him, that is Her right and we mustn't deny Her."

"You have to help him, Na'amah." Her whisper held a whimper. "For me, if no one else."

I refused with a silent gesture and turned away from the

unbearable sight of dread and power. "It is like my father's blood-father lying in the River of the Mother's Hand," I said. "Father always wanted to be great like Eben. That desire all but crushed the life from him. And now he is great. We should rejoice. He will enter the stories we will pass from generation to generation, whenever the dread of this day is mentioned. But no mortal may move him—at least, no mortal woman. If I could run for our men, perhaps, but I'm not at all certain they would come."

I stopped my babble; it was growing shrill. And I could tell Eve was sparing no further thought for me. She licked her dry lips and rubbed her cheeks with nervousness. But she took a deep breath—and ducked into the men's cave.

The Earth twitched, another, slight aftershock. A scream strangled in my throat. I braced my feet, certain Earth would move again and again. I buried my face in my hands for another blast of lightning. When neither happened, surprise fixed me instead, caused my breaths to come too fast, too shallow. My head grew light and faint.

Slowly, I regained control of my breathing and, with it, my senses. When I dared, I peeked into the cave again. I saw nothing but Eve's struggles. She had my father caught under his arms and was trying to drag him. Gasping with sobs of terror, I found myself with her, hurrying and helping for no other reason than to end the horror of the profanation.

As I entered the cave, I felt the power of the place under our feet. It was like the power a woman may feel when she sits on a man's lap and the Mother in her calls to the god in him. Only here, the power was the cumulated maleness of generations, the very god himself. It tripped my feet into clumsiness.

But I kept moving.

Fifteen

I divided my time between the old people at the big Cave of the Dead and my father outside the men's shrine. Except for the fact that they were supposed to be dead, I decided I ought to have stayed mostly with my grandparents, because Adam had Eve. But precisely because Adam had Eve, I didn't dare leave them alone.

I suppose I ought to have been able to leave my grandparents alone. We had sung the song of parting for them; they were dead. But Grandmother, having found the place in her mind where she stored knowledge of food gathering, would wander off to find it. And I couldn't bring myself to eat without offering to the elders first, as I had always been taught to do.

Now that we didn't have a hunter, there was lots more gathering to be done. The fact that the Valley had been foraged out, at least as much as Mother allows, made the task that much more difficult. The spring foods wilted past their prime or vanished altogether. Hunger began to inflame the illnesses.

Eve helped me, of course. She couldn't let her patient die of hunger, having defied heaven and earth to bring him this far. But of course, she often hunted thyme or valerian—blooming vividly purple at that season—for remedy instead of food. She said, and I knew, that a blow to the head did better with a stiff,

meaty broth than the tiny spears of bolted spinach and tough
grape leaves we brought. Eve's eyes always wandered to the
animals we saw, as well as to other things that weren't allowed.

Figs from the blasted Tree did not escape her eye, for the
rain had put the fire out rapidly and half of the Fig still stood,
shadowed with ripe, purple, forbidden fruit. But who would
eat from a Tree the spirits had so clearly marked? Even if we
hadn't seen the strike, we would have avoided the fruit when
we came on it, scarred with the black ash of spirit anger.

My father, once he regained his senses, suffered raving
fits. He had wanted to stay behind to join my grandmother, I
thought. Well, now he has his wish.

Eve, however, doubted the fits from the first and soon
stopped giving him mind-clearing herbs. "It is a vision he had,"
she told me. "A true vision, sent by the God, the spirit of the
aurochs whose name is Bull of Heaven. Your father mixed
some of the aurochs dung he found with his hemp and let it fer-
ment. He learned the recipe from the old man, and no one has
been able to make it for decades because there was no dung. It
makes the voice of the gods much stronger in a man's ear. The
voice came and told him. It is the Bull who moved the earth."

"Nonsense," I said. "Everyone knows the Earth is Mother,
and it is She Who moved."

"You wouldn't know this." Eve looked at me almost pity-
ingly. "But they teach it to you at initiation. A woman shakes
when her man moves over her, as the storm moved over
Mother Earth on that day, full of virility."

After that, I sat and listened to my father sometimes. His
words did seem lucid enough, though strange. He didn't remember the earthquake at all. "But a Voice. The Voice of the
Bull. I knew it. I'd heard it before. While trailing the aurochs
this spring. One afternoon when I was lost and had been without water for two days. The Voice came and led me to a clear

source. Like the lead bull may sniff the air and lead his herd to drink.

"The Voice of the Bull came to me. Not only did He bring me to water, but there was more. 'A new way is coming,' He said. 'A new creation.'"

"'What way?' I asked."

"'A way where men need no longer hunt aurochs to see their seed flourish, innumerable as the stars.'"

"'How will I know this way?'"

"'A sign. I will come to you. With a sign.'"

"And the sign came to me, daughter. As I chewed hemp in the men's cave. The aurochs spoke to me again. The time is near. Very near."

I listened, as I listened to Granny's ravings. But I didn't know what to say. I couldn't hear my father's words with Eve's evenness and favor. They brought darkness to the edges of my brain.

Just as worrisome, and seemingly more pressing, was the swing of the night sky overhead. The dark of the moon was coming fast. What was I going to do, with five mouths to feed throughout the power time? What was Eve going to do, for that matter, with a sacred Tree blasted so that no one dared come within fifty paces of it, let alone retreat to it?

An even greater fear edged the shadow spaces of my mind: suppose Eve didn't retreat at all? She had come close to doing this our first month in Eden, affected by my father. How would she do without the lure of other women to weigh against Adam? I certainly had no power to force her. What would happen to the world then?

I was thinking on such troubles late one afternoon when the time for these events could not be more than two or three days away. I was sitting through the blistering heat of the day with my grandparents. The bitter smell of plants starved for

water stifled the air and hardly a bird struggled up to embed itself, motionless, in the equally bleached and parched sky.

I knew Eve was up on the hill with my father and that I
should be seeing to them, but the heat had made me lazy. Dust
tightened about my throat like a band of rawhide and set a
rough polish over my skin.

I was longing too for the cool night pastures, and scratch-
ing idly at the bites caused by nights full of mosquitoes. Surely
Eden was never meant for human life at this season. Eve
thought she had pulled Father and my grandparents from the
grave. Hadn't she jumped into the pit with them instead? And
pulled me in after her?

Such were the thoughts that itched my brain at a place I
couldn't reach when suddenly Grandfather called my attention
to a human figure laboring up the Valley on the far side of the
river.

The figure came to the log ford, crossed it. Surely this was
no one we knew. Our clansfolk would come downward, not
up—from the mountains, anyway. If they would be so foolish
as to come.

"It's a woman," Grandfather said, astonished.

"A woman," Grandfather repeated, "traveling alone." Was he
astonished that his eyes could still see so far? Old as he was, I
had imagined he had seen everything.

Grandfather was right. But she was no ordinary woman.
This was apparent almost at once, and grew ever more so as
she drew nearer. Her long black hair snaked unbound from
her brow to her hips. She was naked to the waist, with heavy,
rounded breasts. And snakeskin belted that waist. Sacred black
vulture feathers cuffed her legs at mid-calf. More feathers
formed a sort of cape—or wings—beneath the hair at her back.

She carried a walking staff, curled with a snakeskin and more feathers. Otherwise, she had no belongings at all.

The woman shifted the direction of her climb to come straight toward us, and so the sun, which had been at her back, caught her face more directly. Her eyes remained in shadows still, due to the rather heavy ridge of bone under which her eyebrows rode. And in this light, I could see how dark her skin was, the wheat color of my people's skin left until it scorched.

Then Grandmother spoke, and the strange clarity of her voice, like the strange clarity of Grandfather's vision, let me know that for once, she spoke true.

"It is Lilith," she said, rising with joy, yet a little fear. "It's Mother Lilith."

Sixteen

Lilith," I repeated, feeling cold for the first time in weeks. "I thought Lilith was— Well, just a story."

"Just a story?" Grandmother said, scolding gently. "Your own mother is just a story?"

"I only remember Aunt Gurit," I said, asking pardon. Then I repeated, "I thought Lilith was just a story."

"Have you so little respect for the craft I taught you that you think it's all fluff from old women's dreams?" My grandmother's words had more force because I was aware they might be the last clear thing she ever said. Like a sudden solid stone appearing in a swirl of river.

"No, Grandmother. I just— Well— Lilith? Mother Lilith? Alive?"

"Of course alive. Didn't she plant our Fig Tree? Didn't she plant you on this world?"

"Yes, but then she should . . . she should be dead." I stole a fretful glance down in the direction of that Tree, then quickly returned my gaze to the nearing figure. I could look nowhere else. I watched her pause at the foot of the hill and regard the blasted Tree, but with what feeling I couldn't tell at this distance. The thought that had recurred frequently over the last days came to me again: *we* might in fact be dead. That was why this apparition of a dead woman appeared to us so easily.

"Dead, child? Bite your tongue. Mother Lilith, die?"

"Well, at least . . . at least I expected a . . . a much older woman."

Granny hummed a little, to suggest I was a child and couldn't possibly understand such things. She hadn't had the wits herself to do that in a very long time.

But the main focus of Grandmother's attention was not on me but on our approaching guest. Granny waved now, a formal, respectful gesture. Lilith waved back, a sweep of vulture wings. Then Grandmother got up and walked down to meet the woman, half the rest of the way that remained between them. Grandfather too seemed to forget his frozen joints and bounced after his wife, hardly leaning on his stick. I had no choice but to follow them.

This *is* death, I thought. I knew plenty of tales that told how dead ancestors came to greet the dying and lead them on their final journey to realms unknown. The old and ailing regained youth and vigor when the peace of death claimed them, that was in the stories, too.

As I approached, the snakeskin wrapped around Lilith's staff dislodged itself, dropped to the ground, and slithered off toward the Tree; it was alive, so we must be, against all reason.

Grandmother was kneeling now. I followed her example. Lilith touched her gray head in blessing, then raised and embraced her, kissing her on either wrinkled cheek. Granny, surely, was weeping, although I saw only the back of her head. Tears stood in Lilith's eyes, black, birdlike, and piercing though they were.

"Daughter," I heard the strange voice say—and in strange accents.

"Son," she said then, repeating the act for my grandfather. To hear anyone call the old man "son" seemed so wonderful, I wanted to laugh. But the strange woman did look on him with a hunger one might well credit to a mother savoring the long-lost features of her child.

"And this?" Lilith asked, turning those fierce, swimming eyes at last on me.

"This is my granddaughter Na'amah," Granny said. "Your own daughter, Mother."

"Na'amah," Lilith repeated, lifting my face as if to fix it and my name in her mind. "And the last time I saw you, you were so tiny and wrinkled, I could hardly tell you from any other."

The shiver down my spine at the sound of my name on her tongue rose again and became a sort of airiness in my head. Yes, it seemed I could remember being held by this woman be-fore. I could remember the strange tones of her voice, as if half the open sounds were slurred into one.

Mother Lilith spoke again. "I've always thought Na'amah is one of your clan's most pleasant names; a pleasant name for a pleasant girl." I felt her look right through me, her eyes sharpened by tears. Why should she be crying? I asked. She left me, she—

"Mother," I managed to stammer out at last.

I couldn't remember a time when I'd had anybody to give that precious name to. But all at once I had such a one. I knew it was right. My face stung with tears. What Lilith had given me by allowing me to say that name "Mother" was greater than anything I gave her with the gift of that word. That she had left me to grow up without her suddenly seemed part of her gift to me, as well.

Lilith raised me, kissed me, reaching up, for in spite of all impression, she was small. Her arms went around me with a rustle of vulture feathers and held me greedily while my tears beaded into her hair and released its smell of heat and life. The touch she gave my wet cheek was like the brush of vulture feathers, yet burning. I felt she'd chosen me with that touch, chosen me of all Earth's children—for some mission I did not know.

But perhaps every soul felt the same in Lilith's presence, chosen—and perfectly loved, just as it was. Such a thing seemed not only possible but very likely. I had only to look back at my grandparents. But I didn't want to think that way, not at this moment. I was too jealous of my newfound love.

"Please, please, Mother. Come and join us," Granny said, gesturing the way.

"What, my children, here? Outside the Cave of the Dead? Not within?" Lilith hesitated just a moment, looking around, remembering, before she accepted the invitation and sat.

"Yes, Mother. There was an earthquake, you see, and we—"

"Ah, yes. An earthquake. No doubt that is what I felt. Calling me." I blushed and hung my head. *I* had called on her, not even truly believing in her. But I could not let her see my confusion.

"And aftershocks?" Lilith continued to quiz my grandparents.

"Yes, Mother."

"Part of the disruption that drew me to this place of all places in the world. But an earthquake, my dears? The Mother must love you dearly, to seek to draw you to her in such a quick embrace once your time has come. You rejected her embrace?"

"We . . . the girls, Na'amah and Eve . . . they thought we should come out. For safety."

"You move to the Cave of the Dead—and then fear death." Lilith did not ask but stated it. And it certainly did sound ridiculous coming from her.

"Na'amah is with us, you see." Grandfather seemed to beg pardon.

With this reminder of my presence, Granny gestured quickly that I should offer our guest some refreshment. Had I forgotten every scrap of manners and could only stand and stare like a fool?

There was nothing but mint, so I began to brew tea.

"I see."

Some doubt draped Lilith's voice, some hint of displeasure. But the eyes with which she watched me showed nothing but love and kindness—at least toward me. I managed to make the tea without a disaster, though nerves shook my limbs.

"And just how," Lilith said, "did such a girl-child—and my daughter—come to be sharing the grave with you?"

"Ah, Mother." Grandfather sighed. "It's a long story."

"I have no doubt it is." Amusement danced in Lilith's voice now—and in her face.

"And confusing," Grandmother faltered. "And sad and all out of kilter."

From the stammer in her voice, I sensed the old woman's mind was crumbling again.

"That's why I am here now," Lilith soothed. "I felt a slip in the Earth's balance as far away as I was. I was in— But that is of no consequence. Here is where I felt the slip. Here in Eden."

"I never doubted you would come," Grandfather said vigorously, attempting to prove himself the only male present.

"Oh, Mother," Grandmother cried. "Can it be fixed? I thought only for the best, but—"

"I suspect balance can be restored. It's never failed before.

Like the time with the Fig Tree. When we planted it. Daughter, do you remember?"

I felt a little twinge of jealousy and dropped the fire-heated rocks into the skin of water on its tripod. I knew of the Tree's planting only from legend so I assumed Lilith couldn't be speaking to me. But suddenly I wished for no other soul in the world to get the name "daughter" from this dark woman.

Grandmother seemed just as anxious to claim the name. "I remember the story, Mother," she said. "Very well. But the Tree, you should know—"

"There, daughter, I know. I saw it on the way up. Lightning, was it?"

"That's just one of the disasters." Granny wept like a child.

"There, there, daughter." Lilith laid a comforting hand on Granny's shoulder. "But before I can help, I must hear the whole tale."

"I . . . I can't say where to begin."

"Begin at the beginning," Lilith urged. "'Once there was— and once there was not . . . '"

Lilith gave her the words, but Granny failed to find them. "Let Na'amah tell it," she said at last.

"Na'amah?" The birdlike eyes turned at last to me, bright under their heavy brows. "A storyteller? She has that of me, then, even if she looks so much like her father?"

"Yes, Mother." I stammered as if I could never tell another tale. I remembered my image in the river, the image that looked like no one else in the clan. I might be looking into the river now.

"And like your grandmother?"

"I hope half so gifted as she is—Mother." I added the name, greedy for it, loving it.

"So tell me. How does one young as you come to be here,

with your grandparents in the land of the dead? You're not even a woman yet, are you, child?"

"No, Mother."

Lilith must have sensed my impatience with my own body for she said gently, "Soon, I guess. Very soon. If we can win you back from this place of the dead, this place for those who have had their lives."

The tea was ready. I served it up, pressing the ram's-horn cup into Lilith's hands like an offering to spirits. Our guest breathed the sweet steam with delight and once more made me feel I'd given her the best gift on earth. I served my grandparents, then myself, saving the cracked gourd for me.

"So, child," Lilith said, drinking out of politeness, it seemed, rather than thirst. She watched me closely until I took my first sip. "Tell me how it was."

I told the tale, from the beginning, and as if charmed, for I had the full attention of a mother. I, who'd never had it before.

When at length I finished, Lilith set down her emptied horn. "Adam again, is it? Yes, I doubted my magic would hold him forever. Adam." She looked up the hill toward the men's cave where I'd gestured time and again throughout my tale. "And Eve?"

"Yes, Mother." It had been long since anyone had put as much space between those two names as Lilith managed. Comfort filled my heart and it rested after the anxiety brought on by the world of the story.

"I see. Well." Lilith fingered the shed serpent skins at her waist. "We shall have to see what we can do about Adam and Eve."

Seventeen

We visited the Tree first. Mother Lilith would have it that way.

"The Tree is not dead," Lilith confirmed. I stood beside her in the strange openness where shadows ought to have been. "The blast destroyed the storks' nests and frightened them away. But it was a spirit warning, that's all. This half will surely live. And the birds will return."

She touched the Tree as she said the words, the very tips of her fingers seeming to pulse life into the charcoal-smeared bark.

"I do think, however," she continued, "we should give it a rest for a while. I'll put a ban on the figs for this fall." She pointed out the tiny wasps, busy about the caprifigs for that coming crop, as if insects were her children, too. "Will you tell the clan?"

"Yes, Mother."

"Come. You will help me set the spell. And help me re-sanctify the Tree for women."

"I, Mother?"

"You worry that you are not initiated?"

I nodded.

"I shall make that of no consequence."

"Yes, Mother."

"And Eve." Lilith set her face like one about to do battle. "Eve should come, too." Then the tautness in her face eased somewhat. "Go get her for me, will you, child?"

"Yes, Mother."

All those years I'd been waiting for Lilith, thinking there was nothing I could do without her. Now I saw there were some tasks for which she needed me.

———————

My father was sitting up, propped against a fall of stone with a horsehide at his back. The spray of betony leaves I was used to seeing bound to his temple with twine, holding on a poultice of boiled onion, was gone now. A blend of hardened scab and purple-green bruise marked the place. The wound still looked angry, but was closed and healing well.

Eve sat beside him, very close beside him. She was running a hand through his curls, hunting for nits. For a moment, it seemed he sat on her as well as on the horsehide. I think they must have been holding hands, although my father moved away as soon as he saw me.

Eve had no such shame. She slipped her free hand down until it rested lightly but pointedly among the black curls on Adam's chest. Then she met my eyes steadily and dared to say, "What are you staring at, Na'amah?"

I stammered "Nothing," and looked away, down the hill as if for help from some source now out of sight. I licked my lips, even drier than I should have been from the climb up the hill under the direct press of the westering sun. I heaved my chest up for the deep breath I needed and said, "Eve, you're wanted down the hill."

That caught her off guard. Her laugh came just a heartbeat too late, just a bit too loud. And the laugh, joined by a toss of her hair, seemed to be for my father more than for me. "Down the hill? Why, Na'amah! What can the old people want from me that you cannot give them? You are their flesh and blood. Surely it's your company and help they want, not mine."

"It's not my grandparents who are asking for you."

There was no breath of wind, no birdsong. But I nonetheless felt something. Heat curling up my back from the powdered yellow earth, from the powdered blue sky, and I knew the feeling. Lilith was with me. She had always been, even when she'd been visiting her children on the other side of the world.

Something in my face made my father start. He removed his hand from Eve's and shifted his shoulder away from her as from a fire grown too hot.

"But no one else is—" Eve didn't finish her sentence because she felt Adam move from her.

"My mother wants to see you," I said in the pause.

"Lilith," my father said, so low I feared he might be losing his senses again.

"That's impossible." Eve's voice was also hushed, but much more danger, much more fight hid in the lowness of her tone.

"That's impossible," Eve repeated, her voice gaining force. "Lilith is gone. She never really existed. Except in your stories to frighten children into good behavior."

"She's come back." I shrugged. I could think of nothing else to say but the simple, unelaborated truth, though I couldn't explain it myself.

"I knew it. Didn't I tell you, Eve?" My father still spoke crushed with quiet. "I could tell she was here."

"You couldn't," Eve insisted to him. "It was your wound. You could tell no such thing."

My father began to try to get to his feet. "I'm going hunting," he said.

Eve's hand shot back firmly to his chest. "You shouldn't," she said. "You shouldn't move. Adam, you're not well."

My father shook her from him and was on his feet. He had none of his weapons at hand but an old, worn spear in need of retipping that he'd used as a crutch in the last few days. He grasped it firmly as a hunter would, for all the sway his weak legs put under him. "I'm going hunting," he repeated, gave Eve another shove, and was gone.

The slope of the hill made me stand below her. Eve could hardly look at me without dropping her chin. But stubbornly she lifted it to the sky, tossed her head, then looked at me steadily. A shrug of her shoulders into the shells of her necklace told me to lead the way.

———————————

"This is Eve? Blessings, daughter."

Lilith opened her arms for my friend, but Eve, who hadn't knelt, didn't move. Lilith moved into her instead. The one-sided embrace was brief.

"Just what I would imagine for Adam." Lilith didn't speak aloud, but I could hear her thoughts as if she did. "Just the sort of girl-child he would like to flatter his first streaks of gray. Haven't I seen it a thousand times before?"

Aloud, she repeated, "Blessings, daughter."

"I'm not your daughter." The force required to say the words in the actual presence of this powerful woman brought tears to sting the corners of Eve's eyes.

"But you left your own mother so early."

Eve couldn't find words to deny the statement, though her eyes continued to flash a dare.

"Not that I can blame you." Lilith's accent gentled her words to a lullaby singsong as she gestured for us all to sit. "My daughter Rimona—your mother—suffered a hard blow when

fever killed your father and you were but a child. She needed a
hunter. She took on your stepfather—for your sake, child, so
you wouldn't go hungry or cold for want of furs. She knew he
was a difficult man, that no other woman would have him. Perhaps he has made her difficult, too. But she did take him for
you."

Eve blinked furiously. She found no words to counter
Lilith's telling of her own story. Still her eyes dared: "How do
you know this?"

"I know this," Lilith replied, just as if my friend had asked
it aloud, "because I was with your tribe when it happened. I
was with your tribe, married to Adam, carrying my daughter
Na'amah."

Her hand reached out to brush my shoulder in an endearing gesture. I would have slipped closer but the way we sat,
side by side, mother and daughter, already seemed too much
opposition to Eve.

"My mother's not your daughter, either." Eve found words
at last, tight, spat words.

"No," Lilith agreed, nodding with a rustle of vulture feathers. "She was, as I recall, a daughter of Semadar who was a
daughter of Nitza."

Eve had to nod, from sheer wonder.

"Yes, Nitza was a girl when I planted the Tree in her clan.
And I remember her father . . ."

So did Lilith chase Eve's generations back from tale to tale
until our separate clans rejoined and there was the common
ancestor, Tzvi.

"Yes, Tzvi," Lilith said. "Tzvi was my own son. I carried
him under my heart, gave him the breast. In time I saw how he
married Tamar and brought their growing family to this side of
the Mother River as the desert crept in upon their traditional
lands. Tzvi found a place and a way of life that circled with the

aurochs and about the mountain valleys as the glaciers with-
drew."

I didn't know what a glacier was, but I sensed cold in it.

"So what is that?" Lilith continued. "Forty generations?
Forty-three? I lose count. Does my daughter Na'amah not tell
you the stories?"

"I . . . I do my best, Mother," I said. I was burning with
guilt, for I had never understood just how vital the stories were
until Lilith put them in this light.

"She tells them." Eve came to my defense, but her tone was
hardly comforting. "Oh, she tells them."

"Perhaps you don't listen." I think Lilith only thought this,
but I heard it. Then she spoke aloud. "You should have no
doubt that I am your mother, Eve. Your great-great-great-
many-greats-grandmother. But still you are my child, as is every
soul in the world, for I have engendered clan mothers and fathers wherever I go. I am your mother, as I am the mother of
every other soul in the world, and have only your interest at
heart. You should not feel yourself alone, feel that you have no
mother, that you are the only woman in the world. Or that only
a man and his bull of a god can create life for you."

Eve was crying now, shaking with sobs that only grew
more violent as she tried to suppress them. I had not imagined
these things about my friend, but Lilith, whom she had never
met, knew them well.

That night Eve slept at our fire by the Cave of the Dead,
and in the morning joined us for a long and private day at the
Tree.

Eighteen

In the morning, Eve avoided looking at Lilith directly, this woman who had first and eternal claim on Adam. And once in a while, when Eve did cast a few sidelong glances at her rival, I read a glimmer there, as if she imagined rubbing the older woman from existence. As one might rub out something drawn idly in mud at the riverside. But then the memory would come to her: Lilith's claim on Adam not only came before hers; it would continue even after death. So Eve only dragged her feet a little to do as my mother bade her.

First, from carefully chosen, river-tumbled chert, Lilith had both Eve and me chip new blades. "Slightly curved, like the form of the moon," she explained as she showed us how to form the cutting edge along the inside of the curve by taking off many tiny flakes with an antler point. She made us haft axes, too, usually a man's tool.

When this rite was done, Eve said she wanted to go check on our charges up the hill. In particular, no one had seen Adam since he'd "gone hunting."

"We left them with enough food." Lilith refused the suggestion. "And we are fasting. Besides, there must always be at least three together at all times, for any women's ritual. Three, for the three stages of our lives."

"That should be a virgin, a mother, and a crone," Eve complained. "I don't think we three qualify."

"Since your grandmother has been sung to the dead, we must represent them here, virgin, mother, crone." She pointed around to us, me, Eve, and then herself. "Eve must be the mother, as her name signifies, though she is still a virgin. Such symbolism works for a rite."

"And so you are a crone, Mother Lilith? At last?" Eve spoke with a quickness that caused me to think: She is no virgin at all. Or certainly wishes she weren't.

I would have made more of this, but Lilith gave her reply with a similar, evading quickness: "For the purposes of ritual." How would the magic work, I wondered, if I was the only one who was what she seemed?

All the long, sticky-hot afternoon we used the new blades on the Tree. "Pruning" was the word Lilith taught us for our task, cutting back the damage and bringing some balance to the limbs that were left.

"It's like dressing a bride for her wedding day," Eve said. No doubt she imagined she would be next to claim that role. That gave her patience.

Or did she imagine it was Lilith she so vigorously chopped? Lilith's past with Adam and all the claims of time to come? That chopping, then, was also against me. I tried to think of other things.

Dusk fell gray about us and the mosquitoes rose. Still fasting, we went down to the river's ford where the animals came to drink. We frightened away the vanguard of a herd of ibex as we each gathered a basket full of the various kinds of dung we found there and carried it back to the Tree. There Lilith had us spread the dung around the trunk and scrape it into the soil with burnt branches.

"If we are to revere this Tree," Eve commented, "I don't see why we should abuse it so with excrement."

"For the same reason that you will come here to bleed," Lilith said. "The same reason this valley ought to be left for so many months of the year. The same reason the old die—so the new can be born and replenish."

"Everything can't have the same reason." Eve still puckered her nose in distaste.

Lilith said gently, "You should come to your own understanding of that. Think about it while you sit here alone during the dark of the moon. If no answer has come to you when that time is over, speak to me again. I will try to explain it better."

Eve said nothing, but I could tell she thought less of Lilith's skills as a teacher than of her own as a student.

Night fell and stars appeared in a hot haze of dust blown off the summer desert. The air stifled us where we curled up beneath the Tree. The night was too warm for a fire, but smoke would have been nice against the bugs. The constant humming in our ears and stinging on every exposed bit of flesh helped us keep the vigil. Nonetheless I had fallen asleep when Lilith gently shook me awake again.

It was moonrise. I could tell by the cooled air, crackling with dark's peculiar clarity around me. Father Mountain's great black hunched back never let us see the moon until after it rose over the plain. The moon seemed like a thin paring of wild horse's hoof. The night insects sank into a brief doze. The roar of the river ordered attention more sharply than ever during the day, as did its scouring smell.

Lilith kindled the pile of wood we'd gotten from the Tree to honor the rise of Mother Moon. She did it with new fire, not even caught from flint but in the old way, from wood spun on wood with a sinew bow. This task was hard in the weak,

ghosted ivory light, and then there was more smoke than fire,
for most of the wood was green. Once fire came, Lilith encouraged Eve and me to stay as close to the stack of sticks as we
could, letting the purifying smoke fill our nostrils, our eyes, our
hair, our every pore. Lilith tossed herbs on to add to the smoke.
I couldn't tell in the dark what they were. The scents too
seemed foreign, sweet and pungent by turns, though none of
them smelled of men.

Then Lilith began to sing. She hollowed her palms to give
her accompanying claps sharp echoes. Not all the words she
sang were in our tongue. And even when I did understand her,
her accent made them seem ancient, as old as Earth Herself,
like boulders groaning together from deep within the mountain. No matter how fast the rhythm, a sense of lament clung
about the chant, a cloak of loss.

Lilith encouraged Eve and me to join in the clapping and
when she had repeated a chorus. They were choruses full of
the words "dark," "moon," "cycle," "rest," made up on the spot.
We also sang of the moon as an aurochs, sacred to Mother
Moon who controlled calving and tides and seasons as well as
the moons of women.

The unearthly polish of Lilith's dark face enchanted me —
her eyes half closed, tranced between her shadowing brows
and thrusting cheeks. Thus invoked, fear came to muffle my
heart and stomach as smoke muffled my lungs. I grew more
afraid, even, than I'd been on the rock face in the storm. This
fear had an edge to it. The edge spoke to me, as a thorn pricks
in the smothering softness of a pile of furs: "You are Lilith's
daughter. You too may claim this power for your own."

I clapped as I was bidden, clapped until my hands were
numb. Eve did, too, although her hands seemed to grow numb
much faster and more often than mine. Lilith, on the other

hand, kept it up without pause until the prunings were all white ash. The horn cup of the moon had tipped past its zenith then, pouring the white ash of another hot day over all the earth.

With ash from the fire so hot it raised red on our skin, Lilith marked our breastbones with moon-white symbols. And the purification was complete.

Not two days later, no moon rose at all. Then Lilith and I walked together, away from the Tree, after leaving Eve to spend the dark of the moon on her own.

"There," said Lilith. "That should keep Eve for a while." I had the sharp impression of a mother settling an unruly child with a pile of shiny pebbles so she can get some tanning done.

"Mother? You don't bleed?" I somehow found the courage to ask.

"No, child," Lilith replied.

The age of the stories I knew about Mother Lilith would, of course, have led to that understanding. Her body, however, belied it. There was some gray at her temples—in some lights— but she certainly didn't look like a woman past childbearing to me. Still, I was glad to hear that, for all her evasion with Eve, she was indeed a crone. I didn't want to have six to care for all by myself during this time.

Lilith knew every cranny of our Valley much better than I, much better than Granny, even. She found many hidden plants and even foods of which I'd been ignorant. Our hunger had ceased since her arrival, though "You must not stay here too much longer," she constantly warned. "These foods I show you, you must never consider them more than famine foods." Barley, I remember, among them. "And I cannot promise you that our taking them now, out of season, will not sorely hurt your Eden—hurt her beyond repair."

Her promise that she wouldn't bleed delighted me, besides the promise of food and in spite of all her warnings. I didn't want to give up a moment with my newfound mother.

Something beyond denial lurked in her words, however. It made me — no, not uneasy, not yet. Full of wonder, though. But then, everything Lilith did was wonderful to me.

"Now," she said, taking the hill up from Eve and the Tree with purposeful strides and the swing of the talisman on her staff. "Now, let's go see about Adam."

Nineteen

I was out gathering when my parents remet.

At first we couldn't find my father. He wasn't with his parents at the Cave of the Dead.

"We should go find him," I'd said to Lilith.

"You said he went hunting."

"He did, but he must be back now. It's been two days."

"I haven't seen him here. Have you?"

Trying to blunt the glint of amusement in her eyes I said, "I mean back up at the men's cave."

"Do you usually go to fetch men from their cave?"

"No."

"Or go after them when they're hunting?"

"No."

"Then leave him. He will come in his man's own good time."

No protest that he might still be weak or suffering moved her, either.

I hadn't wanted to be away when they met again so I hadn't gone far. I was certain I would hear the noise of their reunion, but I didn't. All I knew was that Adam sat near the Cave of the Dead when I returned that afternoon. A clean-scraped food leaf and the empty horn cup by his side, he was fiercely knapping weapon points. Hunting must not have gone well, with the Valley hunted out and only a worn spear to hand. He'd obviously stayed away and gone hungry as long as he could. He had also not dared to raid the newly sanctified women's space about the Tree to get Eve to help him in his distress.

Lilith was equally absorbed in her work—weaving a new gathering sack according to the oldest of our traditional styles, loose single knots around a spray of hemp fibers—and chatting with my grandparents. She ignored my father as intently as he ignored her.

They both ignored me in the effort it took to ignore each other, the product of their last union. Well, I was used to such treatment from my father, but it hurt to have Lilith catch the coldness from him. Indeed, it frightened me. Her powers must be limited if they could be affected so. It didn't take me long to realize only in my father's presence was she less of a mother. Perhaps dealing with the cold knot of my father required her undivided attention. So I did my best to stay out of the way, vowing to be all the more grateful for the times when he would be gone and we could be mother and daughter again.

I didn't have to wait long before she confided to me, "Now that we are all at one hearth, it will be easier to keep an eye on those two when Eve's moontime is past."

Such was my faith in the power of Mother Lilith's wisdom that I assumed she knew from the start what the cure for my father's pride would be. I was surprised, then, when nothing seemed to happen, neither then nor for some time afterward.

"So—husband," Lilith said pointedly to Adam as we sat around the dying fire that first night of the dark moon. "I understand you have been hunting aurochs."

My father scratched the thick, cracked callus of one foot

with the toe of the other. This rasping sound served as all his answer. My throat choked with anger at his silence; it seemed like rudeness. I hardly considered that my anger and his might have a great part of fear in it. But his silence did recall to my mind that Adam and Lilith were husband and wife, not just mother and son. Silences between such couples mean more, perhaps, than between any others. No man would like to hear this from his wife. Her speaking the actual name of the beast to him said plainly she hoped he would find nothing in this quest.

But could Lilith herself fail? Her gentle prodding did seem to have some of a jilted wife's gloom in it. My spine crawled as if I'd heard fingernails on slate. And if she failed . . . ?

"Where did you go?" she asked.

Father only waved, as he'd done for the rest of us, off in the general direction.

"West," Lilith interpreted. "And a little north?"

Father nodded, picked up a spear to mend, and turned intentionally away from her.

"And did you make it to the sea?"

Actually, our tongue had no word in those days for "sea." What did we mountain folk know of "sea"? Lilith named the foreign concept twice, once in a phrase which in our tongue meant "all-encircling lake" and then in another, shorter term. I did not understand the shorter term then but I now assume it must have come from a different language, the language of a people who lived by such a place and so had given it a name.

Adam nodded, ill at ease to meet someone with knowledge of things he'd been pleased to consider his own private mysteries. Things he kept close for the voicing of his own private god.

"Did you cross the sea?"

"It can't be crossed." Adam snapped his words like a braided whip. "It's the end of the world. And, as you say, 'all-encircling.' I followed it throughout the full of the moon. My old dog died there of thirst because the sea is poisoned with salt. Nothing can live in it or by it."

"No aurochs?" Lilith's question was gentle, feeling Adam's defeat.

"No aurochs." I could tell my father hoped this surrender would close their talk.

"Yes, the beasts have almost vanished." Lilith nodded. But that did not close the talk in her mind. "In that direction," she added, almost as an afterthought. Then, "Did you pass by the great mountain lake shaped like a nestling bird? The natives there call it Van?"

"Yes," Adam said. "The water is numbing cold. But what did you mean, 'In that direction'? There are aurochs? Elsewhere?"

She did not return to the subject he was after, however, and he could not force her to it. Instead, he followed her lead and they spoke of this mountain, that valley, this people and that. In the dirt between them, they sketched the way until dark grew too intense to tell mountain range from river.

Lilith knew the path he had followed like the back of her hand. "I have traveled it myself," she explained with a shrug. "Oh, a thousand times."

Adam asked, "And the people in that place — they mark their faces so fiercely with blue-black tattoos — they never tried to cut your throat?"

"Of course not," Lilith said. "They are my children as well as you."

"I barely escaped with my life," Adam murmured. He tried but could not conceal his growing wonderment with this stranger, his wife.

"How fares the headman of this other tribe?" Lilith asked, pressing the journey forward. "The one they call Humbaba."

"Dead last winter."

"Ah, I feared that would be so." She made a sign before her face and over her heart with her hand which I took to be a sign of farewell to the dead, but it was not known as such in our tribe. Perhaps it belonged to the departed Humbaba's tribe?

"His people do not bury their dead like normal humans," Adam said, "but expose them for the vultures. Even the head-man got no more honor than a fallen beast. They showed me his half-eaten carcass."

"Yes, I taught them that," Lilith said, stroking the vulture feathers at her shoulders. "Because the soil where they live is too rocky to dig."

"Why would anyone with any sense live in such a place?"

"Because obsidian is there," Lilith replied, reaching over to stroke the blade of my father's spear. I knew he had traded many skins for that black blade.

Adam pulled back as if the stroke of her hand might move from spear to himself.

Lilith retreated, too, but not from caressing with her words. "Perhaps you noticed the mountain in that region. At times it smokes."

"I saw no smoke."

"Then it sleeps now. But at other times it belches forth fire and death. When the fire cools, obsidian is made."

"Still, what people would not give their dead a proper burial?"

"Humbaba was dear to me. I'm certain his spirit returns to his ancestors as well through the craw of a bird as through the gullets of worms. He was a fine man, a great upholder of his people's traditions. A dear son."

And it seemed she wept, though the angle of firelight prevented my seeing for certain. She seemed to give Adam every chance to comfort her. He did not take it.

"It never gets any easier," she soon said, begging pardon. She dried her face with the edge of a vulture's wing. "Especially when he was husband as well as son."

"Husband!" Adam burst out, then struggled to say no more.

"Yes, Adam. I married Humbaba years before I married you. Probably before you were even toddling."

My father made a garbled sound, like a man wrestling to put down a foe as strong as he is. When he had more control, he said, "The craws of vultures suit Humbaba well. You know I never liked that—that you have many husbands while I—"

He turned full from her again and seemed about to get to his feet and saunter off in the direction his gaze led.

What Lilith said next certainly couldn't please him any more, but it did keep him squatting with us. "The sea can be crossed, you know," she said.

I heard, more than saw, the shift in my father's body, the struggle between anger and desire. He said nothing.

Lilith went on. "I suggest you attempt the crossing first at a place where you can see the opposite shore. Indeed, there are a few places where that is possible to the west—follow the shore north instead of south as you did. And certainly take a log out with you. Or a boat, such as people in the area can teach you to fashion, with an adze and fire.

"You needn't seem so startled, Adam. Or is it offense I detect? I have children across the sea I must visit, too. It was I who led them there. And I tell you, the journey is much easier going west than over the ocean to the east.

"The aurochs, I might as well tell you—" she declared finally, taking up a stick and idly jabbing at the fire, a movement my father might have felt in his own flesh. "The aurochs are thriving much better on that side of the sea than they are here."

Twenty

I thought I caught a glimpse of what Mother Lilith's veiled wisdom was about. She girded up the rules of balance that were already in place. The vision of it, both the fragility and eternity of her purpose, sent a chill down my spine, a chill I welcomed on such a close and overheated night.

At her moontime, a woman sat under a fig tree. And if she didn't season-move with the clan, she sat there alone. Beasts were drawn to the smell of her, to the smell of her blood on the leaves. The narrowness of Adam's eyes as he looked down the hill told me he considered this, as well.

As for the man, Lilith's wisdom set a quest, a quest with honor whose allure he could not escape. But a quest from which he had so little chance of returning. The closer the balance was to toppling, the less chance he had of success.

Still, I could see: if Father took his seething passion—his kicking against fate—if he took all this together on his quest, my grandparents would be free to die. And Eve and I could go off to the summer meadows, where we belonged. I could see the great wisdom of this and I longed to embrace it, sorrow though it would be, for the whole and final good.

Mother Lilith unflinchingly pushed her children toward such fearsome things, for all her tears at Humbaba's death, for all her avowals of an equal mother's love toward us. But a mother, after all, has seen further than her children—and that is why she corrects—or pushes—them. For their own good. And for the good of all her children. For she doesn't favor the one who buries his dead more than the one who leaves his dead exposed.

Father saw Lilith's purpose, too, I think. Maybe he even felt the awe, as I did. But he certainly didn't like it. He did begin to prepare to return to the sea in the west the very next morning. He dragged his feet about it, however, and had made very little progress before Eve came back up the hill to join us.

Eve had kept off beasts with a fire, I suppose. But she did not sing and dance on her return to the everyday world. It seemed a sad, lonely thing, without other women. I think she was almost ready to come with me to join the rest of the clan.

Until she saw Adam waiting for her.

And once she returned to us, my father stopped hearing anything Mother Lilith said. He made no further plans for the aurochs hunt at all.

Something was going to happen. I could feel it in the air. I thought I could smell it, too. There was a smell of thyme. The clumps of growing thyme were all dry on the hillsides and re-leased their scent when we bruised them. But this smell—of rain, of wet plants—pervaded the dry white stalks of wheat, the wilting pistachio leaves, everything. The smell, I noticed, was strongest when Lilith was nearby, and seemed to be grow-ing stronger every day. As if she herself were a bud ready to burst with sap.

What this might mean, I couldn't tell. Except that the moon was growing near the full and Lilith remarked on it every night.

Every night when Adam and Eve were near. As she remarked on the herds of aurochs months and months away.

Apart from this, I could not name what I felt drawing near.

Adam couldn't, either. Or if he did, he laughed about it with Eve as they walked off together. Once I caught them, hand in hand, though they drew apart sheepishly at sight of me. Lilith and I divided the watch of those two between us.

"You'd think you had a reason to be jealous, as if you and I were man and wife," Adam snapped at Lilith, annoyed.

"We are," Lilith said.

Adam had no answer but to speak in louder and louder tones about the bull god he had heard.

One day, Adam threw his net over a whole covey of quail. There was a bird for each of us, with one left over. Adam looked straight in Lilith's eyes, defying her, as he gave the one left over, the wife's portion, to Eve.

"Son, you must remember who deserves most honor here," my grandfather said, gesturing toward Lilith and blushing almost youthfully at his son's bad manners.

"Never mind." Lilith eased the tension. "One bird is all I can eat tonight. Besides, a man must hear his own voice spirits. If he does not, they will desert him when his net is cast, or when he throws his spear. Only he must not let such spirits drown out the Voice of Mother Earth—when She speaks. I suppose She hasn't spoken loud enough for Adam to hear."

"There was an earthquake," I said.

"Adam needs something louder. Don't worry. She will. She will speak loud enough even for him."

These words seemed to embolden my father rather than make him bow with humility. I gritted my teeth with anger.

Later, when the quail had been eaten and small creatures crunching at the bones competed with the sound of the cicadas in the blackness around us, Adam dared more.

Eve was sitting with her legs straight toward the fire in front of her. I blushed and turned my eyes, mostly because I knew Adam could not or would not turn his. She was picking the last of the crumbs from her legs and, in the process, picked a bit of the fraying ends of her rabbit skirt. I looked away, but smelled the acrid burst of smoke as the tuft of fur hit the dying fire.

And I heard my father murmur drowsily, "I will hunt a sheepskin for you to tan for a new skirt, Eve. Tomorrow."

I looked desperately toward Lilith, sure she must say something to put a stop to this. Lilith only looked up at the moon. As it ivoried her face, her lips thinned in a silent smile. And the strange smell of thyme overcame the smell of smoke.

Father left in the morning and was gone two days. He returned in the mid-afternoon when Lilith, Eve, and I had gone down to the stream for water. My old goatskin had sprung a leak. I'd tried to mend it, first with pitch, then with a careful stitch or two of thong, finally with a knot that limited the amount of water I could haul. I'm the one who needs a new skin, I thought. Anger burned my eyes whenever I looked in Eve's direction.

We took a cooling swim against the almost unbearable heat, and that eased my anger enough so Eve and I could splash and dunk each other like old friends again. I noticed the thyme smell faded in the water, too, and I filled my lungs gratefully with cold, damp, scentless air.

But my anger—which was really only a cover for fear— returned as we made our way back to camp and found my father waiting for us. The smell returned, as well, springing like the bloom of sweat on the low, flat bridge of Lilith's nose.

The shaggy gray curls of a large ram stoled my father's shoulders. We gave him the usual greeting to a successful hunter—"Better luck next time"—so success wouldn't go to his head.

Adam dumped the carcass to the ground, circled his shoulders to rid them of the cramp, then squatted and opened the leather flaps of his tool kit to begin the butchering. I knew from the first cut the skin would not come to me.

The uncomfortable leak of water down my leg, now crusted with dust, lost all the cool, clean effect of the stream. I clenched my teeth with anger again. Though I'm not sure what angered me more, my father's usual carelessness for his daughter or my continued hope that he would change. I had let myself go so far as to imagine the pleasures of a day's trek down to the closest acacia tree to gather bark to rub into the skin, to make it waterproof.

To hold either water, or air as a float, a skin must be taken with as few cuts as possible, peeled back from the anus in one sweep. Adam's chert attacked the belly for gutting first. The fleece rolled off, wide and flat, for a garment.

There is no hope, I thought. Eve will have her way.

And Adam his.

But I'd failed to give proper weight to two things. The first was a strange aversion in my father's eyes, a peculiar stiffness in his movements. His torso jerked as he stood from squatting; his arm jerked from tool kit to bloody belly and back again. Had I given this any thought, I might have supposed he had taken a fall on the hunt—and pursuing mountain sheep can be dangerous. Maybe he was favoring a cracked rib.

Or a bruised groin.

His nose seemed to give him trouble, too. He sniffed testily from time to time, and shook his face like a dog fighting flies. Or a man fighting a winter cold.

The second thing I failed to think of was Lilith's power. I'd paddled in the stream with her and watched her scratch mosquito bites while I scratched mine. It had been too easy to forget that she was, in fact, Mother Lilith, a force of Earth. Divine.

Now she poured a wooden cup of water for Adam before Eve thought of it. Mother Lilith's walk to him with the drink was slow and deliberate. Eve would have had plenty of time to beat the Mother to the act if she'd thought of it. If she could have thought of anything, enchanted by Lilith's movements like the rest of us.

Lilith's bodily change must have been coming on gradually over the past phase of the moon, as does that of any other animal that goes into heat. But this was the first time I'd noticed it, so it seemed dramatic and sudden to me.

Her breasts had swollen and seemed pink and soft. Above them, tiny, tender eruptions picked out the shape of flying geese on the skin below her throat. Her hair sprang glossy and full of life from her head. Her wide, dark eyes had gone to black and were starred like the northern skies in winter. She walked with a rolling gait, as if between her thighs was a thick, moist, and uneasy swelling. And everywhere, from every pore, escaped the smell of thyme.

Lilith bent and gave Adam the water. Their fingers touched, but more, their eyes grappled. I could see the breath come quicker in the hollows where my father's shoulders met his neck. For all the power in those shoulders, he could not escape the hold she had on him, no more than a man could break the pull of earth, spring into the air, and fly like a bird. It was she herself who made the break, slipping away as smoothly as water over a flat stone. But before she turned fully, she caught the edge of his loincloth where it lay, differing only in its hairlessness from the leather of his thigh. She caught at his loincloth with her big toe and gave a playful tug.

Then Lilith went back to her place without a word. And when the fresh-killed fleece slipped free of the last web of white and pinkish tissue, Adam bunched it up—and tossed it, not to Eve, but at Lilith's feet.

"Thank you, husband," she replied, her voice almost as deep as a man's with the pulse of life moving through her.

Twenty-one

The full moon throbbed in the sky. Stars parched away from it like drops of water spattered by the fireside. And just so did the details of my anklebones vanish beneath the swelling of a poisoned mosquito bite. In fact, this bite might have been from a bee or even a wasp grown vicious with the heat. But surely I would have noticed such a sting when it happened.

I had not let my ankle slow me down all day. Too much depended on my mobility. I'd gone on tiptoe through the berry thorn when I'd lost the ability to bend my foot.

But now, by moonlight, I longed for a pack of cool, wet moss wrapped in leaves, perhaps a bunch of quenching, green borage with it, or a few springs of thyme.

I only thought of thyme because of the smell.

Nobody volunteered to run that errand for me and now I was beyond running it for myself. Even Lilith, my mother, had been too busy today working magic on my father. Neither of my parents sat by the fading fire that now blew ash more than smoke. Certainly the clan expected a married couple to leave the fire together from time to time. My concern had been that Lilith hadn't gotten my father to do it sooner. Still, they had been gone the better part of a day. And I had been so long without a mother that when Lilith left me —

I stopped my thought right there in its tracks. Merely thinking my mother's name now softened the edges of my senses. The moon and my ankle throbbed until it seemed I could hear them, a low, steady, tuneless hum. Above and beyond the constant drone of crickets and frogs, they grew together into one voice.

The moon gave every black figure around me a ghost, an outline the color of scraped bone. It also seemed to embolden the local hyena pack and we had no man's dogs to scare them off. I could hear the animals, snarling and giggling, no farther off than our midden, where we'd tossed our bones. Perhaps where our feces were poorly covered. I could smell the animals' doggish smell: nose-wrinkling, moldy thyme. I caught sight of the arrogant yellow eyes. Yet another reminder of why we should move on with the seasons: so as not to have to live in the midst of our own waste like this. The Valley needed time to clean herself up between our visits.

Because we had failed to do this, the Valley—the hyenas were but one unfolding of Eden—was slowly but certainly swelling with rot around us. It was like the berry thorns in my arms and legs, how the flesh puffed soft and yellow around each one, trying to expel the tiny invader. It was like the swelling in my ankle.

Grandmother's mind had taken a turn for the worse in this atmosphere, yellow pus trying to push her from this life. The very dead might have risen up out of the cave and come to sit in the moonshade by her; they were clearly more real to her than we were. All day she had been searching and calling for Eben.

"He will certainly come home from hunting today. Eben, with new skins for me to clean. He is never a man to return empty-handed."

I don't know how many times she shuffled by me, muttering words to that effect in girlish tones, but tones spoiled by the ruin of her ancient teeth.

I assumed this was what made Grandfather so uneasy, so short-tempered.

"Eben's dead, fool woman," he'd snapped, just as often as she'd called the dead man's name. "The great bull got him. Didn't I hear the story from your own lips more times than I can count?"

"You?" she'd reply, blinking down at him in all innocence. "Who are you?"

"He's your husband, Granny," I'd say.

But a deep, girlish flush would rise to her cheeks and she'd say, "What, this old man? This man who should be dead and in his grave? No, no, I am married to Eben and he loves no one but me." Then she would pull a hank of her limp white hair flirtatiously across her face and say, blushing still more, "He loves my thick black hair, Eben does. He loves for me to wear it down when we go out into the bush and he lets it rain down upon his great, broad, naked chest."

And Grandfather would snort with impotent rage, curse, and, I could tell, want to hit her. "Eben's dead!"

She did not know her husband of over thirty-five years but remembered instead the man who had . . . who had had the courage to die when the Earth called his name. No doubt this swelled Grandfather's own edginess. He couldn't pace any more, but his eyes did the pacing for him. They sent more and more frequent glances off into the bushes—in the direction Adam and Lilith had disappeared, the direction from which came the continuous smell of thyme. Yes, and now that it was dark, in the direction of the hyenas. Rightly, the hyenas should have come and found the old couple in the cave long ago and . . .

Or was it Eben that Grandfather expected, on his wife's

word, to appear from that direction? Riding the aurochs between the horns, riding in glory.

"I should comb out my hair for Eben," Grandmother said, and began to do so, with an imaginary comb.

Grandfather fairly spat at her in disgust and struggled to his feet.

"Shall I help you out into the bush, Grandfather?" I asked.

"You think I need a girl to help me pee?" he snapped, and snatching up his stick, staggered off.

He had allowed me to help him any number of times before this. We should all have been used to that indignity by now. I liked to think he was considering my swollen ankle, though nothing in his words or tone made me think that. I clung to this meaning simply because I was tired of being the only one to care, not only for myself but for any other.

As Grandfather disappeared into the moon-flattened shadows, Eve huddled close to me and shivered. She jarred my foot as she did so, by accident, I'm sure, but the night was too warm, too close, too thick with the smell of thyme, for huddling.

Still, now, in the dark, I could hardly blame her. Our only remaining male had vanished into the hyena-haunted dark, too, and our only other companion ghostily combed out her hair for a ghost's arrival. I clamped my teeth down over my complaint and stolidly accepted her arms.

Eve said nothing, but by moonlight, I could see fresh tears standing in the corners of her eyes. I fought against catching them from her, like a cold. From time to time she drew a ragged breath, as if her heart were as swollen and tender as my foot and left little room within her ribs for anything else.

"Ah, Eve," I wanted to scold her. "He's not your husband. He never was. You always knew he never could be. Just be glad he's reunited with his true helpmate again . . . and try to

get on with your own life. Maybe you could go down the Valley instead of up, rejoin your own clan in their summer meadows until your stepfather makes a good match for you."

Surely this was the best advice, but I knew I could not
have borne to hear it myself, in her position.

"My stepfather make a match for me?" I could almost hear
her scream. "That vile man who only wants me for himself?"

If I'd been my grandfather, or Grandmother not consumed
by young love of her own, I might have said such words. They
would have been forgiven their crotchety tone. Credited with
wisdom in any case.

As it was, I said nothing, and answered even the begging
touch of her hands with but a halfhearted hug around the
shoulders. It is too hot for more, I thought. And my foot aches.

Across the blackened fire pit, Grandmother began to sing,
a song of lost loves and youth. As a storyteller she had always
had a better sense of what her hearers wanted than that. Eve
let her tears drop, rapidly and unchecked, onto my skirt. The
leather would stain. If I tried to stop Granny, stubbornly she
would sing louder, and my helplessness in the face of it all
would make me cry, too.

Suddenly a growl and a crash shook the underbrush not
six strides away. One of the hyenas dashed in and made off
with the leftover haunch of ram which my father had wrapped
in leaves and hung from a low branch over our heads. Clearly,
he hadn't hung it high enough, and Granny's presence right
under the limb hadn't stopped this dogged beast. Clearly, the
hyenas were growing bolder.

I hoped the beast would drag the rest of his kin off with
him along with the meat, but apparently there wasn't enough
to feed half their number and they knew it. Most of them never
even left to join the vicious, snarling feed, and those that did
soon returned.

I leapt to my feet, my heart pounding, and yelled out into the dark at them. "Off with you, dogs!"

As if in response to my dare, one hyena now stepped into the pool of moonlight centered around our open fire pit. I heard the click of his toenails on an exposed stretch of stone; the eery light washed out all his natural tawniness and made a bone-colored ghost of him.

The beast stood to my waist at his shoulder and was within easy leaping distance of my throat where I felt the blood throbbing vulnerably. For all the noise I made, stamping on my good foot and waving my arms, he stood his ground, snarling. Shadows behind him told me he had the backing of all his kin in this argument. And out of the corner of my eye, I could see he'd even sent some of his cousins to circle round my flank.

Bending might offer a dangerous show of weakness, but I did it anyway, swiftly grasping for the first thing I could lay my hands on. The pack leader snapped viciously at the two sticks of wood that hit him. I bent and threw again. He started back then, on fury-stiffened legs, his ears flattened to his head. His bared teeth webbed with saliva. The sound that came from deep in his throat terrified me more than all the louder laughs and coughs had done. And I heard it echoed behind me.

"Get the fire going again, Eve," I yelled. Why did the girl, two years older than I, have to be told the obvious?

Too late, I realized the sticks I'd thrown had been useful pieces of wood. I couldn't afford to repeat that mistake. I considered the stone I held now carefully before I aimed. I threw it with a force that ripped through my shoulder with pain. But it landed true between the hyena's eyes.

He howled with anger and pain and skidded back. I saw the stripes along his flanks plainly. So did his clansmen, I suppose. They all retreated, but only till two bounds would bring them to my throat instead of only one.

"Build up the fire," I snapped again at Eve and snatched the kindling out of her hand. She'd been staring at it, tear-blinded.

"What, haven't you ever coaxed coals to life before?" I snarled, rather hyenalike myself, and bent to work alone.

"Why shouldn't we just let them eat us?" Eve suddenly burst out in a wail. "I've no wish to stay here any longer in this horrible valley of the dead. I welcome death."

"Well, fine," I said. "But I don't, yet. So hand me that log and then get out of the way."

Eve did as she was told, but went on to wail such yelps that the hyenas seemed attracted, as if to their mates in season.

I missed Uncle Ari and his steady supply of torch wood. But there was no time to suffer more than a pang. I had to make do with a simple staff of twisted, dry oak. It burned quickly once I got it going, more quickly as I blazed it in one direction, then the other, the flame fed by the motion and my shouts. The hyenas became waves, one side rolling up even as the other rolled back. And, as in a flood, each swell was just a little closer than the last.

The animals were close enough now that I could smell sparks singeing the fur raised in their hackles. I could feel the heat of their breath. They were coming for me rather than the easier targets of Granny or Eve between whom I wove the flaming sticks. Hyena teeth snapped at my ankle and I couldn't tell if the pain came from swinging my foot out of the way in a hurry or if they actually touched me. I pushed the sensation away from my brain and shafted it along moonlight through the world, just so it wouldn't distract me.

I didn't think, when I sent it, that my thought was a plea. But to my surprise, a chorus of almost-human wolf calls answered, as if it were. The howls rose off the great jutting ledge of rock down by the river.

The hyenas' ears shot forward at this. "The wolf is the

hyena's chief," as the saying is. The pack whined, skidded on their toenails, then loped off one by one. I don't think they went far. I heard them scuffling in the dark from time to time during the night. But we did not catch sight of them again.

I stood, panting, torch in my hand, waiting for the terror to clear from my head. It would have gone faster, I think, if somebody had praised my actions. But nobody did.

"Eben is such a brave hunter," Granny said.

And Eve buried her face in her huddles knees, saying, "I just want to die."

My terror did clear, slowly, but of its own accord, and helped by the sight of how fast the untallowed wood was burning down toward my hand. I tossed the stump back into the fire and watched the flame curl around, then slowly consume it.

"Grandfather," was the next thought that came to me, and I said it aloud, further clearing my mind. "I ought to go see if he's all right. He's been gone too long."

As startling as the lunge of a hyena, Eve unfolded herself from her hunch and leaped to my side. She'll come with me, I thought happily and with some relief. Those hyenas hadn't gone far.

But my moment of cheer was a mistaken one.

"Don't go," Eve pleaded.

Granny said something about Eben taking care of everything, but that I could ignore.

I couldn't ignore Eve. She clung to my arm now, her fingers sticking painfully to my sweat-swollen skin. And she joggled my foot again.

"Please don't go. For my sake, Na'amah," she whimpered.

"He's been gone too long." My mind filled rapidly with images of what might have happened to him, hyena teeth thick as thistle spikes among these images. Lest words conjure these images to reality, all I said was, "The old man, he ought to have returned by now."

"Na'amah, I'll die if you go."

I wanted to remind her that not twenty heartbeats before this she had been asking for her own death. But I only shook my arm clear of her hand and said, "I won't go beyond sight. And I'll take a torch. I promise."

Raising my new, fast-burning torch, I found no sign of the old man in the direction he'd gone. Eve's panicked calls told me I'd gone farther than my promise. I swung around, close enough so that Eve's shouting ceased, turning uphill and to the right. For all the moonlight, my sense of smell seemed most keen, and thyme dazzled it. Every plant I brushed against in the dark must have had that plant's tiny, fragrant, mouse-eared leaves. Or so it seemed.

But then I heard a footfall on the upward path where moon-shadow fell in blurred bands like the markings on a hyena's flank.

"Grandfather?" I called up the rib-bone slide of path I could see.

One footfall, but then another, two very close together and with different rhythms. "Father? Mother? Is that you?"

It was none of these people. It was my uncles Ari and Dov.

Twenty-two

"Uncle Ari! Uncle Dov!" My heart rushed with gladness but also unguarded surprise when I recognized the pair.

"Greetings, niece," they said in chorus. But that was all they said. Their eyes never seemed to meet mine, though mine were hungry after such a long parting.

Somebody ought to say something. "Grandmother's right down here." I began to lead them, holding the end of my torch high to light the way but careful not to shed sparks into the tinder-dry grass at our feet. "Here, down by the fire pit. She hasn't been well today."

I felt foolish. What did my uncles care about the health of their mother? In their minds, she had been dead and buried since the last full moon. To find she was not might well disturb them, even anger them to silence.

I yearned for escape the moment someone else picked duty up off my shoulders. These two kinsmen, emblems of all my longing for balance and the-way-things-ought-to-be hoarded over the last month, they were all the relief I needed. In a moment I'd gratefully lose control.

And yet, the more I tried to settle them in our place so I could let go, the more unsettled they became.

"Hello, Mother."

Dutifully each man mouthed the words and bent to send a kiss in the general direction of the wrinkled cheek. But nothing connected, the kisses no more than the words or her sons' presence, in the old woman's mind. She didn't know who they were, and it unnerved them. Ari and Dov might have kissed the ghost she seemed to be, in the bone-white light.

"What brings you here?" Eve asked. "Away from the summer grounds? So late at night?"

Her attempt at casual greeting seemed to make them even more uneasy. The men would not look at her, as if she were something under a ban.

"We were hunting."

"Yes, hunting."

"At night?" Eve asked. "Without your dogs?"

"Yes."

"No."

The brothers looked at each other, then quickly each took the position his brother had just abandoned.

"No."

"Yes."

Another look, then Dov seemed to find uncommon interest in the nail of his little toe and let his older brother straighten the matter out.

"We were hunting," Ari said, still without ease, "and . . . and we got lost."

"Lost?" Eve's disbelief gave her more speech than usual among the clansmen. "Lost, in your own summer meadows?"

"Well, not lost so much as —"

"As this was closer." Dov left his nail in favor of this sudden thought. "By the time we realized it was growing dark, this was closer."

"But on a moonlit night?" Eve persisted. "Men will sometimes hunt all night on such a night as this. Full moon is not a time to lose your way."

"Full moon." Ari breathed in deeply on the word as if smelling the fragrance of cooking food after a two-day fast.

"Yes," Dov echoed. "Full moon."

"I think there has not been such a moon since . . ." Ari rubbed himself absently.

"Since Adam married Lilith."

These words silenced Eve, so now I had to take up our end of the conversation. "I'm sorry, my uncles. I wish I had food to offer you. My father had a good, fat ram's haunch here, but the hyenas stole it."

I hoped the word "hyenas" would rouse them to duty. It did not.

I began to speak with a strange, desperate wildness now. "Won't you come looking for Grandfather with me? Or for me, so I can stay with the women. I don't want to break in on a man's privacy. I've a sore ankle, too, and I don't want to put any more steps on it."

Ari and Dov shrugged, one after the other. What did they care? Of course, they had sung their father to his death just after the last full moon. They had not seen him, cared for him, coaxed the faint life into him day after day in the meantime. Still, their distraction seemed inhuman. They made no move to go after the old man.

Having worn out my words on this subject, I returned desperately to Grandmother. "Granny hardly needs a long story told. You must see her for yourselves. All day she's been expecting Eben to return—"

My uncles remained unmoved. But they were not unmoving. They fidgeted like young boys who've been told they must sit still and therefore cannot. They shifted from knees to seat, to haunches to feet and back again.

In my hope and relief mixed so awkwardly with fear and confusion, I began to speak of Adam. "My father was wounded during the earthquake. A rock fall."

Eve caught my eye and I stopped just before telling them how she and I had broken the men's refuge to get him out and save him.

"Did you feel the earthquake in the summer meadows?" I asked.

My uncles nodded, but no more than twice apiece.

"Who calmed the children's fears with stories afterward?" I told them briefly of the Tree. "Do you miss your storyteller?" I asked. "How are my aunts? My cousins? Is little Boaz behaving himself? Is Kochavah growing fast? Has Devorah managed to rid herself of the child she can't carry?"

At first I waited for answers between my questions, but answers never came.

"Where is Adam?" Ari finally posed a question of his own. He gave Eve a sharp look, from which she flinched, but he was back on his feet now, pacing. He had not even set down his spear shafts but rattled them together now as he paced like a man before a big hunt.

"He's . . ." I stammered. "He's with his wife."

"His wife?" Ari and Dov said it together and Dov instantly joined Ari on his feet.

"My mother," I nodded. "I'm . . . I'm not certain where they are." But I did wave off in the direction I'd last seen them.

"You mean Lilith?"

"Mother Lilith is here?"

The brothers spoke together so I couldn't tell who said what, although Dov made a lunge at me and I thought he would bite my head off like some hyena. The desire larding that name on both tongues made me suddenly light-headed.

Behind me, Eve began to weep aloud.

My uncles were up and gone in a moment. They didn't even bother to reach for torches, although Ari was usually so careful about his light. At least, I thought, Adam had gone in the same direction I'd last seen Grandfather.

Twenty-three

Eve continued to cry. Annoyed—and a little afraid—I tossed another log into the blaze though the night was already so hot and had grown hotter still with my uncles' arrival. Then Grandmother made things even worse by singsonging "Lilith, Lilith," over and over and over again.

"Please stop, Grandmother."

Eve joined my pleading through her tears.

"Tell us some more about Eben."

Anything but that name. That name of unbeatable rivalry to Eve. To me, the name was holy, terrible, ineffable—and maddening as the full moon's bone-white beams.

But, "Lilith, Lilith." Grandmother would not stop.

Eve jumped up and, before I could think, slapped the old woman. I don't think she put much power behind the blow. She shook too much with sobs, and knowledge of what she'd done instantly puddled her to her knees again in misery.

I said nothing. I would have been shocked into speech— but the old woman's jabber had brought a flash of murder to my own mind. She was, after all, supposed to be dead already—

"Lilith, Lilith," over and over. The slap did not make her lose a beat.

"Lilith, Lilith."

I seemed to have grown a second, painfully throbbing heart in my ankle. Double the hearts charging them, my limbs sprang to flight. I ran in the direction of all the men.

Eve, with the cry of a wounded animal, scrambled up from her slump and after me. She brought me down, hard, on my swollen foot. I wanted to smack her—but then answered her clinging embrace with my own arms.

We were not out of earshot. Neither did our combined sobs drown out Grandmother's otherworldly chant, pounding and hissing at the same time.

"Lilith, Lilith."

And then I knew I could not escape. It was my fate. The name, my mother's name, caught me helpless, just in the belly.

I should tell a tale, I thought desperately. It might calm Eve. It might cover Grandmother's singsong. It might calm me.

Once there was—and once there was not—

But I could think of no story but Lilith's.

Then, because there was no escape, I turned slowly, as if turned by the force of a sand-filled desert wind, to face the name. Lilith, I remembered, meant "wind," "night wind," "spirit," all at once and together.

Lilith. Lilith.

A great, heavy breathing fanned the name through the Valley from top to bottom, heating rather than cooling the night. Slowly I began to notice: the pulse of the word matched the pulse in my infected foot—which matched the pulse of the moon grown large and yellow at the peak of the sky.

I felt the rough earth beneath me, three largish rocks in a waving row ending at the point of my spine. Their grit went up into my teeth. I felt the lay of leather on my thighs and across my almost-woman breasts. Sweat trickled under each arm and my horse-tooth necklace pressed into the hollow of my throat,

as if there were still horses' jaws behind the teeth, biting. I felt
Eve cling to me, and felt my arms return the embrace, lacking
any will behind them.

All these things I felt. I knew Lilith couldn't be there, not
the whisper of her vulture wings nor the hiss of her snakeskin
skirt. And yet—

Yet the smell of thyme spread, as thick in the air as a bear-
skin blanket.

And I knew, in truth, Lilith was everywhere.

Eve kept me pinned to the ground. Even if she'd let me up,
the pain in my foot and the weight of mixed emotions would
have kept me down. Nonetheless, wafted on the word "Lilith,"
my spirit began to travel. I moved out in long, vinelike tendrils
throbbing with life. I moved over this next ridge outlined by
moonlight like some frame of bone. Then I moved on, to things
I couldn't see—except, I could.

I had grown a new heart in my foot? Well, now I felt one
beating over there in the core of that oak. In the throb of these
moth's wings. In the hunch of this wildcat, in the heartbeat,
then the death throes of his cornered prey.

Lilith, Lilith.

Leglessly, motionlessly, I continued to expand my being.
Like a snake, I slithered, feeling the very life of the Valley rising
up through my belly until it encircled my being like my own
ribs. The source drew me on, in a slipping, waving line.

At the same time, my soul moved out in all directions at
once, feeling each surface, licking, bathing it, like moonlight,
until I held all Eden in a throbbing, lustrous, white caress.

Lily petals touched my temples, my cheeks, then my lips,
till they felt heavy as bee legs with pollen. The swelling spread
down to my throat and pressed saliva forth, like hunger at the
smell of good food. I opened my mouth like lily petals, inviting
the bees to burrow, inviting every blessed, creeping, crawling

thing to enter and find life. My lips moved wordlessly, groping hungrily like a baby's mouth for the breast. And my breath became the rapid, heavy panting of the Valley wind.

Strands of Eve's thick hair clung unnoticed to my parted lips.

Lilith, Lilith.

The flush of damp heat spread lower, to my breast, where my heart thudded violently. My back arched, pushed by the bursting of my heart, pulled forward by my breasts that had knotted like buds of fruit, tiny, tight, but teeming.

And I felt my thighs and buttocks kneaded; licked like his midnight fur by the panther's rasping tongue; mantled like the raven's feathers; smoothed as the curves of the foothills are of their tight darkness by dawn's light until they open and smile.

All the Valley seemed a quivering womb and we, her children, still bathed in the pure milky film that covers us at birth. A life-giving spring rumbled, gurgled, then burst between my thighs. And with the white rush of spring water, my vision thrust forward over the final stretch of summer-parched soil, washed even more of color by the moonlight. With the soar of the swift I shot forward until I saw them, four figures—no, five—seated, lying against pools of moonlight.

The scent of thyme enveloped me, a heavy, animal smell. And the very instant I recognized a face among the figures, said to myself, "Lilith. This is Lilith," I had to amend those words. For I had rushed up through the crushed and powdered grass, up the dark, well-muscled legs into the soft mound at her core.

I had to say, "No. *I* am Lilith."

As once before but a single heart had beat for us both, now again she cradled me within the vibration of her pelvis. At the same time, my own pelvis, which had become the entire Valley, contained her.

A freeing burst ripped my soul from navel to hair part, like

the bolt of lightning through the Fig Tree. I screamed, but it
was Lilith's throat that carried the air.

And when I opened my eyes from their flinching, it was
with Lilith's eyes that I saw. I knew the other figures about me
with a recognition that teared my eyes. These were all my sons.
And all my lovers.

Yet as Na'amah, I still knew them otherwise: This was
Adam, my father. My uncles, Ari and Dov. And my grandfather.

The men were howling, answering Lilith's—my—quick
little bays. I realized these might have been the howls that
frightened the hyenas away, so wild were these sounds, echoing off the moon-sheered cliffs. So unhuman.

Moonlight cobbled out the ridges of their spines, found
the heights of chests, shoulders, naked buttocks. And it formed
itself tight around each manhood in a rigid, white-hot sheath.
The only darkness, the only hollow in the whole night, seemed
to lie in the recess wedged between Lilith's—my—legs toward
which not only all the men, but all creation yearned.

This place was not only black but also achingly empty. I
swam there in its depths, like a blind fish in the depths of a cave
pool, tickling like hunger pains, and more ravenous myself
than I had ever been before.

I couldn't think of anything but that hunger. It made me
scrappy. My chest pulsed with a short and demanding temper.
But in the connectedness of all the world in that night, I felt the
hunger too of the white-pink marrow of Lilith's bones, like the
cores of the rocks beneath her. I heard the roar of her blood,
which was the same as the roar of the nearby stream that
joined the roar of Mother River, which was even the same as
that mystery called "the sea."

Skin was a sheer thing in such a world. Smears of male
seed floated on Lilith's flesh, on the coat of dewish sweat like

oil on water. Indistinguishably hot when it hit, the vital juice had begun to cool now and glistened like snail trails on broad forest leaves. And even older layers had collected a roll of fine dust that Lilith could feel like leather bands constricting the panting breaths for which her hungry lungs clamored.

Whose seed, I couldn't tell. Perhaps there were trails of all four. But Adam had most recently peaked, for he shifted position now to Lilith's head, cradling it in his lap where his manhood continued to stir uneasily like a bird on its nest when berry pickers are nearby.

Adam ran his fingers through the unbound thickness of Lilith's hair, massaged the roots, searched for nits, though in this light such a task was only a further demand of intimacy. Through half-closed eyes, Lilith saw the quiver of his lips between rigid beard and moustache. She pulled them to her again, felt the touch of lips on bruised eyelid, first one, then the other, then her cheeks. After that, her mouth beckoned, swollen like fruit the moment before it drops, ripe enough to crush. With a groan, he could not resist the taste of it, that juice. And having tasted once, tasted again and again, nibbling on the tongue.

In the hollow under each of Lilith's arms also lay a man, Dov to the right, Grandfather to the left. Lilith gripped each around the shoulder and offered a breast. Grandfather licked at his raised knob of nipple like a tentative child at some strange food. His labored breathing steamed the dampness on the spot. Dov was more vigorous in his suckling, and both freed a hand to grope blindly, farther down, to finger, press, and spread thigh and buttock.

It was Ari who claimed the prized void now. I could see the attempt to linger in his half-hazed eyes. But Grandfather and Dov helped lift and press, knowing that the sooner Ari spent himself, the sooner their turn would come. I felt the burst of his rigid boundary's sudden release, felt it both in myself and in Lilith like a tiny swallow, a brief sigh of satisfaction. But this was a sigh that quickly grew ravenous again.

Ari, exhausted, almost weeping with joy that was at the same time a kind of defeat, rolled away. Dov helped him with a little shove and rose on his knees to lay claim.

But Lilith shook herself free like a bitch of her pups. Presence of mind was difficult to come by in the heat, and I suppose even more difficult for me. But I did hear a thought roll through her mind: "Adam. This must be for Adam, in spite of the rest."

She shoved aside Dov's claim and raised her head out of Adam's lap. The movement flooded the dark air with the smell of sex-dampened thyme so thick that it scalded my lungs like smoke. Breathing in through my mouth filled my belly like eating.

Twisting onto hands and knees, Lilith began to crawl up Adam's body like sap up the trunk of a tree. Lips and chin led the advance, tickling their way first through the thick hair on Adam's thighs, then rousing his organ off its nest like a startled quail, then following the marked line up to dip in his hollow mark of her motherhood. Her hands claimed his manhood, crammed it into place while the place gulped with wet hunger.

Adam lay back and groaned helplessly. But then, at a point where his eyes should not have met hers, they did. His eyes suddenly flew open and hardened, like warm bitumen plunged all at once into cold water.

Adam struggled, wordlessly, a fish hooked below the jaw. This was an old battle between them, I could see, and between more than just this immediate man and woman. There were no words, but I heard them anyway. And the words I did hear were only moonlit shadows of the real struggle, a battle as old as that between winter and spring, as old as coupling. As old as the unbreakable bond between the lust of life and the necessity of death.

"No," Adam flared. "You will not have me like this."

"Ah, but I will." Lilith's voice held the compulsion of the night wind breathing heavily down from the mountaintops.

"Not again. Never."

"Foolish man." The words growled deep in her throat like the hunting call of the wildcat. "You cannot escape me."

"I am not a man to be one among many."

"But look around. You are. The world is well peopled with men."

"A curse on Humbaba and his kind."

"All are my sons."

"A curse on my brothers and this old man who calls himself my father."

"And all are my lovers."

"Get off me now, you bitch in heat."

"Ah, yes, so I am." The look in her eyes darted like a snake. "And I want you, Adam, to slake that heat."

"She-demon, off!"

For answer, she grabbed his stock and began to work it again, her legs almost split, just at the point where sparks could not help but kindle, while Dov moved on her from behind.

"No!" Adam screamed the scream of the falcon thwarted in his hunt. "You will not mount me. No other beast in the world lets his female mount him. Must I be lower than rutting boars or rams? You will not."

"But I say I will," said the voice of the earthquake, the roll of thunder.

I saw the gleam of Lilith's sharpened teeth in the opaque blackness of Adam's eyes. And then, in the world where I was everywhere at once, I saw what he saw pressing him, mother and wife at once. I even think he saw me then, so here was lover and daughter, as well.

Adam's eyes flinched shut. With the bellow of an angry bull, he gathered all his strength behind those closed eyes and shot it into his arms and legs. Violently, he thrust Lilith from him. Superhuman in her strength until that moment, she crumpled back now into Dov. Dov did not mind the burden; in fact, he took it in a tender, hungry caress, as a gift.

But Adam scrambled to unsteady legs and bolted.

Soon I found my mind had dwindled into itself once more. I felt the burden of Eve sobbing in my arms. I felt the throb of my infected ankle, taking a rhythm different now from the thrum of moon, which seemed quite silent and everyday.

A sudden scuffle in the summer-dried brush made me think: hyenas again. But it was not. It was Adam. The haphazard clutch of loincloth about him poorly hid his state of arousal.

"Eve," he barked. He might well have been a hyena. "Eve," he tried again, no gentler, but I felt the burden in my arms stir and grow lighter.

"Come," Adam said. "Now."

She went, and let him grab her by the shoulder as if he'd crush the little bones there.

Not long after—I hadn't moved—I heard the cry of pain as Eve lost her maidenhead to that dark night. The sound united with the howl of wolves, of lovers, rippling up and down the Valley of Eden.

Twenty-four

Four days later, dawn entered the Valley with an echo-ridden quiet. The moon, now plainly on the wane, made a pale reflection in the sky opposite the already-hot sun, like the scar to a flaming wound. I could see the bones of my ankle once more; the bite had shrunk to an itchy nub. But that was the least of my worries.

I woke alone outside the Cave of the Dead. Eve—always late to rise, her hair tousled into her face when she did—I no longer expected to see. She and Adam had done the unthinkable. And they had set up a camp of their own, down close to the Tree.

"The voice of God," my father had said to me defiantly. "The thundering Bull . . ." He'd said more, but I didn't stay to hear him out.

This morning, too, Grandmother was gone, leaving the hollow she'd dug to sleep in lined with crumpled mats and skins. I went to relieve myself, but still found no sign of her when I returned. She must have wandered off in the night. I would have to go and look for her.

There was no meat in the camp. In normal times, light at night would have invited the chase. But no man had been hunting since the hyenas dragged off the last of Adam's ram, not since the moon turned full. So I had braved the thorns and picked blackberries again the day before. A couple of handfuls lay mushed in the bottom of my basket. Grandmother hadn't helped herself to the fruit, which was unusual.

I picked the berries clean of goatgrass seed and ate them, the very sweet but slightly spoiled taste rising to my nose. There was a bunch of immature grapes, too. Stewed, they would have given a pleasant contrast to mutton, but raw I couldn't eat more than two. They were too hard and tart.

I got up and started my search.

I had meant to avoid Lilith. My untamed mind had been drawn to the men's howls, whether I wanted to or not, several more times during the past four days and nights. I knew that Lilith and her lovers drank often enough, but hardly ate or slept. This did not require too much shifting, although their wild romping did move them from place to place. The silent contact of our souls always gave, or so I thought, a sense of where I might find them, even if I could avoid being the throbbing center of their hearts.

Obviously, things had changed in the night, the first night I'd slept much at all since the full moonrise. For though she was precisely the one I took most care to avoid, Mother Lilith was the first person I found that morning.

She was alone. This startled me. I found her curled like a naked infant under an oak on grasses rolled almost to powder. I meant to leave her. It didn't matter how intimate we had become under the wild light of the full moon. That very intimacy made me shy—and not a little afraid. She had power I couldn't understand. And what was more, when I was near her, I had power, too. Power I could neither fathom nor control. She was my mother. And to see her naked like this was dangerous.

But, as in all things with Lilith, I had very little command over what I did. She seemed asleep. Then, as my footsteps didn't stir her, I felt she was in a state deeper than sleep. Even death crossed my mind. I lifted my head to the pale, gritty sand-colored light of that morning. Yes, there was a smell of death; the smell of thyme was gone.

She was alone. And seemed vulnerable. Dried bits of vegetation matted and tangled her hair. Raw red patched the skin on her knees, her elbows, her forearms, her buttocks, where demands of the moment had made her ignore the burn of rubbing grass or dirt or stone. Now, the demands of weariness made her ignore the flies that settled on the wounds.

I crept closer and waved the insects away. I touched her arm.

Slowly, slowly, as if returning to me from a great distance, Lilith opened her eyes. Then, as if she hadn't the strength to see and smile at once, she closed them again. Her lips stretched in a grimace.

"Hello, dear child," she murmured in a voice also conjured from far away.

"Are you all right, Mother?" As soon as I said it, my heart remembered its delight in that word. I said it again: "Mother?"

Lilith took four deep breaths to say, "Fine. I shall be fine. Nothing some sleep . . . won't cure."

"But you'd like some clothes?"

What I had seen with no shame when my being filled all Earth, or rather, when Earth filled all my being, now made me turn away, bewildered by the sight of my own origins.

"Yes, I suppose . . ." Lilith still spoke lazily, her teeth and jaws lisping over her words rather than hitting them straight on. "I suppose my snakeskins are ground to powder. I shall have to find more . . ."

"But would you like a leather skirt until then? I have an extra, my winter one."

I took her silence as agreement.

"And would you like something to eat?"

She nodded weakly. "I am very thirsty."

"I'll bring you water."

"Thank . . ." She could not even finish the phrase.

I rose to go. In my torpor, these tasks might fill my whole morning. And I must find Granny. Grandfather, too, I supposed, since he was no longer with Lilith. And one could hardly avoid either Adam or Eve in Eden . . .

The touch of Lilith's fingers on my still-discolored ankle brought me up short.

"And I will need to get rid of this child," she said.

"Child?" I was her child. What did she mean? Did she mean me?

Gently Lilith touched the hollow between her starkly protruding hip bones, above the dark fringe wedged between her legs. A sudden confusion of emotion swamped me. Could she indeed be carrying a child? A little brother or sister for me? A son, perhaps, for Adam? But she would not carry it to term? I'll care for it if you won't, I wanted to tell her. I will be an Aunt Gurit if you'll just stay with us till it's born.

Yes, but who was to say the child was Adam's? I had been there, at this getting, more than at my own. Certainly, there was doubt. Was there every bit as much doubt around my own conception? Was that the reason I'd always felt myself the clan's child as much as Adam's? There was truly a child? What would Adam say?

"Where . . . where are my uncles, Ari and Dov?" This was as close to my real questions as I dared.

"They slunk back up to the summer meadows, I suppose," Lilith replied. "As soon as the spell released them. I think they are shamed and may say nothing of this to the others." She worked a tiny globule of saliva onto her tongue and lips.

"Let me get you water," I said.

"Tell me first where Adam is. I think you know better than I."

I looked away, but avoided looking down the hill, toward the Tree. "With Eve."

"And have they—?"

"They have."

"Yes. I heard it happen." Her closed eyelids seemed bruised over her eyes.

"The whole Valley heard it. Oh, Mother! How terrible will your jealousy be!"

Lilith sighed, as if talk of jealousy were the only part of my storytelling that was truly myth. I stepped away and this time she did nothing to stop my going.

Twenty-five

Nothing drew me from serving Lilith. If she'd planned my actions herself, like the priestess in the vulture rite at the turn of winter, I could not have been more distracted. Not long after, I was sitting with her again.

High clouds flecked the heavy blue sky — like the scales of a silvery perch in a still, deep pool — but they offered no shade. The climbing sun weighted the back of my head. I shifted out of this burden to sit closer to my mother, closer than I'd ever dared, our thighs stretched out side by side, almost touching, mine slightly longer than hers from the knee down. We sat under the shade of a pistachio where unripe fruit hung in their pale green clusters.

I had never seen the nuts in this stage before, for always we had been in the summer meadows at this time of year. It seemed a secret, dark sort of thing to see, shameful, like the sight of my mother's nakedness. She had covered up now, my skirt laid loosely across her lap. The tree knew no such modesty and I kept my eyes averted. Lilith's breasts were heavy, the nipples large, round, and dark. I had suckled there, I thought. But the thought — like the suckling — was not long.

A clan of partridges worked the underbrush not far from us, their feathers almost invisible against the unvarying dun.

Insects hummed idly in the waves of heat all around. If they moved, it was to glide rather than make the effort of flight. The black outline of kites' wings slipped over the ground from time to time, making more of a shadow than the thin clouds.

As if all this surrounding life possessed and entered her, sinking to the heart of her pelvis, Lilith touched it again tenderly.

"I must give back this child," she mused. "This must be my first task."

Another slip of kite wing, like skin sloughing off a scab. Kites meant death—somewhere. And I continued to smell moist, sour death, too. It came when the breeze shifted from the north and scattered the parched-grain smell of hot, dry grass.

But I continued to hope.

"There my be no child," I urged. "Surely it is far too soon to tell."

"There is a child."

Lilith idly watched a horsefly land and bite her arm. She made no move against it, didn't even flinch at the pain, though when it came to take a turn at me I was quick enough to swat it dead. Lilith turned from looking at my deed as if from something she would not condemn, but which she could not watch. Yet here she was speaking of depriving me of a sister or brother.

"There is always a child," she repeated. "With me. Unless I hide myself away from all men at the time, as I have learned, with much suffering, to do."

"You are not too old?" I was thinking of other ways out. "You are not a crone?"

"No, child. Not in the usual manner of speaking, though I am old. I am so old that . . ." Some inkling of that age showed now in her face, though neither in wrinkles nor grayness. "You don't understand."

"Mother, I confess it is a mystery beyond my grasp."

"Almost beyond mine," she agreed. "Even for me, who has had all these lifetimes to try to get my mind around it. I would not burden your young life with it. Except—except you are my own daughter. And I know you are different—from the others. I know you came. You were with me these last few days, at the moontime. I felt you here, with me. That much you do understand."

"I was. But I don't understand. I . . . it only happened. Without me. So I was afraid."

"You say without you. But with you, child. You were there. And that is the best of understanding. What did you see?"

"I saw . . ." I blushed and looked off toward a circling of vultures, now joining the kites.

"What do you know of the full moon?"

"Nothing."

"Nothing?"

"The wise women say it is a time when childless women are most likely to conceive."

"Yes."

"And women who don't want to should put off their husbands."

"Because it is the exact opposite of the dark of the moon, when women bleed under the Tree."

"I see."

"You know the rutting seasons of beasts?"

"Of course. The elk bellow and charge. The bear are dangerous. The deer dance in the meadows for their mates."

"Once, long, long ago, human women knew a season, too. Only perhaps I am wrong to give us—them—the name of humans. They were close to humans, very close. But creatures like me."

"You are human."

"I may appear so. But in many ways I am not. I was born in a time when . . . in a time when women still came into heat, like the beasts. Over the years—many, many years—things have changed. It is the way of our Mother Earth, to change. To birth, to live, to die. Were it not so, were life to freeze in some good form mortals imagine, it would cease to be life. The fact is, I go into heat. That may be a sign to you just how long I have been alive."

"I . . . I cannot grasp it."

"I am, in fact, the last woman ever born to do so, which is the key to my power. I am also pleasing to men nowadays, you see, which women before were not—usually. For generations before I was born, women had been growing more and more open to men, more and more of the time. A woman who was so, you understand, could keep a man with her more and more of the time. Such a woman, with a man's help, was better and better able to care for her infants, which were born much more helpless than other creatures'—but much more teachable."

"That seems to be a very good thing."

"Perhaps."

"I mean, rather than living by yourself, trying to find food on your own, with a baby strapped to your back all the time . . ."

Lilith nodded, sighed, then went on. "This change does have its drawbacks, however."

"Such as?"

"Women who are open all the time may keep their mate, but they may attract other men, as well—and at any time. That means you may be forced."

"Oh." The chill of a vulture's flight slipped over me.

"No man even considers mating with me . . . unless I am signaling him and he cannot resist."

"You enjoy . . . all that?"

"Of course. Probably more than the men do. It is nature, better to appease than go hungry."

I looked away, uneasy. "I see."

"There are other drawbacks."

"Yes?" There was already drawback enough to make me wince.

"Women now can give birth to more children than they can care for."

"Alone. Yes, I see. Her man can die."

"Or — he can leave. For his attraction to stay with a woman whom he can constantly mate waxes feeble — if another female presents herself. Caring for her child is fixed in the body of a woman. But for a man it is mostly a matter of what he is taught. And what he is taught, or what he learns — from his own gods, perhaps — changes, whereas a woman cannot change what her body is, paint it with ocher or kohl as she may."

"I see."

"Women how can have more children than they can care for — even with a man's help. More children than even our Mother Earth can care for and still renew Herself in Her own dark of the moon. That is my task, since I am from the old time. I go throughout the world and among each people I kindle rites that may balance the evils of this new way of being women, since they are so easy for me to see — and become easier with each year I live. I form the powers that bind men to their women and children. Magic, curses, whatever I can."

"Like the aurochs."

"Yes, like the aurochs. I began that rite here when the great beasts began to fade. The snows grew less, the trees more. This is no longer as good a land for the aurochs as once it was."

"But why demand that men hunt aurochs just in a place where they are difficult to find?"

"Precisely for that reason, daughter. I present a different challenge in lands where the aurochs still thrive. If the quest is too easy, men are too quick to come and go. I have been known, in fact, to make up beasts that don't even exist—or at least, not any more. Dragons, for instance."

"Dragons don't exist?"

"There are some very large lizards, but dragons? No, not any more. A man must simply slay a dragon first, before he wins a bride. A second bride, rather."

"But how can women, tied to the demands of their bodies, live by such myths?"

"You, a storyteller? You must ask this? Every woman must agree to the myth, must hold out for the dragon and not bargain herself down, else—" Lilith's voice faded as she looked down the hill, through the rounded pistachio leaves, to where we both knew Adam and Eve were.

"I see."

"Tell the story, Na'amah," she murmured.

"What story, Mother?"

"The story of Adam and Eve. At the Tree."

"I don't know. I wasn't there. I was up caring for Grandmother and didn't—"

"Tell it, Na'amah. You are a storyteller. You know."

She closed her eyes, waiting. And I told it.

Twenty-six

*O*nce there was — and once there was not — a woman named Eve. She awoke to full sunlight and found herself caught in the crook of Adam's arm, pressed against his earth-hard ribs. They were both naked. This, she thought, finally. Finally this is where I belong.

"Bone of my bone, flesh of my flesh."

She mouthed the words — words Adam had given her last night — back into his warm flesh, letting the curls of his hair tickle her. They were words his bull god had given him, he'd told her. Words that would bind them closer, more powerfully than any chant in any common marriage among the clans.

And she did. She did feel she was still part of him, as she had been that night, breathing with the same deep, gasping breaths. She felt the warmth between her legs — not really pain as they'd told her in initiation it might be — but a heat, a glow. So might a slight festering feel. So might muscles feel after a day of exertion. So might something growing feel, in spring in the damp of last year's mold.

Such thoughts separated her from Adam — for surely Adam did not feel what she felt or he wouldn't have been so rough last night, so beastlike. So she stopped them. She tried to think only of Adam, the ease that now smoothed his face in sleep so that beard and moustache seemed only a mask, letting him play at grown-up for a while when he was actually still a child. She listened again for the rumble of breath, the slow, even thump of his heart beneath the wonderful strength of his chest.

Surely such strength could never die.

Another rumble, lower, told her he would wake hungry. She was ravenous, her lack of interest in food, in anything supporting life during the past day or so, had vanished and now her stomach demanded revenge. She should go and gather something for Adam to eat when he awoke. Lilith would have managed something wifely like that.

Lilith! Eve burned with anger. What did she care what Lilith might do? Lilith, with all her witchcraft. It was not Lilith who had made Adam her own, after all. Eve had done it herself.

Unfortunately, she couldn't think of anything to be gathered — except that vicious berry briar Na'amah kept dragging her to. That was so far away in any case. It would take all morning to go there and come back and she'd have to go up to the old people by the Cave of the Dead to get her basket. Wouldn't it be lovely, she thought, if I could make things grow where I wanted to?

Like Lilith can.

In order to stop that thought, Eve sat up, moving quietly and slowly so as not to disturb the arm flung around her shoulders.

The first thing to meet her eyes was that Lilith Tree. Again. Adam had brought her down to this place in the moonlit dark. Very close. Too close.

That cursed Tree.

Ripe figs dangled among its branches now, taunting her. A wild dissonance of birds were taking their fill of fruit, and their shaking, flitting, scolding knocked some of the half-eaten pink rinds to the ground.

That cursed Tree, which lets birds eat and not people. What are birds to thinking, loving people?

Eve was close enough that she could see a tiny gray mouse creep to the edge of her sight within the fig's shadow. She sat so quietly, he came out farther and began to feed on the fig rinds. Even a mouse could break the ban but she —

She had helped to put the ban on that Tree herself. "In the day that you eat thereof, you shall surely die."

The mouse didn't die. With a twitch and a nervous look around with bright, shiny eyes, he darted to the next fig, open and gleaming juice.

I never put the ban on that Tree, Eve thought. Lilith did.

Lilith.

Adam's god had rejected Lilith. She only prohibits us because she thinks we are not as wise as she. She thinks she is like the Mother, to know good from evil. Ancient Lilith, worn-out Lilith. The bull god has chosen a new way.

I am the way he has chosen.

The mouse did not die when he ate. There are figs enough for all, left on such a big tree.

Eve got to her feet, leaving the imprint of her body next to Adam in the grass, and quietly approached the Tree. The mouse did not hear her, but continued to nibble away.

Even Lilith moves no quieter than I, Eve thought.

She reached up into the closest branch, bushing aside the handlike leaves, and wrapped her fingers around a forbidden fruit. Its flesh gave ever so slightly with wonderful ripeness. She was quite certain she didn't even give a tug. The fig was so ripe it dropped of its own warm, dark weight into her hand.

Eve brought it to her lips and felt the wonderful firm warmth like Adam's kisses. The smell was sweet beyond resistance. She bit into it and crunched the many, tiny lives of all the seeds.

She picked another—and screamed.

Adam was beside her in an instant, swinging a stick after the snake that had frightened her so, the snake that had made a legless lunge out of the shadows and caught the mouse in its unnaturally stretched jaws.

"Cursed creature!" Adam was shouting. "Cursed above holy cattle

and above every beast of the field. Yes, crawl off on your belly. Eat dust all the days of your life. You and your lady Lilith."

"You . . . you didn't kill it, did you?" Eve whimpered when she could whimper anything.

"No, it got away. But would it bother you if I had?"

"You must not kill a legless one." She carefully didn't speak the creature's name. "They are subtler than any beast of the field. They live forever, shedding their skins. Unless impious people kill them."

"Lilith would have it so. But when I hunted the aurochs, I lived for a time among people who caught snakes and ate them."

Adam clearly didn't care if he spoke the word "snake" any more than the word "aurochs." How fearless he was!

He continued, "I'll bet if you asked her, that she-demon Lilith would tell you she was the one who taught them to eat that food. And she comes to us, toting that snake wrapped around her staff like a holy thing."

"You think that was her—her snake—just now?"

"I have no doubt. It was different from the dirt-gray variety we usually have here. So, don't be afraid. I won't let Lilith and her frigid jealousy touch you, my love. My wife."

His hand was on her neck now, up among the roots of her hair, and she shivered with delight at the many tiny, sharp tugs.

He bent and kissed her, then snorted before he was far enough away from her face. She felt it. "By the Bull, I tell you. I wish I had killed that snake. I'm hungry enough this moment to eat it—raw, head and all."

She felt a little queasy at the thought—she couldn't help herself. She wasn't as brave as he. His god had never spoken to her. She didn't think Adam would like it if the god did.

She wondered if he'd tasted the fig on her lips. He didn't seem to, but dropped all contact with her and looked about the Valley distractedly. She knew he was wondering where he could find something to eat before he fainted with hunger.

Eve reached up and another fig fell into her hand.

"Eat this," she offered, as enticingly as she could.

"Figs?" Another snort. "That's woman's food."

"Only Lilith says so. Lilith—and your daughter."

"Her daughter. Not mine. I intend to have sons."

Eve felt his eyes on her, on every part of her, for she had never stood before him thus, naked, in daylight. His eyes darkened with the sight, dark like the skin of the fruit he took in his hand. He opened his mouth, uncovered the endearing gap where his tooth was missing, that she had tasted with her tongue that night. That she would taste again. Forever.

Fig after fig went between his lips and he picked the high, sunwarmed ones for her.

And when they were full, they went back to their imprints in the grass to satisfy other needs.

Such is the tale. And within it are contained three apples, one for you, one for me, and one . . .

Any other story might have had a "happy ever after" at this point, but mine did not.

My mother spoke. "So they think they are in paradise"—I didn't know that word she used, but she made it sound the same as Eden—"when actually they have left it behind. Forever. And may carry all the world with them."

"I'm sorry," I murmured to her as the story faded from my mind.

"Sorry, child? For what?" In spite of what she'd said before, the drowsiness crept over her again.

"Sorry to tell you something that upsets you."

"Why should you be sorry to tell me something that is true?"

"It isn't true. It's just a story. I made it up."

"But you made it up by sending out your spirit and sensing how it must have been. That is your gift."

"I guess . . . I guess that is so."

"I tell you it is so. It happened all very much as you told it."

The silence between us stretched until finally I prodded it. "Could you not lift the ban? Just once? For Adam—for my father. He is so lonely, and you—you are never here to care."

"You think I don't care?"

"I—" The eyes she lashed toward me held a dark, feral, hunted look. They silenced me.

"It is precisely because I do care that I—" Emotion stopped the words again, then brought them out in no more than a whisper. "I cannot love one child—even one grown to manhood—above another."

"Nor even—nor even a daughter." I nodded and turned my head away.

Twenty-seven

The sun was at its most merciless now, paling what colors the season left even further toward a dead white. The vultures and kites must have found their prey. At least they had emptied the sky, as had the clouds. My throat felt dry and empty from breathing the smell of hot earth and, vaguely, death. I fumbled for the waterskin, still my old skin, leaking and unpleasantly flaccid. Where it dragged, my bare legs were cooled—but muddied. I drank the taste of the story away without offering the water to Lilith first.

But the skin also left a smear of dampness on the bare ground. Even the touch of so little water released a darker, more vital smell. Tiny insects had been faster than I to notice the blessing. Ants and a pair of black beetles scurried to the mud, thrilled and busy about their tiny lives. And a dragonfly hovered, the blues and greens on its wings so brilliant, so beautiful, that the breath caught in my throat and tears stung my eyes.

My mind instantly created autumn rains from this wet fragrance, very close to the woman-smell under the Tree at the dark of the moon. With this vision, I saw the naked pistachios harden and ripen, fat with oil, the earth grow lush, life—and love—stir from the pounded mold that seemed only hard and lifeless beneath me. But only—only if I did not try to force it. Only if I embraced it exactly as it was, and expected no happy-ever-after ending to it.

Then I dared to look at Lilith again. She was looking back. She closed her eyes—so she could smile—then opened them again and I saw myself taken into their black, lazy depths. I passed her the skin.

"Be careful of the leak," I warned.

She smiled again—but let the water leak down her chest, remuddying the dirt-crusted tracks.

"Adam should get you a new waterskin," she said. "I charged him always to care for our child."

She licked her lips, drank more water, and sighed, so that a blessed cooling breath of air came down the Valley—and away from the scent of death.

"But there are many things, I suppose, that every man ought to do. And I cannot force him."

After a pause, she began to speak again. "I come to understand each place where people live, sometimes jungle, sometimes desert, sometimes forest, sometimes savannah."

Like the word "sea," I didn't understand all these words. "How can you come to such an understanding?" I asked.

"Part of it is having lived so long. I saw such and such a fertile plain before the mountain exploded and spread ash and pumice all over it. This dry canyon I knew while the carving stream still ran at its bottom."

She breathed deeply through her exhaustion. "But it is more than that. It is an ability of my soul to spread out into the world and become every stone or beast or blade of grass I seek to understand. I do not take this understanding; they give it to me. It is a gift of the Earth to me, and mine only as long as I obey Her will. I can't explain it better than that."

"You don't need to," I said. "I have felt the same myself."

Lilith looked at me as hard as her weakness allowed. "Yes, you were there. I suppose it may be, since you are my daughter . . ."

It seemed easier for Lilith to ramble carelessly through the far-flung fields of her children with dreamy, vague words, touching each one with love. "To some of my children I forbid men and women to unite at different seasons. Some I teach to build upon the lust Mother Earth has given them for each other, men with men and women with women. Some I teach to circumcise—at an age when the rite can be dangerous to a man's vigor. Some men I even require to be always celibate or to castrate themselves and so to form a holy priesthood. Always, everywhere, I initiate women in the holy things that control their own fruitfulness. I show them what holy herbs can prevent childbearing, or end the clot of blood if a child nonetheless begins."

"All these things are holy? You keep saying that word."

"Of course they are holy. Anything is holy that would turn men and women against such things as self-love would make them seek. Holiness is all that defies reason, for only such things can stand up to the dissolving power of one man's mind. Holiness is what keeps a man in tune to what he cannot change, what is greater than himself. But what seems, against reason, less. Like women."

"I wish—" What did I wish? Some deep longing opened in my heart, but I couldn't at first give it a name. At last I spoke as close to the purpose as I could. "I wish I could help you, Mother."

"Perhaps you can, my child. But first—" She set aside the waterskin. "First I need to regain my strength."

"Of course, Mother. I will not keep you talking any more." I bunched my knees up under me to rise.

"You do not know the plants I will need to return this child to the earth, Na'amah?"

"No, Mother." I stopped in my rise, aware of the unpleasant mark left by the muddy waterskin on my leg.

"I will keep no thing alive that does not serve its purpose. And the purpose of this child was to bind Adam to his duty." The defeat in her voice echoed with the empty blueness of the summer sky.

"You have not spoken of it to him?"

She shook her head and closed her eyes.

"Then you may, and change his heart when you do."

"But the force of my jealousy must not change. For if it did, who would believe the ban on second wives again?"

"I see."

"You don't know the plants?" she asked me again.

"I am not—"

"Ah, yes. Not yet initiated."

"Aunt Afra knows. I could run and find her."

"No. I shall be well enough to teach you the plants myself before you could run up to the summer meadows and back down again. I can wait, though every day the strength of life within me grows. Besides, there are plenty of other things to occupy you here. Your grandfather, Na'amah—"

"Oh, yes." Sudden guilt at my forgetfulness shadowed my mind. "That's why I first set out, to find Grandmother. She's wandered off again."

Something in the bunching of Lilith's flesh at her heavy brows told me she knew this.

"You have seen her? Earlier today?"

Somehow I knew the answer was yes, though she didn't say.

"And you didn't try to turn her back to the safety of the camp?"

"What is safety, Na'amah?"

"I—" I didn't know, but I wouldn't say.

"I pray the Earth she may have found your grandfather by now. I think we have given her enough time."

I was on my feet now, dusting off the gritty, drying, tightening mud. "Enough time to—"

"Your grandfather is dead, Na'amah."

"Dead?" My heart stopped, and my hand, in midair.

"My heat proved too much for him," Lilith said simply. "Life brought him the death he craved when nothing else would."

"You—? You let him—?"

But I halted my own tongue. Tears stood in Lilith's eyes. I could tell that, no matter how many children she watched die, it never became easier for her. Life was a greater burden to her than to those of us who must die.

Still, I wanted to get away. Her power, joined with my sorrow, sickened me. "Where is he?" I asked.

Lilith closed her eyes and pressed the tears down her cheeks. She merely nodded in the direction.

I didn't have far to go to find him—and the source of the smell of death that had begun to invade everything as the day's heat pressed harder. I thought Lilith must be wrong. The mound still moved. But it was the carrion birds. My approach frightened them off. They didn't go far, but sat low in nearby trees and on rocks, watching me, waiting. A hyena's wicked laugh told me I'd frightened one of that tribe, too. But not for long.

Still, there seemed to be breath, with the bone showing through half his face— A maggot dropped from his nose into his grizzled old beard. Grandfather had at last become one with his aurochs hide.

I tried not to think of how it must have happened, how

death could have crept up, with Ari and Dov present but oblivious, under the full-moon spell. How Earth had called the old man to Her finally, not as the Mother, but as the eternal Lover.

I hurried away, my gorge rising. There was no choice. I had to find my father. And confront him.

Twenty-eight

Grandfather and Grandmother lay side by side in the Cave of the Dead. Gold and bone-colored yarrow, the last of the broom mustard with all but the very tips of its sprays already in pod, wild carrot, and seeding onion heaped the bodies. I'd gathered groundsel, too, though the moment I'd plucked them, most of these yellow flowers had burst into downy seeds. I'd managed to amass enough blooms to cover the sight of Grandfather's decay. Grandmother too required concealment: We'd found her not far from Grandfather's corpse, and not long after. She had wandered to the edge of a cliff, and then off it, Mother Earth calling to her from the heights.

Or perhaps it was the bull bellow of Eben she heard. I imagined she found Grandfather first and was so grieved at the sight of her husband of more than thirty-five years, dead from the embraces of another woman, that she . . . But this is only my imagining, the imagining of a storyteller who must always see more in anything than the simple call of Mother Earth when a woman's days are done.

So I'd picked these second masses of flowers. The species were nearly two months later than the first bunches I'd gathered for the same ancestors, these drier, more brittle plants in dusty yellows, gold, and washed-out whites. Rain was out of season on Eden's hillsides, and my eyes were dry. Mortality was only catching up to the Earth's will, after all.

Though my flowers covered the wounds, they could not, in their vague and herbal scents, cover the smell of my ancestors returning to Earth in that tight and dusty air. Earth, it seemed, was angry at being cheated of Her proper food for so long, and She was going about Her work with even greater greed.

I should cover my grandparents with more than flowers, I thought. It is neither decent nor respectful to watch Mother Earth at her divine feed, maggots her white teeth, rotting juices her saliva. The thought of the day my own flesh would come between Her jaws made me nearly faint with fear—and a deep sense of loss.

At the same time, I also saw Earth embracing Her fallen children, crushing them to Her ample bosom after years of separation. I wanted to shovel the dirt on flowers and bodies, to hasten the long-thwarted, happy reunion.

But after he'd helped me bring the bodies down, my father had told me to watch, as due honor to the dead. He wanted me to wait until he and Eve returned to complete the setting away of our dead from out of our sight. A girl obeys her father, especially in matters of death and ancestors. I had always wanted a father in whom I could have such faith, who could order my life with his. And having found a mother gave me wild hope for a father, as well.

My own heart said Earth had already loosened plenty of rubble, aching to bury this pair. I could move the rubble easily with my bare hands, here in the place where my grandparents had waited—and then been denied. I should help Mother Earth complete Her business and then go see how I could help Mother Lilith with her recovery.

Several times I started to cover them, then backed off.

Several more times, while backing off, I moved to the mouth of the cave. To clear my head. And to keep the contents of my stomach down.

A real watch of the dead, such as my father had commanded, would not have allowed even such escapes. But as my mind wavered, so did my watch. The heat-weighted air gave little relief to my lungs, no matter where I carried them.

At last I saw them coming, Adam and Eve, hand in hand like any bridal couple, up the hill from the Tree. Rather than a lawful couple, however, they looked like a pair of children, playing at wedding. They had crowned themselves with the customary flower wreaths—which only reminded me of the dead behind me. And who besides children made clothing for themselves out of leaves?

"I haven't had time to hunt for anything else." My father shrugged when he noticed the direction of my gaze, which was probably also bunched into a scowl.

Eve giggled. "And I had to have something to wear," she said. "My rabbit skins just fell to pieces."

Even Adam blushed at the memory of those rabbit skins—and their coming apart in his rough hands. "There is so little game in the Valley these days." He thought he was changing the subject. "Hunting takes so much more time than before." He wasn't.

"There's a reason game is scarce in Eden."

My father looked at me in surprise, as if he'd never heard me speak before. As if he thought I couldn't.

"You shouldn't be hunting here in this season at all," I said, just to prove to him I could.

And I would have said more except an even greater horror had registered in my mind to wipe the words away. I had noticed the shape of the large, dark green leaves Adam and Eve wore, like cut-off human hands. She had strung hers together on a twisted hemp fiber, slung low around her hips. And he wore even fewer leaves, baring his thighs completely to the waist where the hemp cord creased the softening flesh of his sides.

Terror caught my words like a hand at my throat so I could only whisper, "Those leaves . . ."

"From the Tree, yes," Eve said brightly. "I've often wondered why our clothes must always be made of skins, which are hot and chafe so unpleasantly. These leaves are much softer. And the fibers we use for baskets and mats—flax and hemp—could be softer still with a little work and care. We might even shave the fur off animal skins, twist and knot it to a finer material. It would go further. Then we wouldn't have to worry so much about following animals at every season of the year."

"But the Tree . . . The ban . . ."

"Lilith is a creature whose curses rebound to herself." I think my father was trying for gentleness, but I was not used to hearing that tone from him, nor he to giving it. Harshness sounded instead. "She doesn't belong to this world's truth."

Eve's gentleness came with more practice, more ease. But this only piled up the meaning of her words; they cracked my heart like ice tossed suddenly into warm water.

"Lilith's curse means nothing," she said. "We can even eat the figs without punishment. See?"

She opened her gathering sack and showed me five blue-black figs in their perfect sweetness.

"Adam and I have been eating them for days. In fact—" She looked up at him with swimming eyes, as if he were, indeed, too bright to look at directly, like the sun. "In fact, we took them for our wedding meal."

I repeated, "Wedding meal . . . ?"

"We've had no ill effect."

"The snake ate the mouse," I whispered.

"What mouse?" Eve blanched. "What snake?"

"We've had no ill effect." My father prodded Eve.

She remembered herself and spoke just a little too rapidly. "And now we've brought the figs here for you to share . . . To let you see . . ."

My father said, "Go on. Tell her the rest, Eve, my dear."

"And Na'amah, there is more . . . Come, see . . ." Blood pounded so fiercely behind my eyes that I saw black. I could only hear that Eve had moved into the cave. "I've sprouted the wheat, see . . . Don't look at me like that, Na'amah . . . Adam ate it. He did not swell up and burst as Afra said he would."

"I love the taste of wheat," Adam agreed.

"It's all lies, what they told us," Eve said. "And what I took from the pits, I have replaced. And dug and filled other pits, away from the dead. There is plenty of wheat in this Valley. It's overflowing with it. The wheat lies hard and dead on the ground until the autumn rains, when it bursts with life. But by then, I'll have gathered enough to . . . Well, so we don't have to season-move . . . Nor ever empty our wombs of children we cannot carry again . . . Little fingers will be good at gathering the grain up off the ground where it has fallen . . . Little fingers will also be good at pulling out the useless plants in between to which Adam has given the new name 'weed.' With your help, Na'amah . . . The birds and animals . . ."

I didn't hear what fate Eve wished for the birds and animals whose turn at the wheat was supposed to come after ours. Her words reached my brain in more and more ragged scraps, and my father's deep tones—which I knew joined hers—cast but a shadow of sound in between.

Now I saw, in the midst of blood-beat black, a flash of

white bone that deadened my mind to words altogether. I couldn't tell where it had come from, but my father had produced the aurochs skull. New-painted with red ocher and henna, but removed from the men's cave, it consumed me with its empty sockets, spitted me onto its tasseled horns. I couldn't tell if my father spoke or the aurochs. Snatches were all I heard, bull-like bellows, speaking to me—or my grandfather—or the world at large.

"There, old man. Your time is past. The time of the aurochs too is past. He has left the earth and ascended on high. He has become a God, lording over the earth and its common things. A God instead of a dung-leaving beast. God . . . In the cool of the day . . . The beginning . . . new . . . The voice of God . . . Keep the garden and dress it . . . Dominion over all creation . . ."

I had never heard such foul language. The rank smell of it overwhelmed such an everyday thing as death; the smell burst in my head like a sun-ripened corpse. I felt my insides leave my mouth and nose. But they found every other opening, too. Heat soured between my legs and dribbled down my neck from within my ears, deafening them. Acid tears burned in my eyes. Rot heaved itself all over the world.

This was death, the smell, the taste, the sound, the very icy grin of death. Not just the death of my grandparents, which I must learn to endure like every other person who has ever lived, but death of the entire world. Not just the death of the aurochs but death even of the flies and maggots that fed on death.

Sorrow ran deep now. It ran boundlessly greater than what I might have felt over the simple passing of two old people who had lived long, good lives. Who had ached so badly they wished only to return to fresh wombs again as quickly as they could. My sorrow was for the hunger-death of the young at shriveled breasts. The anger-death of young men as they fought, not side by side against the world, but against each other. It was the death-unsated of lovers in each other's arms, reward for the pleasure Adam and Eve had stolen before them.

For if a beginning is bred, in that instant so also is an end. And in his sudden, new creation, Adam had broken apart what had been until then a spiral, a circle. By brute force of his own will, he had stretched the arc taut and long, made a line. He had shoved a great stone off its balance at a cliff's edge. Now nothing could stop its fall.

"With this act he has created progress," I thought I heard Lilith say, more words I didn't understand. "History. Hordes of other things for which there are as yet no words. But in that story's closure—"

Adam was no storyteller. He couldn't see. He could only see the "happy ever after" from his point at the beginning and make a willful grab for it. But the storyteller who knew her craft could see. He was going to have to create something beyond this world, a springtime Eden to award to people who obeyed him. For the old saying, "Close the circle, close the circle, that is the best reward. Give up—and gain. Gain return," was no longer enough in his smooth-pounded world. And if he created such a reward, he must also create a punishment for those who didn't obey. The storyteller could see . . .

Blackness.

Nothing.

"Multiply," my father said.

"Replenish," I spat though the globs of vomit on my lips.

"Multiply . . ." My father's voice trailed off, finally conscious of my state.

The storyteller could see . . .

"The End," I said.

Twenty-nine

The End.

The sounds could hardly stir my choking windpipe. But the vibrations seemed to enter my bones instead. They thrust down my bones and into the skeleton of Earth, to whisper, to heave, at last to roar.

With a volley of stifling dust and shards of crystal, the back of the cave swept down and claimed my grandparents. The earthquake came within a finger's breadth of claiming Adam and Eve, too, but my father moved quickly and dragged Eve along after him.

Myself, I stood safe outside the cave, having long ago backed away from the horror it contained. But I felt as good as dead. I fell to my knees, my head hidden in my hands, a hollowed husk.

Then words, like shafts of light, stilled the lurching earth. They entered and filled my darkness.

"Cursed be the ground for your sake."

Lilith's voice.

"In sorrow shall you eat of it all the days of your life."

The soothing tones of my Mother, albeit forming the ancient, timeless words of cursing. It didn't matter what her words were. She had heard me. She had answered the cry of her child. I was alone no longer.

"Thorns also and thistles shall it bring forth to you, and you shall eat the herb of the field."

Now, in the lightening of my brain, I could see her outline.

"In the sweat of your brow shall you eat grain till you return unto the ground."

Lilith stood framed in the mouth of the cave. She was naked, but for her vultures' wings and the mantle of her hair. She stood hunched like a carrion bird, leaning on her staff around which curled earthquake-disturbed serpents, twitching.

"And woman—" She turned ever so slightly to Eve. "Woman, I will greatly multiply your sorrow and your conception; in sorrow shall you bring forth children; and your desire shall be toward your man and he shall rule over you."

Now my pure vision of Lilith in her power grew shadows at one edge. Adam was drawn to battle with Lilith, not when she cursed the land, nor when she cursed him, but when she extended the ancient curse to Eve.

"Go away, old woman," he said, his voice quiet as an aimed spearpoint. "There is no place for you in this Valley any more."

"I am your wife," Lilith replied, quieter still.

"I repudiate you. I repudiate you and have taken another."

"Then you shall know the jealous wrath of Lilith, Lilith, the Mother of all living."

Lilith shook the serpents from her staff. They dropped to the ground and slithered toward Adam's feet. My father moved quickly, shoving Eve to safety behind him and crushing the head of one snake. The others slithered away, out of sight, into crevices and tufts of grass.

"It is death to kill a messenger of the gods," Lilith hissed.

Adam scoffed, breathing heavily. "Like it is death to eat your precious figs or your sprouted wheat?"

"Like it is death to take another woman when the child of your first wife stands before you."

"How can I say she is mine?" My father didn't even look at me. "You have more husbands than stars in the sky and children . . ."

"While Na'amah lives, you may take no other woman."

The force in her voice silenced Adam for a moment. Lilith pushed that force on, beginning a low hum in her throat, slowly raising her hands and her staff as the notes rose as well. Not only Lilith hummed, so did the air thick with cicadas and the earth to its depths. Out of nowhere, clouds seemed to clot the sky and a sharp, black wind rummaged through oak leaf and summer-dried grass.

Reflexively, Adam drew his flint knife out of its tooled-leather sheath.

"You cannot harm me, Adam." The humming sank for a moment to a low drone under her words. "You know this. You've tried it before, remember? I am Lilith, Mother of all living. I cannot die." Then the humming swelled once more, Lilith in the core of every being—but without so much as a twitch of her lips. "Cursed be the earth . . ."

"While Na'amah lives . . ."

Suddenly, the only thing in creation quivering to a different rhythm grabbed me. Adam caught me about the waist and held the cold of his flint against my throat.

"She shall not live." The force of his breath in my ear shot cold down to clamp at the base of my spine. "If I kill her, Lilith, you have no further claim on me. I will. I will kill her and send you on your demonic ways. Leave Eden in peace."

The humming stopped abruptly. Lilith lowered her arms

and grew pale beneath the heavy ridge of her brows. I felt the heartening caress of her mind on mine and knew she cared for me. But I also knew she must call his bluff.

"Your stone knife is nothing against the circle of my being," she said slowly, the rhythm of her voice searching for the hum again. "Kill her, yet I carry another child of yours within my belly, Adam. This one, I think, will be a boy."

I smelled the sourness of my father's sweat and felt it foreign on my own skin. I felt the prickle of his damp hair from my shoulder to my calf. I felt the stiff green of fig leaf at his groin.

"Give that bastard to Dov," he said. "Or to Ari. They have as much claim to it, surely, as I do."

"But the child is yours, Adam, and a son."

Lilith took a step toward us and the flint creased tighter against my windpipe. The slightest move, side to side, would cut.

"Let your daughter go, Adam . . ."

Lilith took another step. I felt myself suddenly dropped as my father made a lunge at Lilith. Side to side moved knife and hand across her naked belly. I screamed and scrambled to help my mother.

"Never fear, little one," she crooned. "He cannot hurt me."

And indeed, where red blood ought to have been flowing, there seemed to be only a darkness and a wind and the flesh closed swiftly in on itself.

"He might as well slash at the ground."

With a bellow of rage, Adam lunged again. Reflexively, I moved between Lilith and the blow. The blade itself did not strike true. It only slid along my chest, then clattered to the ground. But the force of my father's arm behind it caught me under the chin and lifted me from my feet. My head flew down and back, then all but black burst from my nose outward.

Thirty

She's dead."

I became sensible somewhere up in a speck of sunlight where it shifted among the tiny, still-green acorns in the highest branches of an oak. From this vantage point, I saw them, Lilith, Adam, and Eve. Lilith spoke. She was kneeling at my head, feeling past the slick of blood at my neck, finding no pulse.

"I am unbound," my father said.

Wonder more than cheer draped his voice. It may, in fact, have been the chirp of a bird that I heard, for I suddenly found I could understand those sounds, as well. And human speech was losing its meaning, certainly its singleness.

Adam continued. "I have no child. I am at liberty to marry."

"Liar. I carry your child," Lilith said. "A son."

"It is you who lie. Give it to Ari."

Perhaps the words were only echoes in my mind, like the flashes of light here among the tossing leaves.

"I am unbound." Then he invented a new word. "I am free."

"A murderer is never 'free,' as you call it. Nor is a man who uses brute force against anything in creation to enforce his own will."

"Crazy old woman, that is the only meaning of the word 'free,' to have such power, such freedom. I have invented the word. I can make it mean what I want." Adam picked up his knife, sheathed it, then slipped his arm around Eve's shoulders, which were shuddering with sobs. "Come, Eve."

Lilith groped for her staff and stood up from my side. She watched them go, the fig leaves patting their buttocks with each step. She raised her arms to hum and curse again, then dropped them, wearied by the weight of the world. The world pressed harder. She turned back to my corpse and sank to her knees. Letting out a cry of anguish like some cornered and wounded beast, she covered her eyes with a hand on their heavy brow-shelf, bared her teeth, and began to pant out rough little howls.

I floated down from the tree. One with the hot afternoon sunlight, I rippled on Lilith's black hair, still tangled with love. I slid down the sheen of her vulture feathers. I rode the round curve of her breasts, dirt-smeared, snail-trailed, and entered her heart, racing there like an underground spring in a valley floor.

And then, though they were in a tongue foreign to me, a tongue like the click of cicadas or the whisper of wind, I knew the words of her heart.

"Of all the children I have borne," Lilith said in her heart, "so many that one child blurs into the other—this is the only one I have had to see die. I have been careful not to see such death, knowing how hard it is to watch life leave even when I was not actually the one who pushed it forth."

I felt the dryness and dust on Lilith's teeth, the throbbing in her head.

"My child," she said. "My child, my only child."

I felt the half-remembered spasms in her loins, smelled my own birth blood, held the wriggling little thing that was me, newborn. Watched the tiny toes curl and uncurl, as yet never pressed to earth.

"Ah, little one," she said. "Na'amah. Are you there? I feel you yet."

Lilith dropped the hand from before her eyes and ran it over my corpse from head to toe, just a finger's breadth above my cooling skin. Then both hands returned quickly to hover over my belly where she sensed the lingering knot of life, clutched in my womb. She perceived the organ like a soft, ripe, rich fig and flinched at the blasphemy Adam and Eve had committed against such holiness.

Her hands fluttered again, seeking to escape the bitter knowledge they had stumbled on, though in truth she knew, in her endless life, there was no such thing as escape. There could be no escape from anything for the almost-woman condemned to bear the world's sins but never to know the reprieve even of death.

Then her hand returned quickly, as if suddenly sucked into a whirlpool there, just below my navel. The fig, ripe and rich, fleshed with red, sweet juice within. She had said my time of a woman was soon and now she knew just how soon. Even now, the first little speck of life was moving within me, even though my heart and lungs lay still. There, at the core, death came last of all because there, first of all, was life.

The wonder of it! Yet the sorrow! That here was a woman dead who was hardly yet a woman. One who had never known what it was to have new life folded within her like the center of an onion. For her who had borne so much—indeed, all living—for Lilith, the outer, crackling skin of the onion, it was almost too much to endure.

"My only child," she said again.

Then I felt the change, the stiffening throughout my Mother's body as she came to her decision. She gasped at the pain. To die. What no man could take from her, she, like any woman who comes to her time, could willingly sacrifice for the life of a child.

She knew the secret. Endless time watching life ebb and flow had taught her nothing if not this. So, after years whose number she had lost, she determined to end them.

———————

And in that moment, in her throes—the pressing waves that brought death in the same cycling as they brought life—death seemed an easier burden than one more day. Years that no human reckoning could compass weighed on her, pressed her every fiber with exquisite earthward longing. The embrace of Earth pushing up beneath her crouched knees was the sweetest thing she'd ever known.

As Lilith knew the secret then, I know it now. Yet I will not disclose it. On the day the secret is revealed, not only will humankind know good from evil—even Adam knew so much—but they will gladly take up evil to avoid the further need, death. And from such men as Adam—Adam who would choose good only as long as it was good for him—must this knowledge be hidden.

Woman may sense the magic. It lingers, in their own moontimes. Any woman, in the dark of her moon, will know she contains the power, onionlike, within her.

But for men—the less said to them, the better, for they will surely seek to control it as Adam did the wheat harvest.

It is enough to say that Lilith snatched up the stone knife my father had abandoned when he'd seen me dead. My blood still stained the flint and Lilith plunged it deep into the core of life at her own belly. She gasped at the pain. For though she could not die—without the supreme act of her own will—there was no remedy for pain.

Her rarefied flesh instantly began to close in on itself again, as was its nature. But before it could do so, Lilith plucked out the red, bleeding speck, her just-conceived child. No bigger than an awl's point at this stage, lacking even the contrast of brain from heart or sex from sex.

But now it was enough. She pressed it, still warm, into the cooling, congealing, blackening blood in the wound at the back of my corpse's head.

And the magic began.

Lilith was the dark wind of the vulture, whose sacred duty it was to return the dead to Earth so She could birth them soon anew. Lilith was the snake, and taught my cold, senseless limbs how to shed that dumb, dry flesh and take on a jewellike newness.

She who has ears to hear, let her understand.

Later, with fingers slicked with our combined blood, she pierced my hymen. I relearned pain with that stab. She felt me wince, then whimper, and she whimpered, too, from the black depths of her mind-force. For she'd felt the endlessness of her own life begin to crumble in the same instant.

Once more I could read her thoughts. "I never had such a barrier," she said, moving from between my legs.

Her heart seemed to be pumping air now instead of blood, at least every other beat. "My kind had no maidenhood, nor did we need them. Made to conceive, or even to copulate, only when our bodies and our lives were perfectly prepared, we needed no such sign between our mates, the promise of you-and-no-one-else. I take this sign from your body with my own hands as I take the other limitations of your flesh. As you know no death, you need know no such sorrow, no such beholdening, toward any man. But with all the rest of my daughters, it cannot be so. Teach future generations, my Na'amah. In a world after Adam, in a world where the aurochs is no more, it will never serve women to treat their maidenhoods lightly. Woe to our sex in that day. In the day that they do so, they will have so yielded to the view of Adam that even now I weep for them."

I felt her tears splashing so thickly on my belly that each drop fell twice or more. And then, I felt life. Life suffused through every part of me. Life, with all its pain, its sorrow, as well as its supreme joys.

But from the first I knew this life held a difference. I felt it like light, so it was there, yet nowhere near so cumbersome as the life I'd known before. Like motes of light in a sunbeam, it drifted. Light . . .

"Light. Yes," said Lilith. "As my sustaining power was the dark night wind—Lilith—yours shall be the light. When you call yourself no longer Na'amah but Noreah—Light—the power shall be yours."

My eyes fluttered open. They took a moment to focus through a rainbow of shifting lights. Then, the first thing I saw was Lilith. My Mother, twice over. Like an infant, I was as yet beyond speech. Still I tried to say all there was to say with a smile.

She smiled back, but it was a weak smile, no stronger than the life that throbbed as yet but doubtfully at the base of my neck. She had to close her eyes to form it. I could see the gray slowly creeping across her flesh while, at the same time, warmth returned to me. Sweat gathered in the hollows of my prone body like puddles of rain on the face of the earth.

I closed my eyes, rested, willed the rush of light-struck blood to my fingers, my toes, my lips. To the wound at the back of my head where pieces of skull sorted themselves out of their confusion and closed again.

I opened my eyes once more and ran a tongue of light-drenched saliva over my death-pinched lips.

"Mother," I said. "Mother."

But the breath caused by speaking that single word scattered the last clinging ashes of life from Lilith's frame. Helpless to do anything to stop it, I watched her, like a night wind, blow off down the Valley. Her cape of vulture feathers hissed lifeless to the ground.

I lay with my eyes closed until tears came. I lay until the tears had totally ravaged me, and then were past. Then slowly, I got to my feet and picked up Lilith's cape. The light of sunset laid a golden sheen on it. I shrugged it onto my own shoulders.

Thirty-one

For days I watched Adam and Eve from afar, without their knowledge.

I watched Adam digging new pits for more wheat. I watched him lay stone upon stone and plaster them with mud mixed with wheat chaff. He would build, I overheard him say, a house such as no woman in the clan—no, in the world—had ever had before. It would keep out the cold so they would pass the winter in complete comfort together, here in Eden. It would be safe from beasts—and from other, jealous men. Jealous women he did not mention—but I knew he thought it.

"We can store our belongings here, so we don't have to decide with each season-move what to carry and what to leave behind. It can all be ours."

He built the house under the Fig Tree.

I watched the awe Eve fixed on him as he spoke and as he worked. Without others around, she had no need to conceal it.

I watched her gather basket after basket of wheat, hull it, pound it, parch it. I watched her twist hemp fiber and weave it. She seemed not to miss the company of other women, though that ate at my heart the worst. She would raise her eyes from her tasks and gaze at Adam. And that seemed enough for her, a reward for which my death, her own death, the death of the entire world, in fact, was easy sacrifice.

Now, Adam's death, that would be something else again. Or his unfaithfulness. She would not suffer those events well. Much worse than any other woman I'd ever known. And she could no longer claim the threat of a wife's jealousy over him. That cord she had cut with her own hand. The membrane within her she had let him cut . . .

But her life, as Eve saw it, seemed endless. It stretched so far beyond that slash of an instant that such thoughts seemed as nothing.

The dark of the moon came and went. Eve did not seclude herself. Of course, the sacred, separate place was occupied now by this ever-rising dwelling of theirs, to which Adam added a course every day, let dry, then added another course.

But Eve didn't even go apart. She seemed to sense no need. They didn't bicker—and bickering, older women had always told me, was a sure sign that the moon was almost gone and it was time to go apart again.

In Eve's mind, this must have been great reason to rejoice. But I could only remember Lilith's words—"Your desire shall be toward your man"—and knew it was a curse. Perhaps, in time to come, women wouldn't even bleed together, so strong would be their link to their men. And then the urge among men for rape—and other things—would grow yet stronger.

It occurred to me, as it occurred to Eve, that she might be with child. I watched her smooth a hand across the fig leaves on her belly, look up at Adam and smile.

About the same time, the profound changes in my own body struck me. I realized, at one point, that I couldn't remember the last time I'd eaten or drunk anything. I think I'd stopped eating altogether in grief over the loss of the Mother

I'd known so briefly. Now that I thought of it, my mouth was
as dry as the Cave of the Dead and the hollow of my stomach
floated up to my brain. I felt this pain, and felt it keenly. But
the light of my being surrounded these sensations. And though
any other mortal would have died in the time I had been without water in this late summer heat, I did not. My mind remained open to think of other things.

I made myself go to the stream, cup my hand, and let the
water numb it. Flecks of light danced in the spray. I caught
them and lifted them to my lips. My lips numbed, then caught
the dance of light from the water.

"I have been thinking of myself as Na'amah still," I said
aloud. "But I am not. I am Noreah."

I drank more until the water-light danced in every part of
my body. Then I sent my mind out for pleasure, to dance with
the water among the spray.

The new moon was past, the full moon growing bigger bel-
lied each night. I crept close to Adam and Eve's fire on that
night, feeling the loneliness of my light-being so sharply, prey
to a strange, new, beastly hunger. I crept close enough to hear
their speech. I heard Adam sniff the air. Then he shoved himself out of Eve's arms and scrambled to his feet. His form was
black wreathed in gray smoke and outlined by low, red-orange
flame.

"A curse on it," he said.

"What is it, love?" Eve shifted so I saw her neat little outline, too.

"She's here."

"Who?"

"Lilith."

"Oh, Adam." Her voice betrayed more hurt from him than
from her rival.

"She's still here."

"Oh, can't she leave us alone?"

Adam forced himself to sit back down and grappled his body to Eve's as one might rope down a roof in a winter storm.

"Don't worry, my love," he said. "She won't have me again. I have you. Tomorrow I will begin to roof this house. We don't have to fear the wild any more."

I heard nothing else. I had moved off. I realized now that I hadn't just sat carelessly and bruised a herb bush. The smell of thyme was rising up from me.

I went as high as I could up the Valley. Yet, I knew I must avoid the summer meadows, as well. In the place I found, the trees ended and bare gray rock dominated, brutal in the heat of the day.

In spite of all my efforts, and in spite of his vows to Eve, two nights later I knew my father was hunting me in that vile place. I could read his thoughts and heard him tell himself he hunted me — or Lilith, for he hadn't seen me and still thought I was my mother — he hunted me to find some way to kill me. Probably he'd told Eve that, as well.

He had built a roof over Eve's head so she could no longer see the moon. And she had never understood the ebb and flow of her own body at all.

The whole world reeled around me. And the whole world called to Adam.

And I wanted him myself, with a heart-pounding desire I had never known.

But to answer the moon's call on my body? In this place and this time? Lilith had not died so that I could live to be such a fool. And certainly not with the man of this Valley, my own father.

Desperately, I sought to escape him, and had the advantage of my own soul, sent out before me in particles of light, which tracked the ground before me like the best of hunters. Also, I could go without food and water in this unfriendly place, while Adam had to retreat again and again to the closest stream, to a thicket of berries past their prime and shriveling.

My soul, however, warred with itself. Sometimes my desire to escape got confused with the very moonlight charm I sought to flee. I would find myself running, scrambling over boulders—directly toward Adam instead of away from him. I would not realize what was happening until the light of my mind actually reached out and caressed his rigid spearpoint— both of them, for I don't think he could tell the difference between what he meant to do with the one of flesh or the one tipped with stone.

Once or twice he even saw me, but never clearly enough to think that, in the vulture feathers, I was anyone other than his first wife, Lilith, haunting him with jealousy.

"I will kill you," he would howl to the night at such times. Then, in the same breath, "I will do anything to keep you. Lilith! Lilith, night wind! Lilith. My love . . ."

Fortunately, I remembered in time how bathing in a stream had washed the scent from my mother. Then, when crouching in water, numb to my neck, became too uncomfortable, I called on my mother and received another piece of advice on the breath of the moon-soaked night wind.

"Trees. Trees," she whispered.

So I learned the power of certain trees—those with a strong scent of their own—to cover the smell of my heat, or at least to confuse it. Pines are such trees—there were a few so far up the Valley. Acacias lower down. And tamarisks. There are other trees throughout the world. I found I could stoop beneath one of these and Adam could look me full in the eye— just as he had when I saw him and he saw me as I looked through Lilith's eyes at their coupling. We would be so close, yet he would not see me. He would pass right on.

Just as he had when I was a child.

This taught me two things. First, bare rock was not a good place in my condition, despite its allure for hunted animals. It only created a clean background against which my heat stood out like shadows under a cloudless sky. Secondly, I came to understand another reason why Lilith had given her gift to me and not to any other of her thousand, thousand daughters. I was Adam's daughter. Adam's world was somehow beyond her, but not—oh, let it be so!—not beyond my powers to deal with. When those powers should come to their full.

The difficult thing was not to let those powers be snapped in the bud. I must not follow the urges of my own body and leap out like some wildcat, taking him for myself. I wanted to do that, more than anything I'd ever wanted before. But I learned to satisfy myself on the end of a deer's femur bone, left from a wildcat's meal.

So I let Adam return to Eve, satisfied with himself that he had won.

Thirty-two

When the full moon had passed and I could think clearly once more, I decided to leave Eden. I went up the rock face to join the clan in the summer meadows; that was something familiar, a place where I could regain my bearings.

I found the clan on its season-move. The nights had turned cooler in the heights and the game was shifting again. It was time to return to Eden.

I watched them moving from afar, my clansfolk, so familiar—and yet, after what had happened, almost strangers. I packed the vulture feathers in the bundle with the rest of my things so they couldn't be seen and drew near. Still, I feared I was so changed they might not recognize me. Lilith's were the only eyes, I remembered, that had seen me since I'd died.

"Why, Na'amah!" My clanswomen welcomed me warmly.

"We've missed your stories so much."

"Tell us a story, tell us a story," Boaz and Kochavah chirped, both of them hopping from foot to foot.

I set my hand fondly on the little boy's head. "Yes, I'll tell you a story right away. You'll find it hard to believe, as I do. About young Boaz and how he grew like a vine in a single summer."

"But you've grown, too." Aunt Afra confided, taking my

arm. "I think perhaps it's time I initiated you, Na'amah. Don't you think so?"

"Thank you, aunt, but there is no need. I would like to learn all I can from you of the healing arts, but my Mother Lilith initiated me herself after the last full moon."

"Lilith? Mother Lilith was here?"

The clamor of voices sent my mind spinning in all directions as on a whirlwind. I saw and embraced every heart around me, saw in a moment all the joys and sorrows of the summer I'd missed. Saw that Devorah still carried the child she couldn't keep. I knew all the clan and didn't flinch from the sight. I embraced each, rather, with light.

"Yes, Lilith was here," I replied, speaking that love I felt. "She came to set things right. Didn't she, Uncle Ari? Uncle Dov?"

The men too had come up to greet me. From the looks those two brothers passed between them, I knew they had told the clan nothing of what had befallen them during the full moon before last. They had probably not even spoken of it between themselves and certainly not to their wives, who had the awful power of jealousy.

"Mother Lilith?" they echoed with some confusion, and stared at me, hard. "Mother Lilith is here?"

"She is . . ." I began, then altered my thought. "She is gone now."

"Indeed?" Ari did not cover a sigh of relief.

Dov nodded. "But I had the sense of her this last full moon. Didn't you, brother? Something in the air."

"Probably only the first of the signals to move on with the seasons," I assured him.

The men nodded gratefully. "That must be it."

Even so far away, then, I affected the men. No, I couldn't return permanently to my clan.

Not for the first time the thought of leaving them, mixed with a deep sadness, swept over me. I had already imagined how difficult it would be to face my father again, to explain—Better to let him tell the clan he had seen me dead. Would he confess that he had killed me with his own hand? Never. No matter. An evil unnamed could create demons in its wake.

Let Adam believe in ghosts, think that Lilith's curse was just beginning. Let the night wind haunt him.

Still, I decided to enjoy the clan as long as I could.

"I should warn you," I said. "Things are very different in Eden now. Many changes have happened."

"Our parents and grandparents are dead," said Afra, and many copied her in making the sign to speed their souls back to our women's wombs. "But we knew that already."

"There is more."

"Tell us the story," Kochavah begged.

Falling in step beside them, I chipped the story out of raw rock, as the saying is. I first spoke then some of the phrases now known all over the world, though as yet but rough-hewn: "And it came to pass that the gods planted a fertile Valley eastward in Eden . . ."

The word "garden" had not been made up yet. Unless Adam was already using it.

Nothing I could tell, either in story or common speech, could prepare them for what we actually saw as we rounded the final ridge overlooking the Valley the next day. Great mushrooms of smoke billowed up into the sky toward us as if the whole of Eden were on fire. My heart stopped in my throat: it was too similar to the blast on the Fig Tree, only much greater.

"Stay where you are," the men told us, then crept down closer to explore, their weapons ready.

We women obeyed gratefully, yet fearfully. We set down our packs to wait, few comfortable enough to actually sit. Some wept quietly in fear and confusion.

"It's Adam." Dov brought back the news. "He's tending a great fire." A scuff with his heel at a nearby heap of rocks told me how angry my uncle was.

"Adam?" Afra asked. With Grandmother gone, she had taken over without quibble as speaker and leader for the women, and she had had a summer in which to grow into the honor. But even she didn't know what to make of this mad action on my father's part.

"He's burning trees and great heaps of trash. Trash, that's what he calls it. Weeds."

"Adam was always making new words." Rachel's voice never lacked fondness. "Even as a child."

Afra was not so fond. "What do these words mean?"

"He burns them to open up more space for wheat to grow," Dov muttered.

"Na'amah?" Afra looked to me. "Do you know what this means?"

I said: "I told you how my father has discovered good and evil and set a solid mark between them. I suppose if he holds a spear of fire between what was and what is now, like some evil spirit, this will please him even more."

"But what of my asparagus stands? My yarrow? My healing herbs?" Afra wrung her hands together and then dragged them both through her hair so it pulled out of her thin braids and stuck straight up in gray spikes.

"I suppose he names them 'weed' in his new world."

"We must go stop this at once."

We all marched down after Afra and watched as she defied Adam with the same questions. I took care to always stand
behind my father, or to keep a thick cover of blowing smoke
between us.

"But the bark of that very willow was the best for fevers."
Afra lashed out at him. "Our asparagus stand? My herbs?
What do you expect us to eat in spring?"

"We'll eat wheat, as we'll eat it in every season," Adam answered calmly. He stood tending his fire with a forked branch,
blackened at the tips. His face was sweat-drenched and
smeared with soot, but proud, contented, and immovable.

"I for one will get cursedly tired of wheat, day in and day
out," stated Ari.

"If you want to live in this Valley, you will live as we live,
Eve and I, or you will not live here at all." Adam met his elder
brother eye to eye. "Move on, Ari, if you don't like it."

"Adam and Eve—that is evil coupling," cried one voice behind them.

"Give us back our home, our Eden, our paradise," cried
another.

And Dov's hand went to his knife, though I managed to
stop him with a gentle finger on his wrist.

"It is too late, uncle," I whispered to him, other cries keep-
ing our talk from being overheard. "What my father has done
has cursed the soil. Lilith has cursed it. The only way to bring
Eden back to the way she was—now that he has brought the
fire—would be to abandon her totally for two or three years.
Are you willing to do that?"

"What, go and join other clans for all that time? Be be-
holden to them? We don't have the patience. We'd be at each
others' throats, for I tell you, being a beggar would not sit well
with me."

"Beggar." That was another new word.

"That is the choice you must make," I said. "Either join the other clans—or join Adam."

Something in my eyes made Dov think me more than just his niece. To Adam, he shouted, "But Lilith—"

"Lilith." Adam laughed aloud. "Lilith, the demon, will never be found in Eden again. I have seen to that."

A wave of shock and cries of "Blasphemy" ran through the group. But no one moved.

"Or perhaps," I murmured, "it is Eden that will never be found again."

I stepped back from my clansfolk as they stood debating what to do. Devorah I heard, shrill with the hope that she might not have to give up the child in her womb. And Adam's voice boomed loud and compelling, full of phrases that made me shudder: "The end of the aurochs hunt . . . Placed here to dress the garden . . . Dominion over all the earth."

The voices had drawn Eve up from the house. Adam put an arm unashamedly around her shoulder and held the forked stick in his other hand.

"Women," Adam said, "go to my wife Eve and let her teach you what your new duties will be."

How could Afra take instruction from a girl who hadn't even borne a child yet? Who wasn't even properly married? But Eve must have bragged of her pregnancy, for I heard her discussing possible names. "Cain" was all that drifted after me on the smoke. "Cain."

I turned my back, alone. All alone, staggeringly alone. New tears, fed by smoke, caught in my throat and filled my eyes. I wanted, in that moment, to die for loneliness. But death, I knew—death, that best of cures—was taken from me. No wonder Lilith, my sweet night wind of a mother, had wanted rid of her life's burden so fervently, act of love though it was to pass it to me.

And this was but one tiny, little, unimportant group of her children in a world already full to the brim.

It was too much, too much for one so young and inexperienced as I. These were my children now, though I had not even known a man. I did not know all the other tongues, all their ways . . .

Yet the wind of Lilith breathed within me. It had since my childhood, I realized, though I hadn't understood it at the time. All the while, Lilith had sensed this story's ending, perhaps even had been preparing me in the best way she could by leaving me alone. With Adam.

The moment I was out of sight of my clan and had cleared my lungs somewhat of the sorrow and the stench of burning, I set down my pack and opened it. I tenderly took out the vulture feathers, crumpled and the worse for being hidden. I put them on. I wouldn't hide them again.

Then, as I knelt to retie the rest of the pack, I saw the snake, Lilith's snake, a stranger to this Valley. He was sitting coiled up in the hollow of a sun-baked rock, looking unblinkingly, fearlessly, back at me. His skin seemed wet and new, each scale catching the light like a flake of obsidian. Then, at the foot of the stone, I saw why. He had just shed his skin and the old husk lay there, offered to me.

Carefully, carefully, I moved step by step to the stone. I bent and picked up the shrugged-off skin. So light and fragile, it seemed no more than the breath of the wind across my palm. Yet the magic in it weighed like the whole earth.

"Lilith," I whispered. My breath rocked the skin in my palm.

The snake had lifted his head to watch me, out of curiosity rather than threat or fear. The head bobbed a nod—yes, the skin was meant for me. Then a quick flick of red tongue seemed to urge me on. Indeed, I felt I could almost hear him say it: "Be on your way."

I tucked the skin into my belt of braided deerskin. I would get more skins. In time, I would have enough to need no leather. In a long, long time.

But I had all the time in the world.

I realized I needed nothing else. I left my pack where it lay. Perhaps Afra would find it: extra skins, my tool kit, my gathering sacks and baskets, all. I left everything behind and walked purposefully down the Valley to the rest of the world.

I only stopped to pick up a suitable walking stick and to let the snake crawl up it—as I was leaving Eden.

Author's Note

Readers may think that a "primitive" girl like Na'amah should have matured earlier than at fifteen. "They had to," runs the saw, "because they died so early." My intuition, borne out by anthropological studies, tells me that, on the contrary, the age of maturity has been dropping with time and modernization.

A woman needs a certain amount of body fat in order to bear children. The more sedentary her life, the more fatty the foods she eats, the earlier menarche arrives. My characters lead lives more akin to those lived by modern female athletes, who sometimes do not begin to menstruate until their early twenties. I pushed the ages of my characters downward in concession to modern (mis)beliefs.

This also addresses the ages of Na'amah's grandparents. "Why, they'd have been lucky to live to twenty-five," says modern intuition, "but you have them pushing sixty." I don't mean to suggest a hunter-gatherer life was not harder than most modern bodies could tolerate—or different from what most minds today are trained for. But it was the life for which we evolved. Many views of such lives have been informed by what modern "primitive" tribes have been forced to at the margins of existence. We shouldn't equate what "Adam and Eve's" lives were like to, say, what the Cherokee Nation suffered upon the Trail of Tears. Anyway, this is a portion of the evolutionary background into which I've set my mythological characters: Lilith, Adam, Eve—and Na'amah.

.